The Descent

Dedicated to my lovely wife, Kim, and our three children, Joshua, Jesse, & Rachel

The Descent
© by Cliff Hulling 2018
All rights reserved. No part of this publication may be reproduced in any form without the permission of the author.

ISBN-13: 978-1985271258 / ISBN-10: 1985271257

Check out cliffhulling.com for other books by the author, free devotionals, and more.

The Descent

Contents:

Prologue	*Hamartia*	5
Chapter 1	*The Assent*	7
Chapter 2	*The Entrance*	15
Chapter 3	*The Disease of Denial*	24
Chapter 4	*The First Contact*	35
Chapter 5	*The Crooked Path*	48
Chapter 6	*The Hypocrite*	62
Chapter 7	*The Seductress*	76
Chapter 8	*The Jackals*	88
Chapter 9	*The Beginning of the End*	109
Chapter 10	*The Runner*	125
Chapter 11	*The Final Confrontation*	139
Chapter 12	*Redemption*	163
Epilogue		172

The Descent

Prologue

Having already traveled deep into the mountain called Hamartia, the trip back seemed all but impossible. Every step backwards towards the light of day meant crossing seemingly infinite territories of previous indulgence. Around every bend in the trail there lay a sinewy side path that beckoned me towards not so distant memories of lavish exploration in temporal earthly pleasures; corridors of deceit, conduits of darkness. The rocks beneath each footfall were slippery with the well-oiled smoothness that only comes from thousands of visiting travelers. Each of their previous steps had only served to wear down the sharp edges which used to lie on the surface of the stony trail, sharp edges which *should* have been jagged reminders and warnings of how dangerous this path really was; a trail fully capable of cutting deep into both sole and souls.

But this wasn't so now. The path was broad and darkly comfortable. It was odd how quickly one could forget the light, could turn and embrace the cool darkness, somehow believing that it would cloak you in a sense of serene and sublime comfort. Darkness tended to sell itself to a searching soul. But to further your descent into darkness there were also those odd remembrances and haunting thoughts about the sterile honesty of light that once shone around you, revealing all things in a sort of blinding pureness of reality that was often too hard to bear. Light was certainly cruel while darkness was uncompromisingly tolerant. Light revealed me for who I was, while darkness accepted me unconditionally. How could it possibly be, that the path of least resistance was not the correct one? But alas, I found out too late that the spiraling pathway into the mountain was *deceitfully* attractive, not betraying the barren emptiness that lay at the murky bottom: a pit where hopelessness and hollowness worked like duel pistons in an engine churning out only despair and death within a man's heart.

And though I could see no one else anymore, I knew that I was not alone. Once and awhile I thought I could hear the other voices, *knew* I had heard other voices, but the fleeting echoes seemed to flutter just beyond the realm of recognition in the cavernous and shadowy gloom of empty space. In truth, the voices became more of a torment really, ever summoning me towards a mist I could not penetrate. It was at these moments, and a hundred others, that I realized my mistake. What once presented itself as a journey into complete freedom and liberation, indulgence and fulfillment, had somehow turned on me, and the change was so subtle, to this day I cannot pin it down to a moment in time. When does deception present itself as so? I now know that those revealing moments will forever be disguised, for if the destination had been clearly revealed to me at the crossroad into my oblivion, I surely would have turned and ran back to the light. But it was too late for me now. Depravity of *any* kind is insidious by its very nature, for though it eventually reveals itself for what it is, it mockingly does so at a moment in which you are powerless to choose anything else. At least that is what I thought.

Chapter 1 – The Assent

Hamartia. I'll never forget my first view of the towering mountain. Bathed in sunlight, it appeared as a green jewel floating in a churning sea of olive colored trees. As the warm wind stirred branches back and forth like the froth of an angry tide, the mountain stood defiantly solid, stoically silent, yet speaking volumes simply by its magnificence. It seemed to have an otherworldly presence, calling out to those who might dare to explore all its hidden beauty. Like the sirens of Greek mythology, this peak seemed to draw you in to its rocky shoreline, promising unlimited discovery and adventure. The towering presence simply could not be ignored, at least not by me: The allure was overwhelming; I *had* to see what pleasures awaited inside so great a stone monument. By nature, I pressed forward with a sense of anticipation.

The initial journey towards my goal started out in somewhat uneventful fashion. Pathways had already been hewn into the smooth ascending terrain, but it was interesting that there were so *many* different routes to choose from. Each one looked equally traveled. I once purposefully backtracked and chose a different path upward, wondering what alternate vistas I might encounter as I made the trek uphill. But after a few moments, I found myself right back in the same place I had been only moments earlier. The interconnectedness of each trail seemed to betray a grand design that allowed everyone easy and unrestrained access to the mountain. I wondered who might have taken the time to prepare these passageways so carefully and completely. Whoever the architect was, he had certainly made it convenient for the average traveler who may have lacked an explorer's sense of direction. Someone really wanted to make this journey easier.

As I approached the mountain, each bend in the trail seemed to dim the ambient light surrounding me. Trees grew taller and thicker, spinning cobwebs of branches that served as a canopy further blocking the light of the sun. Brightness gradually gave way to shadow, and shadow to opaque twilight. Night would soon envelope the countryside, and much to my dismay, it was becoming clear that I would not have time to make it to the base of the mountain before the murky darkness would overtake me. Though the path was mostly clear, something told me that the wise course of action would mean making camp for the night, forestalling the final part of the journey until morning light. That became the plan: remove my backpack, lie out the bedroll, and make myself as comfortable as possible.

That night was the first night I heard voices; not something someone readily admits considering the admission of hearing phantom speech in the night watches usually means a trip to the state mental institution. But in the interest of honest disclosure, these voices would play an integral part in all that followed. They would be the inconvenient and unwanted friends who visit at the most inopportune times; disturbing whispers in the mind that cause one to stop and listen to your own heartbeat, trying to distinguish reality from illusion.

At first I was convinced they were indeed illusion, a trick played on a tired, trail weary mind as the wind spun its way over rock and glade, hollow valley and steep mountain pass. And the voices themselves were only slightly discernable, rambled mutterings of positive and negative admonitions of a sort I could not grasp. It was like trying to remember and desperately hold on to the plot of a dream as it quickly fades from memory during the waking minutes where full consciousness emerges from wistful sleep. I only had a vague premonition that in some way a battle was raging in the air surrounding me, pulling me in two different directions simultaneously. As it turned out, the onset of sleep came quickly, so the battle turned out to be merely a skirmish that dwindled into a dreamy truce as slumber gradually defeated the two phantom combatants. Little did I know, the voices would be back.

The next morning brought with it a cascading flood of light that thankfully purged any memories of disturbing voices completely from my thoughts. This was a day of adventure, a day where I could reach my destination and begin my exploration. I set about my journey with a sense of renewed hope that my wanderlust would at least be partially fulfilled as I neared the foot of this hulking behemoth of stone. My enthusiasm meant progress was quick, and by the time I reached the base of the mountain, only half the day was gone. And yet the morning light seemed to fade sooner than the day before. It left me with the disturbing feeling that the day had been shortened somehow, like time had actually sped up. I had a fleeting thought that perhaps this mountain had the mystical power to warp the very elements of our existence, to alter the stage upon which we were acting in this life. I had to laugh silently at that one. A suspicious type I am not. I moved forward.

Finally, reaching the uppermost part of my trail at the base of the mountain, I was surprised to find that it spilled out into a crossroads where *all* the other separate intertwined trails gathered into one. It was odd that all the diverse paths leading up to this point eventually funneled travelers to only one single myopic choice. Up or down. Forward or backward. No third choice. That being the case, I doubt anyone coming this far would choose the option to leave. Standing this close to the summit trail, the mountain seemed to beckon visitors with a sort of persuasive magnetic attraction that was irresistible to anyone with the desires that brought them this far in the first place.

An eerie mist hung lazily in the atmosphere around me; invisible pockets of slithering air made certain portions of the fog react as if drops of water were falling sideways into vertical pools of water on each side of me. It was as if the mist was deliberately blinding you to your surroundings and yet guiding you at the same time to a single distinct trail that was the only choice for further assent. Mist and mountain were working in perfect harmony. At this point, I had no choice. Though many paths had led up to this point, it became obvious that this *single* path was needed for anyone wishing to proceed upward. No problem. This was the purpose for which I began my journey in the first place. Gaining entry to the mountain had always been the goal.

My desire was steadfastly set on the ascension set before me, and though the restrictions of only a single upward route at first disappointed me, I eventually realized that this limitation surely promised that others, perhaps more wise, had found this to be the best way of forward progress. That was fine with me. Not *all* of life can be unique or original. Thousands of other generations have used the self-deluded and seemingly "original" battle cry of rebellion against "the system" only to eventually conform to the norms of their own contemporaries. Silently deceived and blissfully unknowing rebels always seem to end up simply becoming the *new* establishment; something they had desperately tried to avoid. Maybe uniqueness and originality were overrated concepts outgrown by an ever-evolving humanity that improves itself by creating efficient and effective societal drones. This was the lone trail that led up to an opening in the side of the mountain. This is the one I needed to take. It was well worn by preceding travelers. So be it.

Perhaps falling in line with the other drones who preceded me, I had been captivated from afar. The path had been a beacon for my entire journey up to this point, and second-guessing my commitment to complete this quest was now simply out of the question. Desire gives birth to action and action would surely bring about just rewards. I was motivated and ready to move. As a matter of fact, the renewed idea of reaching my goal only caused my pulse to race once again as my strides quickened, moving me closer towards my objective. Despite my enthusiasm, the last part of this journey to the mountain entrance wasn't easy. This solitary route was traversing quite a bit of jagged elevation, so as a courtesy to travelers, it had to be filled with numerous switchbacks. As I moved quickly forward, the multiple changes in direction made me a little light-headed and dizzy. One hairpin turn after another made me feel like some sort of animal scurrying away from a predator who could be thrown off the scent of his prey simply by frequent and erratic course changes. I even thought I heard some guttural heavy breathing behind me from time to time, but I knew it must be another trick of the wind. Being born with a vivid imagination was sometimes a curse. Surely nothing could be pursuing me; I had not seen any human or animal life for miles. In hindsight, I'm not sure why that last fact didn't give me cause to wonder why that might be.

Contrary to my enthusiasm, there was one other disconcerting thing about this trail. The mist seemed to stay with me the whole time, and I don't mean in the sense that the entire mountain was covered in a cloud. Out of the corner of my eye, when I wasn't looking directly at it, the fog would occasionally seem to dissipate, at least in part. But each sideward glance only redundantly revealed the same watery shroud, as thick as ever, still morphing and moving with me like it was some sort of pale gray cadaverous and ghostly veil waiting to wrap itself around me in some sickly ritual consummation. This devouring canopy of mist persistently and stubbornly blocked the surrounding panoramic view of the valley, but I supposed that was fine too. I had already witnessed the majestic scenery that led up to this point. But it was still a bit unnerving that my view was so constricted and claustrophobic, as if I were being transported unwittingly to the top of the trail by some sort of possessive luminous soap bubble. And I also couldn't quite shake the premonition that something was following me further down the trail. *There's that vivid imagination again.*

I had to shake it off. My destiny was at the top of this trail. Things had already been set in motion that made my eventual destination unavoidable. So I pressed on. But fatigue was now beginning to be my enemy; a constant and persistent heckler who kept throwing out taunts mocking my cursed human frailty. I couldn't really argue with him, but he became the incredibly annoying stalker who wouldn't stop taunting, even though his victim had already all but admitted defeat. My calves had started to burn with each rising step, my quivering leg muscles turning into hot bands of burning rope stretched across aching bones. The elevation was also sapping my breath and the constant presence of the suffocating mist only seemed to steal what little air there was left in the surrounding atmosphere.

The brain tends to work in concert with the body, and my mind was beginning to betray me as well. I showed no signs of dehydration, and walking in the pleasant balmy afternoon heat would be one of the last things to generate symptoms of hypothermia. Still, feelings of disconnectedness and mild blurred vision were beginning to set in. An occasional involuntary shiver became yet another unwelcome addition to my guest list of current ailments and disorientation. I would later convince myself that it was this sense of confusion that led to what I perceived next.

The breathing I once thought I'd heard well down the trail had seemed to close the gap substantially. I came to the realization that I must have been ignoring it, considering it to be an echo of my own ragged inhalation and exhalation as I was making my labored assent. I might have *continued* to miss the sound if this strange and not so distant breathing had not been brought back to my conscious mind because of an odor that wafted up from a lower portion of the winding trail. It wasn't constant but intermittent, with the time between olfactory assaults on my sinuses eventually dwindling down to mere seconds. The odd thing was; the smell was actually growing stronger when it should have been fading in the distance. I was, after all, heading *up* the slope and the stench was definitely coming from directly behind me. Each step forward *should* have taken me further away from any rotting animal carcass I might have unknowingly passed on the trail. But now, in addition to the vague impression of lightly veiled breathing and foul odor, I heard other sounds.

At first it wasn't anything too alarming, perhaps just an occasional sound of falling rock on a well-worn trail that contained thousands of loose rocks. Wind, water, and other natural forces had undoubtedly loosened untold hundreds of small rocks from their calm nesting place in the hillside. The randomness of nature was the only factor determining when one of these stones might just gain the advantage of erosion needed to break free from its encumbered position of captivity within the mountain walls. But these new noises were uncannily close to the sound of footsteps, though they would express themselves as a step followed by a dragging noise and then a pause. Step…drag…pause…silence. It was too regular to be a natural occurrence. It was the synchronized regularity of the sounds that caused the hair on the back of my neck to stand at attention.

I consciously extended my stride, but the weighty weariness of dead muscle would not cooperate very well. It felt like one of those childhood dreams where you're running from some terrible menacing beast only to look down and see the ground beneath your feet moving unnaturally slow; limbs straining and bursting with energy but moving as if they were running knee deep through thick black tar. In reality, my pace *was* still fairly swift and it unfortunately exceeded my own capacity to keep up. Two separate times I fell forward, the first giving me a substantially deep road rash on the heel of my left hand, and the second was worse, leaving me with a sizeable gash in an already sore right knee. After the second fall, I arose pathetically and simply watched my own blood as it trickled down both sides of my body, disappearing into the parched hungry ground.

It's funny how the mind works, because for a brief moment I contemplated a terrible image of the trail sucking *all* the blood from my body while at the same time, the mist finally enveloping me, burning off my skin in a virulent acid bath. The snapping sound to my right brought me completely out of my oblivious morbid revelry. I was used to the sounds *behind* me, but whatever was pursuing me had started to use the *side* of the trail for what I could only imagine was concealment. Dried wood made brittle from sun and wind made an ominous cracking noise that betrayed a creature of substantial size and weight just outside my field of vision, just on the other side of the fog. I had the dreaded notion that if this thing were able to get in front of me, the deadly game of cat and mouse would be instantly over, and the end I envisioned for myself was not good. *Did I mention; sometimes a vivid imagination is not a good thing?*

An infusion of adrenaline coursed through my body, pumping air into flat tires and gas into empty tanks. I raced up the trail with a renewed vigor I thought impossible only moments before, hoping that whatever blood I was trailing behind would be enough to sooth the appetite of the brooding beast that tailed me. Unfortunately, *not* appeased, the pace of the footsteps behind me increased in equal tempo with mine. Not good. The proximity of this feral threat was real. I was like a scared forest animal running desperately for life and limb, afraid to look back for fear of finding that the pursuer had already taken hold of its victim's tail and was merely waiting for its prey to run out of breath. I dared not risk the slower pace required for a backward glance. In futility I tried to redouble my already exhausted physical efforts.

My pulse pounded in an odd synchronicity with my head creating a feeling that both heart and cranium could explode at any moment and bring this chase to a brutal and bloody end. To make it worse, disorientation and dizziness were now my ever increasing and intoxicating companions. Reality and terror had joined in a sort of unholy matrimony. Blurred perception was their profane offspring. My *own* perception was one of rapid movement, but a brief moment of sober clarity revealed a noticeable stagger had entered my formally swift steps. The reality of a slowing pace was more than a little disturbing…but there was something far worse possible. If there was one thing for certain, it was the fact that a fall *now* would quickly usher in the gruesome finale to the final act of my life. No applause. Just the silent curtain falling on the fading light of my consciousness after God knows what sort of unimaginable pain. Morose thoughts like these kept me going; an engine completely empty and running only on the combustible fumes left in the tank.

At one point, it definitely felt like the beginning of the end. Blood had started to pool inside my right shoe, trickling down from the gash in my knee. Sweat coming down my forehead and temples seemed to pour directly into my eyes like tributaries of salty waters pouring directly into two once calm clear freshwater pools. My already clouded eyesight was being reduced to mere pinpricks of light. Reaching up to rub my eyes and clear my murky vision turned out to be a mistake; it only served to add a mixture of blood and earth into my eyes, inducing a rapidly approaching opaque blindness. Reaching for my canteen and blindly running forward splashing water in my face seemed the only option to clear my vision.

It was then that I saw the cave opening. A slight flicker of hope burned in the nearly extinguished and dying candle of my soul. Somehow I had reached the top of the trail; in record time I imagine. Perhaps if I could just make it inside the cool dark cavity of the inner mountain, the monstrous apparition behind me would vaporize back into the mist from which it came. A silly hope, but at this point, perhaps my last. I summoned every last drop of strength and headed straight for the opening, but the pitiful attempts at keeping up my pace were made worse as my goal seemed to stretch unreachable before me. This was one of those horrifying movie scenes where the camera recedes backwards as the goal of safety moves further away to a distant point in the victims' forward field of vision. No vivid imagination needed here. This was not a movie trailer. This was real.

This whole journey had taken on the element of the surreal. Bright sunshine turned into menacing darkness. The thrill of adventure turned into a flight from ominous and unrelenting terror. Healthy muscle and skin turned into useless spent sinew surrounded by tissue caked with sweat, blood, and dirt. Not what I had signed on for. The breach in the mountainous wall was almost within my grasp. A few more brutally tired bodily exertions would bring me to the precipice where I could throw myself towards that hopeful fissure in the rock. The only new sensation now was that of putrid breath and greasy saliva landing on the back of my neck. There was no more time. Last chance for action was now. The leap forward was pitifully weak.

Chapter 2 – The Entrance

As it turned out, my jump hadn't exactly propelled me *into* the cave; at least not *all* the way in. My position was a pathetic "half-in – half-out" awkward compromise that was the result of unbelievably extreme fatigue and a pitiful underestimation of jumping distance on my part. Still, I had the sensation of falling forward into the cave. But perhaps the more accurate way to express it is that the earth beneath me was *carrying* me forward. An odd sensation to say the least. It was definitely some sort of artificial movement propelling me forward because as I lay there, mouth panting against pebbly earth, I knew that there was no strength whatsoever left in me to move even one of my lethargic muscles. Unfortunately, there were loose rocks at the mouth of the cave that felt no obligation to support a bloodied and weary prone man who had just finished running for his life. How rude. I was in for a ride.

Though happy to be moving forward and presumably continuing to distance myself from whatever was chasing me, it was not long before the realization set in that I had no idea what I was falling *into*. Shortly after this realization, pain jumpstarted my exhausted muscles as I realized I was not always simply riding on *top* of this massive magic carpet ride of gravel. At times I was "becoming one" with the mass of tumbling rock. Claustrophobia began to set in as the possibility of being buried alive presented itself as a very logical conclusion to the perilous situation unfolding around me. Though most of the stones were fairly small, collectively they were beating and bruising an already tired bleeding body. And the few larger rocks mixed into this earthen stream threatened to break more than just my stamina. The flattening of my head just might be on the agenda of this malicious moving earth. Fear once more reared its ugly head, spitting at me with small daggers of venomous stone.

Pondering my choices, there really seemed to be only one option available. It wasn't easy, but I managed to work my way over to the side of the cavern wall, dragging my now bloodied hands against the jagged sides to slow my descent. After awhile, I was even able to nearly stop my downward spiral altogether. But fate would not allow even the smallest victories to be mined from this earthen graveyard. As soon as my mind contemplated a brief moment of success, my soul descended to a new level of despair as I lifted my gaze to the cave entrance above me. Part way into the opening, silhouetted against a fading blood red sun was the beast that had chased me. It was hard to make out any distinctive features other than the fact that my initial estimations had been painfully correct:

It was real. It was big. It was angry.

No way up and uncertainties below froze me in an eerie state of panicked limbo. I could hear the creature breathing heavily. Thankfully it was at least *partially* tired out from the chase. With an unsteady sense of false bravado, I vaguely remember yelling some sort of expletive towards the mouth of the cave. I'm not sure how I thought that would help, but my inner mental equilibrium was further disturbed as I heard myself suddenly break into the kind of inappropriate nervous laughter that sometimes surfaces when people are under times of severe stress. The shrill tone of my own voice echoing off the walls seemed to reawaken a realization of the dire predicament I was in. Of course it didn't help that the next thing I saw was the hideous foul smelling ghoul taking a step forward towards me.

My only thought was: *Oh man; it surely can't come down here. The weight of its footsteps on the shaky ground would carry it down to the same doom I was currently facing.* But undaunted, it took another step. *Come on…no way…give me a break.* Of all the ways to die, surrendering to that hideous thing would have ranked somewhere only slightly above diving head first into a massive wood chipper. And that still may not be a fair comparison, because at least the wood chipper would result in a quicker death. This creature undoubtedly had a warped and sadistic thought process, and one could only imagine what prolonged devilish torture this ghoul might have in mind for my bruised and bloody body. Unfortunately, I *do* have an active imagination and I didn't like the direction my thoughts were going. So the decision was made. The one and only solid thing in my world right now had to go. I let go of the side of the cave wall.

After clumsily drifting downward about another 30 yards, the waterfall of stone began to slow as the cavern grew narrower and as the rocks were beginning to bottleneck through a smaller opening below. Hope began to preach its ridiculous mantra that maybe this mini avalanche wasn't a death sentence after all. Eager at this moment for *any* kind of self-deception, the irrational promise of possible pardon from death brought instant relief to me. But only for the briefest of moments. As sanity returned for a rare guest appearance as of late, it occurred to me that this whistle stop on the rock slide railway meant that the thing above me could now move down freely, leaving me with no place to go. Nice thought. No exit strategy. Brilliant.

Indeed, as I looked up, it *was* moving slowly but steadily towards my position. Even the fresh cool air of the cavern couldn't mask the stench of the menace as it lurched awkwardly forward. More expletives flooded my mind, but the frantic curses became bottled up as much as the flow of rock below me. In fact, I was loosing the ability to express anything. Sensory overload was overwhelming me and my emotions were becoming numb. Is that what happens to the helpless animal torn apart on those nature shows…despairing withering victim driven into an emotional freeze frame so it can at least refuse to watch its own evisceration? For the life of me, I never really understood the appeal of these shows, the attraction of gathering the wife and kids around the television, popcorn and drinks in hand, only to replay gruesome animal deaths as if it were some kind of joyous family bonding ritual. *Look honey, have you ever seen a zebra from the inside out? See the pretty colors?* Now, these shows seemed more obscene than ever.

Back in my own life or death drama, the guttural breathing that had followed me up the trail was now once again an unwelcome audible assault on my senses. Unlike back on the misty trail, the hulking frame that accompanied the voice was visible this time, though its form and features were still bathed in shadow. Truth be told, I was frankly glad for the shadows. I had a feeling that if I were to get a *complete* glimpse of my pursuer, I might just loose what little sanity I had left. Perhaps, in an unholy fusion of bone, flesh, and earth, looking into the creature's eyes would cause me to turn into stone like the unsuspecting travelers from Greek mythology who accidently looked directly into the face of Medusa. Or, for a more cynical thought, maybe Medusa's foul head would actually appear to be the bright shinning face of the Mona Lisa when compared to the hideous fiend that was approaching me. Either way, the beast proceeded boldly. There was no need of stealth whatsoever. Why should there be? The prey had carelessly run into the box canyon. No way out. I pushed my way further down the cave directly towards the bottlenecked opening below me.

Reactions are sometimes spawned simply out of our survival instincts more than anything else. My uncoordinated dive for the small opening below me where the steady flow of stones was pouring through proved that concept true. What was I doing? First of all, I had only bettered my distance between my adversary and me by about 50 feet. Secondly, I put myself in a potentially *worse* position if I were to get stuck only half way through the small opening. Oh well. What's done was done. And of course, according to my run of luck this past day, I *did* get stuck; not a very dignified position, but my dignity had already been lost somewhere between my bloody tumbles during the frantic ascent up the mountain and my ill-fated plunge towards the cave opening minutes earlier.

I couldn't stop now. Somehow, possible immanent death makes dignity finish a very distant second on our survival etiquette priority list. Minute by minute I was gaining a new level of dislike for the nature channel, but what little concentration I had left currently needed to be focused on the most immediate problem. I desperately needed to navigate a passage through the gap of draining stone if I was going to live more than a precious few more minutes. But today, fate had already assigned maximum difficulty to my every action.

Writhing back and forth sometimes moved me further through the opening, but ironically, depending on the movement of the rocks around me, the exact same gyrating movements would sometimes move me in the *opposite* direction; *closer* to the massive brute above me. It was an odd dance to be sure, and would have been comical, if not for the serious consequences of failure. The distance between the descending stalker and me was rapidly decreasing. Equally unsettling was the change in the creatures breathing as it gradually closed in on its prey; a sort of increased panting that comes from the thrill of conquest, *not* from fatigue. You could now see the confident glint in its eyes, an unearthly glow coming from two black holes set in a grotesquely contorted and misshapen face. *Cue camera…evisceration imminent.* Did I mention my hatred for the nature channel?

Not much time left now. I was dangerously close to my own emotional freeze frame. But then an odd thing happened. It started so quietly I didn't hear it at first. The voices I'd heard the evening before my final trek up the mountain returned. They were still garbled and unintelligible, but the volume had increased and was *continuing* to increase…dramatically. The sound is still hard to describe, but it reminded me of the time I had accidently set a book down on top of the T.V. remote volume button. As I walked away, the sound soon reached a blistering level that left me literally running for the remote, my ears ringing from the fever pitch of a crowd scene playing out on the screen; a wild cacophony of sound that oddly enough became more *indistinct* as the volume grew.

Back in my cascading rock graveyard, the reverberant voices echoed off the canyon walls and threatened to split the sides of the cave right open. I stopped writhing and put my hands over my ears. And interestingly enough, the creature stopped its progression towards me and seemed to cry out in pain. A mighty rushing wind then filled the empty space around me, and in the same moment, the surge of draining rocks pulled me through the small gap I had been desperately trying to pass through. My last conscious vision was that of the creature hunched over shrieking in anger and agony as the waterfall of stones sealed up the gap between me and certain death.

When I struck the newly formed pile of rocks on the surface of the trail below me, I reflexively rolled sideways to dodge the remaining flow of loose earth falling through the newly closed opening. Enough larger rocks must have finally congregated above me forming a plug that stopped the rockslide, a rockslide that nearly brought me into a close encounter of the permanently dead kind. On my back, panting from exertion, the voices were no more and a deafening silence filled the empty void surrounding me. It wasn't long before I became part of another empty void we call sleep. Too exhausted to move. Too bewildered to process the days events. Too utterly spent to remain conscious for even a minute longer, sleep overtook me as the silent voices faded off into the maniacal or celestial void from which they came. *One nature channel victim reprieved. For now.*

To this day I have no idea how long I was lost to the normal world of consciousness. What I *do* vaguely remember was a dreamy state where I was spectrally transported into a mist like the one that had surround me at the base of the mountain. I had entered a world of perpetual gray.

Amorphous shapes and indefinable forms seemed to blend together forming a tapestry of blurry multi-dimensional space surrounding me. The sensation was completely foreign to my experience - terrestrial replaced by ethereal, earthly giving way to the supernatural.

I had the strange premonition that this was the *real* reality behind or beyond the five senses of our mortal existence. These were principalities and powers of which I had no knowledge or experience. Was I dead? Though never having had an incidence of an 'out-of-body' experience, this is surely how it must feel, right? No. Not dead. This felt more like a vision. The life of matter and substance, devoid of ghostly haze, would surely once again intrude with its three dimensional blandness and I would exit this realm, whatever it was, sooner or later.

In my newly nebulous and presumably temporary world, the only variations of color came from passing shadows, some ominous, some serene. These ghostly images enveloped me and seemed to carry me randomly. Phantom images of blurred 'presences' who were either *intertwined with* or *part of* the hazy fog sluggishly transported me in various directions. Or was it various dimensions? The realization that I could "*will*" the various directions of movement didn't come to me until many days later. Unknown to me at this time was the fact that this panorama of the mystic realm would be a recurring phenomenon revealing things sorcerous or soothing, terrifying or tranquil, all dependent upon the direction of my drifting. For now everything presented itself as benign or *equally* good.

Eventually, unwanted consciousness rudely awakened a weary body that would have preferred a continued blissful and ignorant dreamy escape from earthly reality. I distinctly remember lifting my woozy head, rolling to my left, and unceremoniously vomiting a foul concoction of earth, blood, and bile from my mouth. My throat was burning from both physical exertion and the unfortunate "earth cocktail" I swallowed during my descent inside the cave. I nearly passed out again. Dizzy and disoriented, I at least managed to get my hands in front of my face as my grayed vision caused me to fall face first toward the hard surface of the trail. The face plant was narrowly averted in favor of more scrapes to elbows and forearms. An acceptable trade. As my vision cleared, I gave it one more shot. An unsteady rise to my knees brought up another wave of nausea but thankfully brought up nothing more.

Being a relatively young man with over average physical conditioning may have helped me up to this point, but my *current* appearance betrayed the person I had become; a mocking specter of what once was. The previously strong athlete had now turned into a bloody mess with multiple bruises and gashes that were covered in dried or drying blood. Not a pretty sight. Fragmented mental acuity was not far behind in the race for instability of the soul. Were someone to look into my eyes, it was likely they would see the vacuous dimming light that often accompanies those who had all but given up hope. I'd seen the look before in the eyes of the homeless city street dwellers; eyes filled with the hollowness of confusion and despair like twin heralds who once enacted cheerful dramas in the king's palace but were now relegated to only performing duets of doom and gloom in dark alleys. For me personally, it felt like both body and brain had absorbed a piece of the mystic grayness from the shrouded fog I traveled through before awakening on the cold cavern floor.

Since I am not usually one prone to melancholy, I was able to shame myself out of my despondent revelry by an unhealthy combination of grit and denial. Looking up to the ceiling, from which this current shell of a man emerged, revealed a well-sealed hole where there had once been a torrent of falling rock. One couldn't help but ponder a close call with death. Considering the small window of both time and confined space that narrowly dropped me into this lower cavern brought on an involuntary shudder. Reaching my hand out to the side wall of the spiraling downward trail provided some stability to shaking knees. Going back was not an option, especially considering what might be waiting on the other side. So with options shut behind me, the decision to move deeper into the mountain won by default.

Surprisingly, like the paths *outside* the mountain, this path was *also* well worn, as if hundreds if not thousands had used this route before my arrival. The walls inside the mountain were largely made out of obsidian and granite. Obsidian was an extrusive igneous rock formed out of lava flows, and ironically, this type of rock was both hard and brittle at the same time. I remembered from geology class that, because of its composition, it could be fractured relatively easily. Early cultures actually used this to their advantage by choosing this type of rock when fashioning their cutting tools and crude weapons.

But though the sinister blackness of the dark obsidian could itself be unsettling, it was the granite that bothered me most. The flecks of granite interspersed throughout the cavern were definitely jagged at one time judging by the pockets of this same stone imbedded in the cavern *walls*. But the portions of granite on the *trail itself* clearly showed a "wearing down" process that shouldn't have occurred without some sort of erosive foot traffic. Granite is actually known for its ability to *resist* abrasion, but this igneous rock had definitely been worn smooth by frequent travel. My mind wandered to the idea and ramifications of other travelers preceding me. It was an interesting thought, but I couldn't help thinking that, though other people may have shared this journey, it was doubtful their passage up to this point had been as eventful as mine.

The final disturbing quality of this mineral concoction surrounding me was that the obsidian portions of the walls were as smooth as glass, giving them a polished, mirror-like quality. Its natural color was a deep iridescent black and this dark coloration and shiny smoothness, broken up by alternating strata of dull granite, gave the obsidian sections of the cave walls an eerie reflective quality that often made you perceive movement that was not there. Indeed, often it was simply a trick of the mind as your own reflection appeared and disappeared as you walked past alternating sections of these two layers of rock; obsidian to granite…granite to obsidian…your reflection appearing and disappearing from the corner of your eye. Then of course the thought was: is it really your reflection or was it something from the other side looking in at you, quickly vanishing just before you fixed your gaze on the smooth wall?

I chided myself for ascribing unnatural characteristics to purely natural occurrences born out of simple geology. I had to stay focused in reality, not wallowing in perceived threats and boogiemen around every corner. In some ways my inbred human defense mechanism was already trying to convince me that perhaps my perceptions of snarling creatures, rockslides, mystical haze, and cave walls infused with phantom life were the result of some temporary insanity brought about by altitude, fatigue, and dehydration. I wasn't buying that one yet. I knew what I saw.

Ultimately, the beauty of this hollow cavity inside such a majestic mountain still called out to me, captivating my senses. Where there should have been stale air, there was a surprisingly fresh aroma not unlike cinnamon and oak leaves. Where there should have been darkness, there was a strange ambient light coming from pockets luminous algae growing throughout the vacant expanse just to the right of the path. It was hard to tell how far the drop off was, but the glow of the algae didn't dissipate until it revealed a fall that would certainly kill any mere mortal. Best to stay on the left side of the trail.

The fleeting thought that my plunge into this lower cavern *could* have propelled me right over this edge instead of onto the trail caused an involuntary shudder to pass through my body. But that potential disaster had not come to pass. Fate had *momentarily* cast her merciful gaze in my direction. First time in awhile. One in a row. A slowly returning clarity of mind helped to create an introspective analysis of my situation; this was the journey *planned* for, just not the method of *arrival* one would choose. Undiscovered mysteries *still* created curiosity and fascination. Exploration *still* held out hope, though hope had now been seasoned with the spice of caution. Ultimately, this was a place of intrigue and ominous threat, beauty and beast combined. Hopefully the beast was defeated for good leaving only the thrill of beauty and exploration ahead. It was time for my journey to continue.

Chapter 3 – The Disease of Denial

Water gently trickled down the left side of the trail walls, and to my surprise, with a little patience, the flow was sufficient to refill my canteen. That was the good news. The bad news: A misguided and disappointing glance at one of the mirror-like obsidian walls revealed a reflection that was less than impressive to say the least. So with a filled canteen now a reality, my bruised ego reenlisted the soldier of vanity to command the repair of an equally bruised and somewhat broken body.

The first order of bodily marshal law was to collect handfuls of water from the cave wall and wash off numerous patches of dried blood I had accumulated over the past few days. The seemingly simple task turned out to be tougher than first imagined and washing off the blood had the unwanted side effect of reopening some of the partially sealed wounds. Somewhat depressingly, I began to loose count of the cuts and scrapes revealed by the full body scrub. Luckily, none of the newly exposed lacerations were overly deep or showed even the most remote signs of infection. At least that was *one* less thing to worry about. Though pitifully insufficient, the slight body maintenance worked to lift my spirits a bit.

Equally invigorating was the thorough face scrub that removed an embarrassing amount of dirt and grime form my unshaven face. But drenching my face with cool water from the cavern wall awakened a voracious thirst that until now had only simmered just below the surface. I found myself drinking frantically like a scene from one of those old movies where the parched man accidently stumbles upon an oasis in the Sahara Desert. The frenzied guzzling sounds were embarrassing and undignified, but in times of severe deprivation, the body has a mind of its own and self-preservation tends to overrule any sense of tact. Emily Post and Julia Childs would not have been pleased.

Dowsing my face with water also caused an eerie sensation of sickly fear to return, creating an oily nauseous feeling in the pit of my stomach that threatened to recall the water I'd just ingested. At first, I wasn't sure where this fear came from, but then the remembrance slowly came to me. The last time I'd thrown liquid in my face, I was nearly blinded by a coagulation of dirt, blood, and canteen water as I raced toward the cave opening. The remembrance of the creature's heated breath and sticky saliva on my neck caused momentary panic. With an automated sense of horror, my body instinctively reacted by swinging around, hands in a defensive posture. But the perceived ogre behind me was nowhere to be seen. Between me, and the sheer drop off on the other side of the trail, there was only empty space. Only the green luminous algae was in view with its ever-present otherworldly glow dimly lighting the cavern walls. *Man…I'm losing it.*

With my back against the cool damp wall, I slid down into a crouched position. Simply sitting on the damp trail calmed my rattled nerves after a time and my thoughts gradually returned from imagined menace to concrete reality. One thing was sure: there was no way my sanity would hold out if I entertained thoughts of brooding beasts around every corner. Something had to give. It was time to move on. And not just physical movement was necessary; clear and logical mental assessments from a once rational mind needed to reassert themselves. Easier said than done. I don't remember how long I sat there.

During the next several days of downward travel, my mind wrestled with events of the recent past. Despite my vivid imagination, I am ultimately a sensible person; I know the dividing line where creative imagination can blossom into superstition and even madness. But trying to reconcile the difference between the rational elements of my journey and a menacing brute surrounded by ominous phantom grayness was beginning to give me a headache.

Perhaps that was the answer: the headaches. I *did* hit my head pretty hard when I fell through the opening into the lower cavern. Perhaps the blow was hard enough to cause a blackout. I had *thought* I fell into an exhausted sleep after falling into the lower cavern, but perhaps it was more than that. There's a fine line between sleep and unconsciousness. After all, both are positions of stasis where you are not only immobile but also mostly unresponsive, and yet certain parts of your brain remain stubbornly active. Most people know what its like to dream dreams that are not even *remotely* connected to logic. You perceive yourself driving a car on a dirt road and inexplicably you look down and discover the car has actually disappeared, replaced by a magic carpet which is now flying over a raging river - nonsense…non-sequiturs…nebulous notions of non-existent realities. Sleep and dreams can create these fictional tall tales of the mind; how much *more so* could a mind that has been trapped in an unconscious state?

I began to piece the scenario together. A trek up the mountain and the discovery of the cave had certainly been real, but perhaps some of the other things had been imagined during my state of unconsciousness while lying on the lower cavern floor. Concussions can cause memory loss, but could they create *new* memories that were not based in reality? I remembered years ago reading about scientific experiments where people could be *induced* into believing that something had occurred to them that hadn't really happened. Test subjects, for example, had been purposefully and deceitfully *convinced* that they were once lost in a shopping center, or that they had gone on a hot air balloon ride as a child.

Perhaps my own imagination coupled with the stress and exhaustion of the mountain assent had seared some false images into my mind that simply stayed with me when I regained consciousness. That *had* to be the answer: What was perceived as mystic grayness was probably just normal fog, present at the base of the final upward mountain trail and continuing to cloak the path all the way up to the cave. The beast? Well…an overactive imagination spawned out of too many movies and video games over the years no doubt. I must have hiked up the mountain, entered the cave tired and woozy from exertion and altitude, and then fell through the hole into the lower cavern while my unconscious state dreamed up the vicious creature and the menacing nature of the fog. It was beginning to all make sense.

I was growing a little tired of all this psychological introspection, and quite frankly, the mind doesn't like to dwell on uncomfortable facts or circumstances any more than a nun would enjoy hanging around a university frat party. So the pragmatist in me decided that the best course of action *right now* was to simply make the best of my situation. Beginning to feel like myself again, the descending path renewed its call and beckoned me forward as the thrill of exploration returned. After quite a few hobbling footsteps, muscles finally began to loosen up and stiffness gradually gave way to more relaxed mobility. This was all going to be okay.

They say hindsight is 20/20. For some reason I had conveniently forgotten that I heard the voices *before* ever reaching the base of the mountain. My mind had been crystal clear at that time. The voices occurring before my exposure to the menacing fog *preceded* receiving the blow to the head, and hearing phantom voices in the air around you is not something that can be explained with rational thought. I was not under any stress due to exertion or altitude at *those* times. A blow to the head did not cloud *those* memories; they were vivid recollections, as real to me now as they were then. Something else was in play here...something deceiving. Not sure why, but it seems that somewhere down deep, my self-willed decision to enter this mountain was irrevocable and despite the warning signs, the choice was sealed in my soul for reasons of which I am only now aware. Hindsight...oh how much grief could have been spared.

Nagging doubts about my *excuses* for the bizarre events of late still bothered me. Being a rational man made it hard to fully admit my apparent unconscious "reinventing" of circumstances. I mean, really? Was it that simple? My well-centered psyche had never deserted me before...but the blow to the head? The mental tennis match between competing possible versions of my story made me dizzy. Personal doubts aside, I nevertheless made decent downward progress into the mountain. But to where? If the wild events of the past few days were merely fabrications of an overactive unconscious mind, then perhaps the best course of action would be to retrace my steps back to the opening into the upper cavern. Perhaps with enough prodding, the rocks blocking the sealed entrance could be dislodged and I could simply climb back up, hike down the mountain, and be done with all this.

There was also the problem of rations. My backpack held quite a bit of food, mostly the prepackaged stuff that tasted only slightly better than the wrapper that surrounded it. But, as plentiful and compact as these consumables were, they couldn't last forever. The luminescent algae could itself be a possible food source, and contrary to what I learned in science class, the green glow they gave off was somehow bright enough to help other types of very small vegetation to appear. Most likely these small amounts of vegetation on the edges of the trail would prove to have some nutritional value as well.

The multiple years of wilderness hiking left me with survival skills well above the average person: I know that cave streams can often bring in aquatic organisms, sometimes even small fish right to your underground dinner table. Insects, worms, and sometimes salamanders are known to be fairly prevalent underground. Bats are not exactly my favorite treat, but they *are* a good source of protein in a pinch. *I can do this.* My pride was in play here, as well as an immense sense of curiosity about where this trail might lead.

Go deeper or get out? That was the bottom line. Though my mental chess match had stalemated, the inevitable conclusion came from how my life had been lived up to this point. *I'm not one who fails to finish what he started.* And as to this adventure? Well, the opportunity to fully indulge, to feel the exhilaration of discovery, even if it did involve some danger was too irresistible to ignore. Perhaps it was time to "man up" and prepare for *whatever* scenario played out down the trail. Brooding beast or breathtaking beauty, foreboding fog or stunning scenery, voices or vistas; it didn't matter, they would all make me feel *something*, and frankly my life was run mostly by various feelings and adventures. It would either be my salvation or my suicide. Fate would make its choice. Either way, in terms of the *immediate* future, it was time to bed down for the night. After all, only so much introspection could be tolerated in any given day.

There were several spots on the trail where the left wall receded backwards into a very small opening. These cavities were becoming larger as the trail sinuously wound its way further down into the mountain and they served as perfect spots for campsites because the moisture from the trail wall did not penetrate into the recesses of these inner caves. I suppose somewhere in my subconscious mind I instinctively realized that these were also more defensible positions, with only one entrance to guard instead of the two open directions of the footpath. For some reason, my mind could not yet completely let go the images of a fantasy beast that may or may not haunt this mountain.

Making camp was quick and uncomplicated; it was a well-worn ritual by now. But sleep did not come so easy. I couldn't shake the premonition of being watched by some maniacal collection of disembodied eyes, multiple spider-like eyes searching this rock fissure from every possible angle. When sleep finally *did* come, it was accompanied by the world of perpetual gray, with all its ghostly images enveloping me once again. The blurry multi-dimensional space surrounding me was of course unsettling, but at least not completely new. I had been through this before in my dreamy state of unconsciousness after falling into the lower cavern.

The phantom images within the fog had returned as well, playing their familiar cat-and-mouse game of hide and seek as they alternately appeared and disappeared just beyond my field of vision. The lazy feeling of floating through opaque nothingness was both liberating and disconcerting at the same time. The weightless sensation made my body feel like it lacked substance, as if the gray mist could pass right through me. Worse yet, the thought occurred to me that perhaps one of these phantom apparitions could move through me and take a bit of my soul on the way out. *Creepy.*

The voices were in this void as well, always on the periphery of my senses, and never detectable as fully recognizable speech. Like trying to pinpoint the direction of wind whispering through trees, any attempt to decipher meaning from these disembodied murmurs was immediately muddled by the nebulous and indefinable nature of the spoken words themselves; sentences thrown in a blender until the puree revealed *nothing* of their original meaning. At least not to me. The effect was a kind of static interference between blissfully ignorant dulled awareness and frustrated desires for objective reality; each one jealously claiming its own territory: White noise of the mind was the inevitable result. It was too tiring to figure out.

In general, it did seem that there were at least two forces at odds with *each other* and with their purposes for *me*. I felt variously pulled in different directions, though the draw was never beyond my will to resist. On the contrary, mild interest or even mere thoughts towards one rival adversary or the other, with no *deliberate* bodily movement on my part, would automatically shift my floating consciousness towards one of these two mystical adversaries.

This was a game of the mind but I was ultimately still in control, and with control came a certain level of comfort. Nonetheless, a decision needed to be made. One set of voices appealed to my sense of adventure and beckoned me towards a deeper immersion in the fog while the other voices seemed to encourage caution. My choice. It was an interesting stand off where I would eventually be judge and jury as to the final victor. One way felt safe but perhaps ended in boredom. The other one felt dangerous but might just contain the excitement and intrigue I so eagerly craved. The vague impression of tension *between* these two forces was one that suggested complete opposition. The opposing powers appeared to act as magnetic poles where one cannot survive in the presence of the other, where one actually *repels* the other if the distance between them deteriorates. And yet, here they both were, two stubborn rivals existing in the same gray mist, while at the same time not comingling their individual substance. Strange. As one who likes definitive answers to problems and questions set before him, my headache would probably be returning shortly.

Now it should be said that I'm no fool. True *life threatening* danger held no appeal for me. There were way too many things in life to live for. Arguably, most of those centered around my personal interests and immediate needs of adventure and self-fulfillment. But though danger and intrigue were appealing, a suicidal man I was not. I was weighing my choices carefully. My senses somehow perceived that the more threatening voices were making an appeal towards the sentiments of adventure I craved, while the more benign voices seemed to want to draw me back to the safety of the cave opening where I first entered the mountain. I tried to remain neutral, but in all honesty, I was beginning to side with the voices that promised excitement and perhaps *some* element of danger. That was, after all, a deeply embedded part of my nature. I was inherently a risk taker.

Eventually, the *gentle* voices, soothing though they were, began to be an irritant, constantly espousing a condescending mantra of peace and security that ultimately threatened my desire for exploration. The more *malignant* utterances on the other hand, though certainly conveying an unrelenting foreboding of danger, promised excitement and excursions into the unknown. *That's* the direction I was leaning. I don't very much like it when my independence is hindered, and though I was still free to choose my direction within this mystic cloud, the *gentle* voices were, in many ways, unsuccessfully tugging at a part of my conscience that had already been buried years ago. Certain parts of my heart felt like dead tissue, seared with a hot iron, gradually moving beyond feeling. It was these portions of my heart that the gentle voices most concentrated on, but it wasn't working. Life was too short to play it safe all the time. I've always admired those people who were champions of their own destiny, those who willfully went against the accepted norms of other people around them and lived life according to the dictates of their *own* heart. Tradition be damned.

Lost in revelry, the subtle change in the surrounding atmosphere had eluded me. In the air above me, small pools of fog began to form that were *darker* than the surrounding vapor. The entire enveloping mist began to crackle with increasing energy, as each water molecule became a conduit for some unearthly electric current. Tendrils of light flashed overhead connecting one amorphous synapse of darker fog to another. At one point, the whole encircling gray mist enveloping me darkened, and the volume of the voices steadily increased. The tone of unintelligible competing speech also took on a more agitated quality. Something was stirring these two foes into action and confrontation seemed inevitable. And here I was, right in the middle of what seemed to be an age-old feud; caught in a battle I didn't even understand.

Then suddenly, a grotesquely withered hand shot out of the ethereal ashen cloud, latching onto my arm as it momentarily pulled me towards the direction of the malevolent voices. As if in retaliation, a waiflike vapor of white smoke wrapped around my midsection and pulled me in the *opposite* direction. The sense of *touch* was something entirely new in this arena of translucent haze and shadows, and it startled me deeply. The truth be told, it sent a spike of fear snaking all the way through my chest and down into my now shaking lower limbs. This dramatic new occurrence gave the slogan "reach out and touch someone" a much more sinister and disturbing meaning than the phone company ever intended.

Fortunately, both combatants released their grip rather quickly, the adversarial magnetic poles perhaps pushing each other away in equal revulsion one to another. But the resulting shock and fear left me more than a bit unsteady. The unwelcome intrusion of physical touch had brought a new and more menacing feeling to this formally dreamy landscape. Also, it didn't help that the air surrounding me was still charged with the same malicious energy that had spawned the intruders in the first place. The dark pools of fog *continued* to loom ominously above me. The threatening airspace that surrounded me in this fantasy realm had become thick, oily, and oppressive.

My only thought now was one of escape. I desperately needed time to collect my thoughts, but the illusion of control I felt earlier was shattered when I realized I had no say as to when I entered or exited this realm. I could only choose my direction once inside it. And even *that* limited idea of directional control was now becoming suspect because both rivals had been pulling me against my will *simultaneously*. What if one side or the other won out instead of repelling each other? My final decision on either of the two directional possibilities had still been somewhat in limbo. But what if one adversary had pulled me unwillingly into oblivion? Morbid thoughts ran through the corridors of my imagination. At this point, I had no interest in supporting either side of this ethereal turf war.

Then something interesting happened. I noticed that as my mind began to center on the fact that *both* these adversaries needed to be avoided, the angry grayness surrounding me began to soften a bit. Dark colors began to give way to lighter hues and the electricity in the atmosphere was starting to dissipate slowly. My rapid heart rate, on the other hand, left me with the now all-to-familiar feeling of that trapped animal on the nature channel again. Which is worse: *physical* evisceration, or *mental* evisceration? And perhaps this mystic grayness promised both - *a "two for one" deal: lose both mind and body in one sitting…no coupon needed…inquire within.* No thanks.

Suddenly and unceremoniously I found myself outside the gray spectral prison as quickly and easily as I had entered. The coolness of the damp cave wafted over my conscious mind and the soothing sound of water methodically dropping from the cavern walls helped signal my welcome return to physical reality. The slightly chilled rocks and dirt that provided the only available mattress for my tired bones, now ironically felt like a warm heating blanket compared to the cold stark fear found in the land of mist. Still shaken and immobile, my heart rate gradually returned to normal and there seemed to be no physical reminders of the oppressive shadow land other than the oily sweat that is often associated with nightmares.

Laying there motionless and trying to regain some sense of composure was the order of the day. Or was it the order of the night? In the recesses of the mountain, with only the luminosity of the algae to provide ambient light, it was hard to keep track of normal life cycles such as mornings and evenings, breakfast times and dinner times, waking times and sleeping times. I had no way of knowing how long I was asleep and how long I was trapped in the alternate spectral dimension. There was also the distressing fear that sleep for me would *now* always mean a return to the ghostly civil war between battling principalities and powers beyond my comprehension. That would certainly be unacceptable. I had been rudely separated from my wristwatch during my tumultuous rocky ride through the upper cavern, so with no reference point, time seemed suspended, and the ever-consistent monotony of sameness threatened to create sensory deprivation.

In school they taught us that there had been studies in the 1950's where people, often university graduate students, were put into isolation rooms, deprived of all human contact and sensory input. Not exactly the "politically correct" experiment one could get away with nowadays. But believe it or not, back in *that* time, a guaranteed $20 per day got no shortage of volunteers. The scientists had hoped to study them for 6 weeks, but to their surprise, nearly *none* of the subjects could last more than a few days. Not even *one* could last for a week. After days in isolation, the subjects were unable to concentrate for any length of time. With many, their mental faculties became impaired to the point where they experienced extreme restlessness and hallucinations. Temporarily after their release from isolation, grade school tests on arithmetic proved too difficult for them, and even the ability to deal emotionally and rationally with others had deteriorated to a substantial degree. It made me wonder about the wisdom of putting criminals, obviously *already* social misfits to one degree or another, in solitary confinement for long periods of time.

But this mountain wasn't a prison and it certainly *did* provide sensory input, albeit some of which I could have done without. In some ways it *was* solitary confinement, but it was still an adventurous choice made by a rational individual who wanted to get the most out of life. That being said, the absence of all human contact was beginning to weigh on me, even though in most ways I tended to be a loner. Human contact was good for social reasons, but not ultimately necessary in my book. Certainly there were the wonderful moments of female companionship, hard to ignore the benefits of that, but we're *all* ultimately here on earth by ourselves, and left to our own devices, whether good or bad. We're born and immediately whisked away into the isolation of maternity ward cribs, and when we die, that will be the *final* sensory deprivation and isolation as you are forced to *individually* stare death in the face, no matter how many family members or friends may surround you. Might as well enjoy the time while you have it. I wanted to *find* my life before I *lose* it. I often wished that my morbid view of life were not so, but literally, *for the life of me*, I couldn't see any way out of our mortal limitations and suffering. *Boy I'm a cheery guy.*

My wistful desire for the briefest of human contact soon turned into a "*be careful what you wish for*" moment as the periphery of my vision detected something running by the mouth of my rocky bedroom grotto. It was silent and quick. It also awakened in me the alarming notion that, if there *were* other beings down here in this mountain, they undoubtedly had been here longer, knew the terrain far better, and if there intentions were less than honorable, I just might be in some real danger. Here we go again.

Chapter 4 – The First Contact

Shaken out of my gloomy revelry by the realization that some-*one* or some-*thing* was disturbingly close by, I quietly stood up and inched my way up to the trail just outside my sleeping chamber. In a rare moment of good fortune of late, I found a fairly hefty stick that was leaning against the cave wall and gladly carried it with me for defense. Earlier, the shadowy figure had run from right to left in my peripheral vision which meant it was, moving past the entrance and descending further down into the mountain. But the figure had been so fast and light on its feet, it was hard if not impossible to tell whether it had simply continued running down the trail, or stopped just on the other side of the opening where I had bedded down for the night. Well…I had *presumed* it was night anyway. I actually had no knowledge of what day this was, let alone what hour of the day it was.

It was a disturbing thought that whatever was out on the trail could have been watching me for quite some time as I unconsciously battled the phantoms within the gray mist. It was even *more* disturbing to wonder if one of the more menacing creatures from the spectral realm had followed me out into the conscious and material world of this cave. Perhaps I was the conduit by which one of these spirit creatures finally gained freedom from its mystical prison, and now freed form the counterbalancing force of its nemesis, could freely wreak havoc on the unsuspecting people who would visit this mountain. Starting with me.

After moving nearly half way to the trail outside my grotto, I began to hear some noise to the left of the entrance. Or was it my imagination? Either way, I steeled myself for the worst. The previously soothing sound of water dripping onto the cavern floor was now an unwanted distraction, blocking any attempts to listen carefully for the possible intruder. I cautiously pressed on further. Eventually the sounds *did* return: scraping noises like claws dragging across the rock wall of the trail. This brought back memories of something I'd already convinced myself never happened in the upper cavern. People stressed by ugly realities often mentally sail into the bay of illusion and denial for safe harbor. For sanity's sake, I desperately needed my reality-ship to stay dry docked in self-delusional calm waters.

At least there was no foul stench this time. Nervous sweat began to trickle down the sides of my face. Edging closer to the trail revealed more scraping noises but when my steps drifted carelessly onto some loose gravel, stealth was lost, and the outside noises abruptly stopped. At this point it became a silent and tense waiting game, each combatant hesitating for the other to make the first move. After several minutes I broke the stalemate. With more attention paid to my footing this time, I moved forward. The entrance was almost within reach, so I slowed my pace to a crawl. But it was too late. I was taken completely by surprise as the intruder charged straight into the opening and right over the top of me, causing us both to fall clumsily onto the floor.

He seemed as shocked as me, which was probably a good sign. This was *not* the moment a vicious stalker or shadow-world menace had carefully planned for his deadly attack. It was more like the moment where a completely preoccupied and unaware man was taken by surprise, having as little knowledge of me as I had of him. And it was indeed a *man*. This both surprised me and put me slightly at ease since the possibility of something far more creature-like and deadly had been plaguing my thoughts. The jury was still out as to his intentions, but he seemed just as nervous as me, glancing at my crude weapon which had been knocked to the ground, still within my reach if need be.

He was older than me, much older in fact, but he seemed in great shape for his age with the kind of body that looked thin and wiry, small but with tightly trimmed muscles. I'd learned from my early fighting days that it was not always the *big* guys you had to worry about, it was often the *smaller* ones who were quick and could bounce back from a punch. These guys were often tough as nails and more than worthy adversaries. This guy didn't appear overtly hostile, but I wasn't about to let my guard down. We both put some space between our previously tangled bodies and began to make eye contact, sizing each other up. At least that's what I thought, until closer evaluation put my estimations in conflict with reality.

The eye contact, which I assumed to be mutual, was definitely in question. He seemed to stare straight through me, as if I wasn't there. It was so disconcerting that I actually took a chance with a quick backward glance in case some other villainous entity was sneaking up behind me. Thankfully that was not the case. But to my surprise, when I moved to face him again, he was already turning around to leave. Not so much as a word. I reflexively reached out to grab him but was astonished to watch my hand pass directly through the top of his shoulder and out the right side of his arm. *Now that's not something you see every day.* But this was no ghost. He had weight, substance, girth…I could see the hard outlines of his body. He was real, and human. He had also completely knocked me flat on my backside only mere seconds ago. No ghost. Something else was in play here.

I followed after him but he seemed oblivious to my presence. I called after him, but if he heard it, he made not the slightest indication at all. I was completely off his radar. Still, this was the only human contact I'd had in a long time and I felt compelled to shadow this mystery man and figure out his story, perhaps gain more information concerning what this mountain was all about. My curious stalking of this poor old fellow took me out onto the trail where my unaware companion picked up a small blade of some sort and continued his work digging into the side of the trail wall. These were the same scraping noises I had heard before his unwelcome dash right over the top of me minutes earlier. I edged closer to him to get a good look at what the old man had found.

Inset into the wall was a bright green gem, probably some kind of emerald or garnet. We used to call the garnets "green gooseberries" in geology class, but they were still considered a semi-precious stone; just not as valuable as some other gems. If it was an emerald, then you were staring right into the face of some serious cash. Either way, the old man had made a worthy find. His hand meticulously worked the chisel around the periphery of the stone, carefully removing the surrounding rock that held the gem captive in the wall. The intensity of his concentration bordered on obsession, as were some of his more frantic attempts to free the imprisoned stone from its earthen prison. In his fanaticism, he occasionally emitted small noises of frustration; a mumbled expletive, a nervous pleading whimper, or agitated snarl. This man was serious about his work. Too serious.

37

A glance towards his feet revealed a small bag filled with other precious stones in a vast array of colors: red, yellow, blue, green, purple…rubies, sapphires, amethyst, topaz; a rainbow of gems in a bag. Some of the jewels in his possession would have made a museum curator drool with envy, and looking at the sheer number of his collection betrayed the fact that the old guy must have been at this for quite a while. It would have surely taken countless hours and effort just to *find* all these gems, let alone harvest them from the greedy walls that held them incarcerated so tightly. I found myself admiring the wealth lying mere feet in front of my eyes. I'd be a liar if I didn't admit that my thoughts fleetingly took a stroll down the dark street of jealousy and ended in a cul-de-sac of possible assault and thievery.

Of course assault wasn't a realistic option given the fact that back in the side cave, I couldn't even *touch* the man. But thievery? Perhaps tailing this guy could fulfill more than just my curiosity. Surely there was a way to collect some of the profits that this mountain had to offer. The seed of desire was firmly planted. It just needed to give birth to action and acquisition. It would be unfortunate to end my journey without some of the crystal treasure resting right in front of me. There must certainly be enough to go around. Patience would provide possibility. Perseverance would provide pay-off.

As he continued to work on the wall, singularity of focus was rapidly turning his efforts into mild hysteria. He occasionally paused his work only to jump backwards, staring at the jewel with eyes full of covetous malice, as if the prized mineral had a mind of its own and was contentiously battling against him in order to stay imbedded in the cave wall. Usually after these bouts of manic repose, he would attack the wall surrounding the gem with a violent frenzy that bordered on, if not embraced, madness, hacking and slashing at the wall with a sickly combination of panic, frustration, and excitement. Interestingly enough, during all his neurotic assaults, he was careful not to damage the gem itself. In his mind, that would have surely been idolatrous, a sacrilegious act of treason against his own hearts desire.

After awhile, I sank down and sat on the trail, weary of watching this obsessive oscillation between frenzied assault and loving devotion towards his prize. But not much longer after I gave up hope on his immediate success, the frantic chiseling stopped. Glancing over at the man *now* revealed a face that shone with the cherub-like purity of devotion, admiration, and worship. The possessive suitor had gained his bride, and she was indeed beautiful. He began caressing the stone with gentle touches as the jewel returned the favor by reflecting its radiance deep into his sunken eye sockets. This was love at first sight. The older gems in his bag had most certainly now been cursed with lower status, as this new mineral maiden became the king's latest lustful conquest.

The old man's reverential love-struck demeanor was just as disturbing as his earlier maniacal and violent efforts to free the stone from the wall of the trail. *Both* behaviors seemed uncomfortably inappropriate to the situation at hand. Enamored with his new beauty, his body swayed back and forth in a trance-like dance of infatuated possession. If eyes really were the windows into the soul, then the vacant blackness found in his betrayed a hollowness of misguided and demented devoutness bordering on fanatical religious zeal. Eventually the glowing embers of amorous attraction began to fade and he once again became nervous and agitated.

He began casting worried glances at the bag lying near his feet, apparently realizing that he must *eventually* put his new concubine to rest within the harem of older jewels. This realization seemed to anger him and his agitated state brought me to my feet, fearful that he might lash out at whomever was closest. That would be me of course. The change in attitude was unexpectedly sudden. He roughly grabbed the bag and thrust the glittering gem inside with a rage totally foreign to his behavior only seconds before. He also began to let out a low-pitched growl that quietly reverberated across the walls of the cavern. The mountain seemed to be singing in tune with his madness. As the pitch of his howl started to rise, I lowered my stance into a defensive posture. But the immanent attack never happened. He was still oblivious to my presence.

Instead of assault, he quickly turned around and headed further down the trail, deeper into the mountain. I weighed my choices, but since there was no overriding reason to stay on this upper part of the trail, I went back to my grotto, grabbed my backpack, and headed after him. Keeping up was actually harder than my pride was willing to admit. For an old man he was incredibly agile and quick. Most of my aches and pains from the early parts of my adventure had passed, but now my body was being tested for endurance. The alternating reflections between the obsidian and granite portions of the walls gave the impression of multiple watchers running alongside us in this house of stone mirrors. The man rudely remained unaware of both me and my efforts to keep up as he spritely navigated over and around various rock outcroppings. Easy for him to do. He knew the territory well. It made me wonder how many years he'd spent scouring this mountain for treasure.

For me it was a bit unnerving moving so quickly and recklessly over terrain that was foreign to me. Unlike the man, I was *unaware* of what lay around every bend in the path. It was a little like the folly of running full speed into an unfamiliar dark room, not knowing where any of the furniture might be placed. Not so smart. Some sections of the trail contained loose gravel, and twice I nearly lost my balance. But I dared not slow down because already there were times when the marathon man disappeared from my forward vision. Rounding one corner, I carelessly ran into a stone ledge that jutted out from the cave wall. This gave me a substantial gash in the left side of my ribcage and it also knocked me dangerously close to the sheer drop off on the right side of the trail. My blood pressure rose quite a few notches as I watched dirt from the path fly outward into the abyss. The shower of dust backlit by the luminous green algae *could* have been my last curtain call in this drama we call life.

Well in front of me now, the man's legs continued to pump furiously and relentlessly. This guy was driven. Luckily, the crooked path had given way to a substantial straight away, so it was at least easier to keep him in my sights. But it was still hard to keep up. Finally, when I was sure that he would leave me in the dust, pitifully nursing my wounded pride for being defeated by this aged madman, he pulled into a side cavern not much different from the chamber I'd slept in further up the trail. I slowed my pace and walked towards the opening. To my surprise, walking inside revealed a large cavity filled with extravagant colors that nearly blinded the eyes.

Lining the entire periphery of his cave were torches that cast light into every nook and cranny of the living space. These torches also revealed and amplified the source of brilliant color that engulfed the senses like a luminescent blanket. Nearly every square foot of space was littered with the same kind of jewels I'd seen in his small satchel. He was a hoarder all right, but not the kind who kept old newspapers and empty cat food cans. No, this was quite different to say the least. Strands of bright stones draped across the ceiling, some dangling from the roof of the cave like streamers. The floor was also lined with a sea of gems whose tide had permanently parted in certain spots to provide walkways to and from different areas of his home. At various intervals, pedestals had been erected, each holding a single but particularly magnificent crystal. The pedestals looked like the altars you might find in an ancient Mayan temple. In reverential fashion, small benches had been constructed so you could sit right in front of each sacred platform, paying homage to the featured jewel. This guy was serious about his devotional mineral worship.

I stood there in stunned silence trying to take it all in, but the sheer immensity of the scene was overwhelming. The value of the riches in this room was beyond belief. It reminded me of those childhood stories in children's books involving buried treasure: kids at the beach building a sand castle and discovering hundreds of gold bars hidden in the sand, children stumbling upon an ancient tomb filled with magical and priceless trinkets formerly belonging to a long lost Pharaoh, treasure chests found on a mysterious sinking island. All the stuff of kid's novels. But this cave was *real*. This was truly the stuff dreams were made of. *And some people would kill for.*

The attraction of the gems was hypnotic, the shining colors wrapping around you, the angular surfaces of each stone radiating various hues of pigmented light outward in multiple directions until the warm glow within the cavern threatened to envelop you in an aberrant fusion of mineral and flesh until the two became inseparable. Entranced by the sheer magnetic power of the stones, I found myself swaying back and forth slightly; an intoxicating dizziness began to gray the periphery of my senses.

In all my preoccupation with the surrounding palace of precious stones, I had lost track of the prince who ruled it all. My thoughts had returned to jealous contemplations concerning the false equity our world often exhibited. This guy had more wealth than most people could even imagine, let alone possess. I scanned the cave to see what the owner of millionaire manor was up to, wondering what sort of mood he would be in given the fact that he was resting amid treasures that could assure comfort for multiple people, for multiple lifetimes.

It was hard to tear myself away from the spellbinding seductive colors, but I finally saw the old man near the back of the cave kneeling down in front of one of his stone altars. I could see him reach into his bag and pull out the emerald he had just recently freed from the walls of the upper trail. He treated it with the typical reverential attention due a worthy relic of such exquisite splendor. This was the *last* empty altar in the cave and it would soon house one of the most beautiful gems in his collection, a collection that was now presumably complete. Judging by his earlier psychotic displays of conflicting behaviors and mood-swings, I prepared myself to witness some sort of awkward and disproportionate celebration.

I had already seen this man go through so many opposing and contradictory dispositions during the short time we spent together. This guy seemed completely out of control. In fact, he often appeared to be driven by something *other* than himself. Or perhaps he was simply at the mercy of damaged mental faculties beyond repair due to his obsessive quest for the wealth this mountain had to offer. Perhaps both. It seemed that I'd already witnessed the entire gamut of emotions he could enact, but he surprisingly allowed yet another actor onto his behavioral stage. This new player could be seen as I neared the back of the cave and was once again able to clearly see his features.

This should have been a moment of rejoicing due to his recently completed gem collection. So I was astonished to see that his face had taken on the dark appearance, not of anger, but of one who had lost all hope. His countenance certainly made no sense given the privileged position enjoyed by this wealthy hermit. Maybe the obsessive drive to *acquire* had dulled his capacity to *enjoy* what he already had. Perhaps in a brief moment of rational clarity, he realized the mountain had possessively seduced him at the terrible cost of his very soul. As well as he knew this mountain, maybe the mountain knew *him* better still, and held him in its sway, a captive within jeweled prison walls.

If that was the source of his melancholy, then it was obvious that he had allowed this mountain to turn him in to a pathetic puppet. Severe depression was now playing its mournful tune across the strings of this poor emotionally distraught marionette. But psychosis is for the weak. I was sure that possessing such wealth would not affect me in the way it had him. In fact, if this wealth had lost its luster, all the more reason I should relieve him of some of it. After all, I'm not so sure that wasn't one of the things on my mind as I chased him down the trail to this spot.

I paced back and forth in continued anonymity even though I was mere feet from the old man. His body stooped awkwardly forward, as if some force had momentarily let go of the strings that normally enlivened this pitiful puppet. His stoic stillness made him look more like a mannequin than a man. The age lines in his face seemed to deepen and already sunken eyes threatened to disappear altogether within his bony skull. I weighed my options. It seemed ridiculous to leave this potential wealth behind. The old man had obviously made his home in this mountain. He was a permanent resident. I, on the other hand, had every intention of leaving one day. A mere few of these precious gems would keep me set for life in the outside world.

The mannequin-man still leaned inelegantly forward, as if in a despondent freeze frame. Why should I not partake of the spoils before my eyes? Why should the value of this treasure be left uncollected? Theses gems, worth a king's ransom, needed to be *traded in* to bring the owner any real profit. They weren't doing anybody any good sitting inside this mountain. The inevitable choice was made. This poor fellow couldn't even see me anyway. The once intense and frenzied man had been turned into a miserable plastic statue. Some sort of haunting and debilitating grief had turned his once lively persona into a frozen caricature of futility. *Not my problem.*

I backtracked to the middle of the cave and approached one of the stone altars. This particular pedestal held a unique ruby, the likes of which I'd only seen in museums. The stone had a bold crimson shade that was stunning, drawing you into its essence as naturally as water is lured into thirsty dry ground. I felt the pull of this gem. It conversed through an unspoken mesmerizing allure of transcendent and mysterious beauty. If I was going to start my own small collection, I could think of no better place to begin. A glance back at the hermit only revealed the same stillness as before. Perhaps the sinister puppeteer had *permanently* cut the strings, leaving his toy to dangle uselessly in the back of this surreal funhouse.

The enflamed bloodshot hue of the ruby was menacing and beautiful at the same time. I had the vague impression that it was dangerous in some way, but that only increased its appeal. Flames from the torches pirouetted back and forth in a choreographed ballet of light with the gentle crackle from their fires adding the appropriate musical accompaniment to the dance. Flickers of color from the numerous gems swayed seductively against the walls of the cavern. Dizziness began to create a sense of vertigo and it felt as if I could simply fall forward into the reflective pool of this captivating gem. I reached out and took the beauty into my hands, but experienced none of the rapture I'd expected. Instead, my revelry was shattered by a piercing scream coming from the back of the cave.

The once despondent and silent statue of a man had been reanimated and was rushing upon his prey. I could literally feel the seething hatred gushing towards me like the heat wave that radiates outward from an explosive blast. The eye contact was *real* this time. No doubt. He could see me now. For some reason, my intrusion into his world, the world *he* cared about, *his* private world of mammon, had awakened and alerted him, creating a jealous and bitter awareness of my presence. Potential loss of even the smallest part of his kingdom had resurrected the man, jarring him from his despairing comatose state and creating a ferocious rage that bordered on possession.

I didn't have much time to react, but my mind still processed some of the details. The man: running, bloodshot eyes, face contorted into equal parts of fury, indignation and vile hatred. Then there was me: just now emerging from my blissful near union with the ruby, in a dreamy state that dangerously contradicted my need to focus on the serious peril of the moment, unarmed, vulnerable, dumbly waiting for the first blows to land. The threat was real and the menace arrived in short order. It ironically reminded me of when I first met this fellow as he bowled me over unknowingly inside *my* cave. But this time was certainly different. The first time was innocent. He could accidentally touch me but couldn't see me because I was of no consequence to his world. Now that I *was* worthy of his attention, for all the wrong reasons no doubt, our meeting was going to be drastically different; it was to be conducted, from his end at least, with malice and with definite designs towards great bodily harm.

So we replayed the same dance from our first meeting as he charged into my left side knocking me to the cavern floor. Trying desperately to protect myself was difficult; he kept the blows raining down on me like an unholy hailstorm. I don't ever remember a time where such calm introspective revelry was exchanged for abject sheer terror on such short notice. This possessed man who now seemed to have inhuman strength was beating me, and beating me mercilessly. At some point, he decided that fists weren't enough to efficiently punish his trespasser, so he reached for a soccer ball sized rock to do his bidding. Thankfully, by the time he raised it over his head, I had come fully to my senses and was able to move out of the way just in time as the rock smashed right down on the spot where my woozy head had once lain. Bits of rock shattered off the stone and stung my face like small buckshot.

I remember the sensation of slick wetness pouring down my left cheek; blood that would simply add one more color to this already colorful room. Even though I had avoided what would have certainly been a deathblow, the *immediate* problem was that the enraged man was still on top of me, still holding his weapon of choice. He raised the rock and prepared to correct his earlier missed opportunity. My opportunities, on the other hand, were running out quickly. Before he could get the rock up to cranium smashing height, I gathered all my strength and stuck the crazed attacker directly on the left temple. The blow served its purpose, knocking him off my chest and onto the cavern floor. Thankfully the weapon had been dislodged from his hands but this assailant was not done with his victim.

He threw himself at me with wild abandon; scratching and clawing like a rabid mountain lion. Indeed, this wildcat managed to extract quite a bit more blood from my arms as I lamely tried to fend of his frenzied attacks. It's amazing how strong vanity is, because I do remember being glad that my face was, so far, untouched by this madman. *His* face, however, had lost all of its humanity; spitting, snarling, and unsettling squealing noises were sounding in a disturbing symphony of madness as his eyes seemed to have a sadistic glow inside hollow haunted sockets. His unearthly appearance sent a shard of fear into my heart as it first dawned on me that getting away just might be impossible. Frantic blows continued. Desperate attempts at defense barely kept the scales of the fight leveled.

Somewhere between brutal blows and skin scraping attacks, I realized that I still held the ruby in my hand. It was odd how, even in all the turmoil, I'd managed to retain possession of the stone. Right now, its value to me was not in the monetary realm, but in the practical. In a brief pause between his multiple attacks I was able to wind up and hurl the stone directly at his face. As fate gently smiled upon me, the stone found its mark and hit him squarely between the eyes, actually bouncing back towards and behind me. Blood gushed from his newly opened wound and mingled with the substantial quantity of mine that had already been spilled onto the cavern floor. He dropped back stunned, lifting his hand to examine the fountain of blood pouring from his nose.

The shock value of my attack was sure to be short-lived so I braced myself for the next attack, at least feeling *slightly* more comfortable as I regrouped and set myself into a more coherent defense posture. But the man's countenance suddenly changed as quickly as you could flip a light switch. He still charged forward, but directly past me. It took me a few moments to realize what was happening. He was moving behind me to pick up the ruby. Once in his possession, all the remaining profane wind was out of his sails and he calmly walked towards the vacant pedestal. With loving adoration, he placed the jewel back in its original position and then sat on the bench near it, idly gazing at its luster.

As for me, now that my self-preservation instincts had enjoyed the briefest of repose, I began to amass my own sense of rage. I wanted to *kill* this psychopath. Some people were just not worth the space they devoured on this planet, and this guy was now at the top of my world-exiting list. If he thought he could get away with his vicious attack and then just go back to business as usual, then he was about to get a rude awakening. Actually it wouldn't be an *awakening* of any sort. His days of being awake were coming to an end. It was time to punch this guy's celestial time card. I approached him from behind, summoned all the strength left in my battered arms, and then chose the best spot of my lethal attack. With a mighty swing I aimed for the side of his neck. A killing blow for sure.

Well, it should have been. But to my embarrassment and surprise, my hand once again simply passed through one side of his body and out the other. The force of my efforts nearly caused me to fall over. This was crazy. I was able to touch him *earlier*. The punch to his temple and the blood streaming down his face was proof of that. But now, some strange concoction of mystical events, brewing deep inside this tortured man's soul had caused him to once again be untouched by the forces that surrounded him. He had retreated back into his own little world. That did me no good. I *still* wanted to kill him. My breathing was elevated, as was my heart rate. But now, it was not so much because of the rigors of the fight; it was because of the hatred and rage that burned inside me. I tried one more assault - a backhand to the face. Nothing happened. This physical encounter was finished. The emotion of unfulfilled revenge lingered within me, a dark ally; one who eagerly *approved* of assassination of those who challenged me. I was not ready to dismiss my dark friend of vengeance just yet.

I stood there for quite awhile, watching this pathetic man as he blankly stared at the ruby. I could find no place in my heart for sympathy. Blood still poured from multiple cuts on my arms and bruises were already starting to form over a substantial portion of my body. Torches still burned and gems still glittered, but right now, I could only find room in my heart for retaliation. I remember reading somewhere that hope deferred makes the heart sick. If that was true, then *revenge* deferred made the heart even sicker. Unfulfilled revenge kills a body like cancer, from the inside out, but the host clings to the malignant emotion as tightly as a shipwrecked man clings to driftwood at sea. Finally, after realizing that retribution would be absolutely *impossible*, I gathered my belongings, and moved my beaten and bloodied body back towards the trail. Perhaps there would be a time when we would meet again. And if he were to ever come out of his self-absorbed stupor in my presence, I would not miss the opportunity to end his miserable life.

Chapter 5 – The Crooked Path

Back out onto the trail, this wearied body resumed the downward spiral toward whatever encounter might be next in this bizarre mountain. Hopefully the next experience would be better than the last one. Of course, that wouldn't take much. The straps on my backpack dug uncomfortably into the fresh cuts the old man had so brutally given me as I struggled underneath him on the cavern floor. This was quite the setback. The physical healing and restoration I had experienced after my first plunge into the lower cavern had now basically been erased by one psychotic lunatic. *Weeks* of progress lost. Aching limbs, painful wounds, and multiple streams of blood - all the unwelcome visitors had returned.

The damage to my psyche was profound as well. Various torrents of pain and anguish had flowed through the streambed of my past life, eroding the outer banks and edges of my crumbling spirit. The newly found corrosive presence of anger and rage toward the old gem collector only served to create a further dull hollowness in my soul. That void was then filled with an unhealthy fixation upon unfulfilled revenge, which in turn, made it difficult to concentrate on things of the moment. It was hard to let thoughts of the brutal attack go. I once heard that an unforgiving spirit is a poison that the *victim* drinks, foolishly expecting it to hurt his *attacker*. Perhaps that was true, but my mind, uncontrollably working like an unending tape loop, kept rewinding back into the darkness of murderous thoughts.

This mountain was taking its toll. Each minute of walking slowly intensified the ugly reality that my body was, once again, broken. But the old man's attack had also reawakened some parts of my broken spirit as well. Memories that I'd carefully kept buried for years began to resurface. As a youth, I was no stranger to hardship or abuse. My father unfortunately trained me very well in those two aberrant areas of dysfunctional family life. Sometimes it felt as if that were the *only* training I received at home. *Here son, learn how to dodge my fists…defend yourself like a man (of course that was hard to do as a child when you weren't a man yet).* When I was young, walking the fine line between submission and self preservation was more like trying to traverse an uncharted minefield, never knowing what the next step would bring, where success simply meant another tedious day of navigating the same hazardous terrain all over again.

Though many of my friends hated school, for *me*, school was a welcome refuge. It was a sanctuary where I could briefly retreat into exploring a world that was quite different than the one I knew at home. Here, there was beauty to be found in books. A welcome sense of tranquility often seemed to radiate from written words that painted pictures of hope. Stories frequently spoke of people who were somehow able to conquer the odds stacked against them. These were things I desperately needed to hear. Science classes also opened up the imagination by offering up the intricacies of an immeasurable world found well beyond the confines of my dismal family life. In a universe as vast as ours, perhaps life *could* be profound and meaningful. In what way, I wasn't sure, but sometimes just the thought was enough. Yes, school was a welcome shelter from dark reality, but it ultimately only postponed the inevitable. Arriving home at the end of the day always forced me to reluctantly resume my pursuit of an advanced degree in the horrifying homeschool of hard knocks.

The fury I saw in the eyes of the demented gem collector had brought back memories of the many one-sided domestic fights of my childhood. These family battles were certainly never as intense as the brawl I'd just finished, but my dad *did* win the prize for frequency. He dispensed beatings with disturbing regularity. In rare moments when alcohol was off his menu, family life tenuously simmered in an uneasy truce. But my brother and I always knew that these pseudo-peaceful moments only barely masked the festering cruelty that would soon revisit our world. Whenever booze entered the picture, which was usually nightly, it was always time to lie low and hope for the best - the best being simply a desperate attempt to stay out of dad's way. At those times, the house became a maze housing an angry inebriated giant who roamed the dark corridors of his castle, looking for *any* excuse to justify the violent rage that always seemed to seethe just beneath the surface of his troubled soul.

More often than not, he somehow found his "excuse" in the two boys trapped inside his fortress.

The vague memories of my mother were pleasant, but she had left dad when I was only six years old, so memories of her were fuzzy at best. My older brother assured me that she loved us, but was simply too weak to deal with the horror of our home. No wonder there. We were barely hanging on ourselves. I don't think I hold any animosity towards her, other than the feelings of abandonment that inevitably haunt your thoughts, even if you understand the dire circumstances that push people to their breaking point. Abuse is hard even for the strong in spirit. But mom, a little farm girl from Kansas, would *never* have survived in the hostile environment she left her boys in. My last memories of her were from a letter we got in the mail, three years after she left us. It was postmarked from the state of Kansas. Dad never knew where she had gone, but it made perfect sense. She had retreated back to her own childhood hometown, forever safe from the brooding giant. The coroner's letter was blandly informing the next of kin that she had passed away from some sort of cancer.

Life seems full of ironic and sick humor. My mother had escaped one tragedy only to find another. Death finds us all. Dad didn't seem moved by the tragic news. He just quietly took the letter, threw it in the trash, and headed back to his liquor. I, on the other hand, cried for nearly a week, but of course never in front of my father; that would surely have brought on another beating. For some reason, the death of this woman, who was really nothing more than a hazy memory, increased in me a sense of hopeless desperation. It was as if what little air was left in the family oxygen tent we called home was now seeping out at an even faster rate, accelerating the asphyxiation of my already suffocating soul. The one and only possible rescuer for me had just abandoned me once again. As a young boy, I guess I still held out hope that she would one-day return for the sons she had left behind. The irrational and unspoken expectation that perhaps mom would come back, with the police or child protective services in tow, was something buried deep within my spirit, offering what turned out to be *false* hope for a potential escape from my childhood nightmarish existence.

So my mother, first in physical presence, but eventually even in spiritual essence was now *completely* out of the picture. As for the man and boys she left at home; they were stuck in an unholy trinity, bound together only by strands of malicious genetic code. We survived that way for five years before the chromosomal connection was further broken. It wasn't a shock to find out that dad had wrecked his own car coming home from one of his frequent drinking binges. But it *was* a surprise to watch him commandeer my brother's car, justifying his action through the absurd assertion that we owed him rent for the lovely living conditions he provided. It never seemed to cross his mind that he was stealing a car that my brother bought with his own money after working hard for over three years.

That car had represented freedom to my brother, a brief respite from the flood of oppression he found at home. Time spent on the open road was his therapy. Even though it may have been for the briefest of moments, in those solitary drives *he* was in charge of his direction and destiny. With that freedom yanked out from underneath him, I desperately watched as the once stronger sibling descended into a tailspin of dark depression. Then, my older brother permanently and tragically signed out of the gene pool shortly after his 18th birthday. He had been forced to ride his bike as an alternate form of transportation and was run down late one night, presumably by another low-life who couldn't live without the bottle. They never did find the driver. When he died that night, yet another piece of me died with him. What made matters worse was that the battering at home gradually worsened. The angry giant now had no need to divide his abuse *equally* between two sons. I won the cruelty lotto and could collect *all* the harmful proceeds from then on.

By age fifteen, I'd had all I could take. As the beatings increased in frequency and intensity, a decision had to be made: either kill this brutal abuser, or take to the streets. I chose the latter simply because I refused to be as violent as my old man. Also, because his abuse was such a well-kept secret, people would *never* have understood or believed. Daddy-dearest had a fairly well paying job as the foreman of a local factory, and everyone around him thought he was a great guy. He was a well-respected member of the community. He was often the one buying rounds of drinks at the company parties: A good old boy for sure. I often felt guilty that I could not see my father the same way as everyone else did, but of course nobody except myself, my brother, and mother saw him as he really was; a bitter old drunk that, for reasons only known to him, took out all his anger on those closest to him.

After being out of the house for only one week, I had already vowed *never* to see my old man again for as long as he or I lived. No regrets. No looking back. I survived the next few years by living with various friends, always coming up with excuses for being absent from my own home. Moving around a lot might have been less than ideal, but it certainly beat the lethal alternative of moving back into the giant's lair. Eventually, I was able to stay in an abandoned trailer on the secluded backside of some property owned by the family of a friend. Their lot was huge and the old mobile shack was hidden in a grove of pine trees near the back of their property line. The parents hardly ever knew *when* and *if* I was there, and they certainly didn't know that it had become my permanent residence. All those years hiding from dad made the deceit easier to pull off. Personal items carried out with me in the morning, minimal lights at night, and very little daytime presence at the trailer served to protect the ruse. *Thanks dad. You did manage to teach me something after all…thanks to your beatings; I learned the art of hiding quite well.*

It was an odd irony that I had actually followed after the example of my mother. She had fled and hid in what should have been an obvious place: her own hometown. Perhaps doing one better: I ran away from home and stayed right under my father's nose in our *own* hometown. There was a perverse sense of satisfaction in the fact that the smaller and younger "David" had outwitted the larger and older "Goliath". It was a calculated risk, but I knew my father's work schedule well. He had kept the same hours for the past twenty-two years. It was easy to make sure my work hours matched his so our paths would never cross. It also helped that I found a job on the opposite side of town. I was determined to steer clear of the man who had cost me my mother and brother; had deprived me of the only *real* family I knew.

There hadn't been many good jobs available for high school dropouts. Factory jobs would have been an acceptable and fairly well paid option, but this town was somewhat of a close knit community, and the *last* thing I needed was for my dad to hear through the grape vine that his wayward son had taken a job in the local factory down the street. With his position in the community, there was no telling what damage he could do even if he was only the foreman of an *other* company's warehouse. Perhaps a friendly call between drinking buddies would land me back on the streets with no job. Plus, I was determined to win this game of hide and seek with my abusive father, even though I wasn't sure if he was seeking anymore. So with the post-escape abuse of my father still affecting and restricting me, even out into the work force, my options were limited. Finally, when a friend mentioned that a position had opened up in a local diner, my application was on their cigarette-stained counter the same day.

The job was far from glamorous, and it certainly didn't pay much, but I eventually scrapped up enough cash to purchase a car. I use the term "car" lightly. It was more like a glorified wagon with wheels that somehow kept moving, provided you were going downhill with a sufficient tailwind. I wasn't even sure of the make or model because all the telltale chrome insignias and trim had either been removed or rusted off by untold years of harsh winters. Someone drawing up plans after a night of Jack Daniels and Budweiser must have designed and created the body shape of this abomination on wheels. The rear of the car was unnaturally wide compared to the slender front hood and the wheel wells arched abnormally high above the tires, making the whole thing look pretty ridiculous. This was definitely no chick magnet sports coupé. It looked more like a *doorstop* than a car…one of those triangle shaped wedges you could prop between the door and the floor to keep the entryway open. Still, ugly though it was, the rusty carriage was a necessary evil since I was rapidly wearing out my welcome asking for rides from friends all the time.

Charity only extends so far. My high school pals were losing interest in a homeless drifter who just wouldn't drift far or fast enough. I could see it in their eyes and bodily gestures as their support of me eventually went from acceptance to tolerance, from tolerance to annoyance, and from annoyance to avoidance. Can't say I blame them. Most of them were connected to good families, so it must have been hard to relate to someone like me who was completely on his own. That position in life seems attractive at first glance, especially for teenagers. But the stark reality was that, without *any* family, there was literally no one to turn to when things got rough. Freedom of one sort always seems to usher in bondage of another sort. My emancipation from a life of cruelty had ultimately destined me to walk the planet as a self-imprisoned orphan.

I lived that way for several years. Times and seasons passed by like disinterested soldiers marching in a circular and unending parade. My life was reduced to simply being a dispassionate spectator of *other* peoples' meaningless pageantry as their lives paraded by my own…*they*, the active ones, *me*, the stoic bystander…*they*, progressing in life, *me*, simply marking time in the hostile world that had birthed me. The treadmill of boredom was both hypnotizing and life draining. Relevance and self-worth had been lost in the battle for true meaning in life due to monotony and isolation. And the war had been lost, not through some insidious victory, but simply by attrition. The recurring sameness of bland daily routines combined with seclusion and loneliness gradually defeated any sense of meaningfulness and purpose. In large part, it was these dull routines of an unfulfilling life that had first led me to think of Hamartia.

Of course there were worse things than boredom possible. I found this out during one of the coldest winters we had seen in years. The morning started out like any other, but degenerated as quickly as the snow began to fall across the frozen landscape. My "car" had been acting up lately, and since it was my only transportation, a trip into town was the order of the day. I had picked up enough vehicle maintenance knowledge over the years to realize that the alternator was about to completely fail. So at the risk of being in closer proximity to my father, I had no choice but to drive to the only automotive store that had the part I needed. It was located back near the center of town, but at least the ogre would be at work, no doubt regaling his underlings with stories of his last epic hunting trip. After scrapping off the icy windshield and brushing off the two inches of snow enveloping my pathetic wheeled-wedge-vehicle, I inched the car out onto the side road that led to the main highway.

The snow had stopped temporarily, but the dark ominous clouds threatened a heavy blizzard sometime soon. My hope was to make it into town and back before the main flurry arrived. The alternator could be safely installed back under the protection of pine trees that surrounded the trailer. A good plan…or so I thought. The roads had been mostly cleared by the huge snowplows and salt trucks owned by the city. But there was still about three inches of fresh powder that had fallen since the plows had done their latest work. Even though the traffic was extremely light, the brutal clash between tire and snow had transformed the highway into an unhealthy brew of watery slush and gravel. After a few miles of travel, the snow began to fall…lightly at first.

In my hometown, people were very familiar with the condition called black ice. It was the dangerous stuff causing many a driver to lose control on the road because of a deadly slim veneer of frozen water on the blacktop, too thin to be detected by the naked eye. But this wasn't the case today. What you had here was a relatively thick layer of melting snow and ice. The road had turned into a giant snowy margarita, the salt from the plows rimming the sides of the road to complete the mushy cocktail. Despite my hopes, the sky was darkening and the heavy snowfall began to hit, blanketing the road. What made matters worse was that as the temperature dropped, the wind picked up, and the slush under the newly fallen snow began to freeze. No wonder I hadn't seen any other cars for the last several miles. Each mile became more treacherous as the car began to sway back and forth on the road. I silently cursed myself for not investing in some snow tires this winter, although it was hardly something I could have afforded anyway. The tires would probably have been worth more than the car itself.

My haste to make it into town and back before the roads became impassable caused me to make a critical error. Failing to adjust my speed according to the rapidly deteriorating conditions, I stupidly ushered in a carnival ride worthy of any theme park. The car started sliding sideways on a particularly icy section of the road, and even though I turned the wheel against the direction of the skid like you're supposed to, the tires had no bite on the slick surface of the now frozen road. With now *no* control of my direction whatsoever, I crossed the centerline and the front bumper slammed into the snowdrifts on the left side of the two-lane highway. The rest happened quickly: My car flipped on its drivers side, spun around a full 360 degrees, slid back to the right side of the highway, and then promptly fastened its big bulbous behind in the embankment of powder left on the edge of the road by the snowplows.

Looking at the bright side: at least I was in the right lane again. But visibility could shortly become a problem: if the storm progressed to whiteout conditions, no one would ever see my car in time to stop. Of course, perhaps *others* would not be dumb enough to be out driving in this weather. There was always *that* embarrassing fact. Either way, staying in the car would pile stupidity upon stupidity. The thought of a fiery metal-twisting clash of vehicles on this mostly empty highway was not pleasant. I'd rather not "become one" with my abomination on wheels. I had to at least get my *body* off the road. The rest of this mess could be sorted out later. The rolling cheese wedge would have to go it alone. Sorry old pal.

Since the car was flipped onto its side, the drivers side door actually resting on the pavement; exiting from that side was obviously not an option. Climbing up to the passenger door was awkward but not that big of a chore. Putting one foot on the drivers seat headrest and grabbing hold of the dashboard did the trick. The problem was that the collision with the snow bank on the other side of the road had pushed the right front side panel of the car backwards into the doorframe effectively jamming it shut. The uncomfortable angle of my position in the car made it difficult to find enough leverage to push upwards to try and release the partially crushed door that blocked my only exit. Of course the glass could always be broken to provide a way out, but the repair costs from the accident were already going to be more than my budget could absorb. Another broken window added to the tab was less than desirable to say the least.

After struggling for several minutes, it became apparent that the passenger door was *not* going to budge. Then the realization came to me that exiting the vehicle was really only the *beginning* of my problems. Once out, there would be a grueling multiple mile trek back to the safety of my trailer. It was also more than likely that I would be on my own because there were no guarantees that other cars would be on the highway in this horrible weather. Discouraged, I sat down on the driver's side window pondering my situation for twenty minutes or so, probably subconsciously hoping that some Good Samaritan would come to the rescue. After awhile, it became obvious that even Good Samaritans had the common sense to stay indoors on a day like this and staying put meant eventual hypothermia or possible death if the storm went on for too long. The decision to break the window seemed like the only option. I could almost feel the money draining from my already nearly empty wallet.

Just as I was about to smash the window, the familiar distant sound of tires crunching against snow and ice was unmistakable. The sound was coming from behind me, well down the highway, and it was gradually growing louder by the moment. Looks like help of some sort would get to me before long. Good fortune. Good timing. A sense of welcome relief warmed my spirit a bit…until I realized that the vehicle was moving rapidly, and in these conditions, might very well not see me until it was too late. Now, smashing the passenger side window seemed like the best financial decision I would ever make. Wallets be damned.

Amazingly enough, frantically bashing the window with the side of my fist was doing absolutely *nothing* towards getting me out of the car. The tempered glass seemed to absorb all the blows as if it were made of unbreakable titanium. Just my luck: the world's ugliest car had the world's strongest windows. The approaching noise of the vehicle behind me kept getting louder, and it sounded like something big. That of course made sense, since only a bigger vehicle should be out in this blizzard. I redoubled my efforts on the window to no avail. Then I remembered the large wrench kept under the drivers seat; a poor mans self-defense weapon. I allowed my body to fall back down to the driver's window as my arm reached sideways under the seat. Of course gravity was following its cruel nature. Since the car had flipped on its side, there was no telling where the wrench had ended up. My hand groped back and forth on the bottom of the car floor but found continuous handfuls of nothing. But persistent frantic searching eventually yielded the prize. The wrench *had* stayed under the seat, getting stuck in the exposed springs of the seat itself. The sound of the approaching automobile was now terrifyingly close with no evidence of slowing speed.

Scurrying up to the passenger window, I let loose with a swing Babe Ruth would have been proud of. It only took one. Shards of shattered glass rained down on me with a ferocity equal to the relentless snowstorm outside. The roar of the approaching nemesis was now deafening. Pulling myself up and through the newly shattered opening added several cuts to my hands and ripped open the right side of my jeans, but freedom was at least now within reach. As I threw myself into the snow bank on the side of the road, fate cast an unusual smiling glance in my direction. The oversized pickup truck careened past me, swerving to the left and just barely missing the front bumper of my recent death trap. I allowed my head to drop onto the newly fallen snow, enjoying the reprieve from several possible outcomes. I was not only alive, but there might be the possibility to save what was left of my car.

The euphoria of my escape was short lived. My gaze had followed the truck taillights as they passed by and stopped 50 feet down the road. A sick feeling in the pit of my stomach gradually spread to the extremities of my body as my limbs became weak and shaky. Though I only saw the truck for the briefest of moments, I knew this vehicle all to well. It was my dad's truck. As a youth, I had used it often as one of my hiding places; because after a day of work, the *last* place dad would want to return to would be his truck. The truck stayed in the garage, and the liquor was in the house. Consequently, dad rarely strayed from the house. Ironically, the vehicle that was once a safe haven for me was now a harbinger of fear and dread.

Now the truck stood still, its red taillights glowing ominously against the snowfall like an angry beast looking back through the blizzard towards the prey it had missed on its first attack run. The exhaust from the tailpipe spewing out into the cold air only added to the macabre picture of a fire breathing menace staring down its victim. Of course, back in reality, there was no way he could have known it was his son exiting the overturned vehicle. Emerging from a car he'd *never* seen came a figure bundled up in a thick hooded jacket that hid the face from prying eyes. His own preoccupation with self-preservation and keeping his truck on the road would have also worked in my favor. No, my anonymity was safe. For now.

I scurried behind my car, for the first time being thankful for its ample fat backside. For some reason, the rock group Queen came to mind, singing their original tune called *Fat Bottomed Girls*. The mind under stress: who can understand it? Humor was certainly not appropriate at this moment. My options were, to say the least, extremely limited. I only knew that the only *unacceptable* solution was to stay in a position where dad would eventually discover me. So with only my pleasantly plump vehicle standing between me and the nightmare figure from my past, I simply ran down the highway using his dismal line of sight and the storm to my advantage.

Before long the swirling snowfall completely obscured my form from the monster behind me. But he must have caught a brief faint glimpse because I heard him call out, asking if I was all right, if I needed any help, if I would slow down. That last suggestion only served to hasten my steps. Oddly, his voice sounded different, softer somehow. But just the thought of my dad offering any compassionate assistance to some anonymous shadowy figure down on his luck seemed completely against his true nature *which I unfortunately knew all too well*. Maybe he thought one of his drinking buddies had indulged in one too many cocktails again and needed to be hidden from the law. Now *that* would certainly be more in line with his character: protect the kind of person who killed my brother. All the feelings and terrors of my childhood came flooding back on that snowy road and the chill in my soul matched the frigid air surrounding me. I still hated and feared this man. And now I hated him even more for trying to leave me with a hypocritical last remembrance of him as a person who was filled with care and concern.

I ran down the newly abandoned highway as fast as my legs could carry me. Torrents of snow continued to swirl through the chilled air and dad's pseudo-compassionate voice soon trailed off as the wind from the storm and the distance from the wreckage steadily increased. Even so, my body involuntarily refused to slow its pace. It was running on autopilot according to its *own* subconscious fears. To be fair, though abuse certainly caused *psychological* damage, it was the body that had to absorb the immediate effects of the *physical* punishment. No wonder it was in such a hurry. Beatings left nearly indiscernible inward marks on the psyche, but left actual *visible* marks on a body. The body was now working quicker and perhaps smarter than the mind. Maybe it had a legitimate concern - what if dad decided to give chase, get into his truck and backtrack towards the person who had nearly caused him to veer off the road? Dad was somewhat of an expert on pay back and revenge, often for offences that only *he* perceived. I kept running.

I couldn't shake the irrational mental picture of the highway behind me morphing into some sort of diseased artery, one that could rupture and pour out a toxic stream of acidic cancerous blood that drowned its helpless victims in vile poisonous plasma. This artery was, after all, connected to a diseased heart – my father. I was determined to exit this infected vein before any of his angry venomous blood clots could catch up with me. My legs led me off the highway and over the embankment on the left side of the road. Digging deep into the other side of drifts left by the plows provided sufficient invisibility until the danger of discovery passed.

I'm not sure how long I waited - probably too long: long enough to be *safe*. Then the mind gradually began to reassert control over the body, gradually perceiving the early stages of hypothermia. The cold was beginning to seep past muscle tissue, settling into joints and marrow. The body responded by eagerly rejoining the mind, it too warning me to get back to the comfort of my abandoned trailer. As a matter of fact, nothing in the world sounded more appealing at that moment. The trek down the highway resumed but the weather worsened. The storm had now escalated to near white out conditions.

Visibility had been reduced to only a few feet in any direction. Slogging through the deepening snowdrifts made progress slow and parts of my clothing were actually beginning to freeze as the snow clung to the legs of my jeans. My tennis shoes were pitifully inadequate to protect my feet, but they *were* doing a great job ingesting snow and making my socks feel wet. My jacket was too thin to provide anything but minimal protection from the wind and the exposed parts of my face felt like they were freezing; it was painfully obvious that I was not dressed properly for this cross-country hike through the Artic. A mild sense of panic set in as the realization came to me that eventually it might become hard to distinguish where the road actually was. Loosing my sense of direction now would mean certain death. How long does it take for a body to die of cold exposure? For now, the built up mounds of snow on the side of the highway served to channel me back into the direction of my trailer. Thank God for snow plows.

The last two miles leading up to my shack were definitely difficult, but doable considering the lack of an acceptable alternative. It wouldn't have been pleasant to exit this life by becoming a human popsicle. I was loosing some feeling in my extremities, but thankfully there hadn't been enough time spent out in the elements to create any real frostbite. Thankfully, no limbs, fingers, or toes were going to be lost today. When I reached the front stoop, I grabbed a broom and swept off the pile of snow blocking the front door and then fumbled around for the keys in my right front pocket. Momentary panic seized me. The keys were nowhere to be found. Had I left them in the ignition of my overturned car? I patted down the pockets of my jacket. Nothing. But thankfully, when I reached into my front *left* pocket, I struck gold. With a wave of relief, I remembered putting the keys in my other pocket because the angle seemed easier when I was floundering around in my wrecked car.

Frozen and shaky fingers made opening the latch much harder than it should have been. My body had paid a much bigger price than my pride was willing to admit. The bitter cold had dulled my motor skills and all my limbs seemed to work stiffly like a rusty machine desperately in need of grease. My sense of humor often has weird timing. Okay, *bad* timing. I can't help it. My mind continually reaches out to find the humor in almost every situation: probably one of many acquired defense mechanisms developed over the years in order to survive early childhood traumas. It was something my dad never quite killed in me, though God knows he tried. Against all odds, I could even get an occasional smile or laugh from my stoic older brother, even though he rarely saw *any* humor in our pitiful life with dad. I'm not so sure it wasn't this inbred sense of humor that helped save me from absolute and total despair during my youth. At *this* inappropriate moment, struggling to get the front door open, I couldn't resist the comical thought of me making it all the way home only to freeze to death right on my front door step. That would certainly be a ghoulish surprise for my friend and his family. Imagine the parents taking a stroll on the back of their property: *Look honey, the kids made an incredibly realistic snowman on the porch of our old trailer. Isn't it cute?* Eventually the key found its mark and I went in, shutting the door behind me.

There was no fireplace blazing, but simply being sheltered from the wind provided some immediate relief. Thankfully, my friend's family had run an electric line out to the trailer when they first parked it on the back of their property. For fear of being detected, I always tried to limit my use of any equipment requiring electricity. Vast changes in an electric bill could raise concerns and prompt an unwanted investigation of my hide out. That's something I obviously didn't want. I needed this place to sleep, *especially* now since my car was out of the picture for the foreseeable future. The situation at hand however warranted a little risk. With shaky hands, I grabbed the two space heaters that were kept hidden under the bed and quickly fired them up. The next step was to peel off wet clothing. Putting on dry clothes felt heavenly and placing both heaters on either side of me immediately bathed me in diffused waves of glowing heat.

Ah, the simple pleasures. It felt like I was in a human toaster. Continuously shifting my body into different positions allowed me to gradually apply undulating sumptuous heat to every square inch of frozen flesh and bone. Submersion in a hot tub couldn't have felt any better at that moment. The extreme contrast in temperature was intoxicating. It felt like I could actually sense the blood flowing to my extremities, as if warm syrup had been poured into my veins. A tingling sensation gradually spread throughout my entire body. I'd never had acupuncture, but this must be how it felt. Although the acupuncturist would have had to be a sadist considering how extensively the pin pricks were spreading throughout my entire body. *My inappropriate sense of humor conjured up the picture of a human pincushion.* Eventually a hypnotizing euphoria began settling into warming bones and one of my more unpleasant life-experiences ended. Sleeping on the dirty shag carpeting of an abandoned trailer felt like crawling under the sheets at the Ritz Carlton Hotel…*minus the mint on the pillow of course.*

Chapter 6 – The Hypocrite

It's amazing how vivid old memories can be sometimes. Thinking back on my near death adventure in the snow, reminded me of the many reasons I left my hometown. At least the fateful excursion into the blizzard was a *distant* memory. So much had happened since that day. And as far as I was concerned, it was all for the better. Leaving my birthplace and all that I knew up to that point in my life helped me focus on taking care of myself instead of wallowing in self-pity, worrying about other people around me. After all, my one-way ticket to self-sufficiency was inevitable. No one was standing in line to look after me. It finally dawned on me after four years of living on my own; *I was already taking care of myself.* The idea of "hometown" sounds deceitfully warm and fuzzy; but in reality, continuing to live in your birthplace can go either way, just like poppy seeds on a bagel are okay, but poppy seeds mixed in a different way can form an opiate that causes you to imagine that the toilet seat is talking to you. At this point, I didn't need my hometown for anything.

It had been foolish to stay in such close proximity to my old man. He had been the one responsible for my brother's death, and I was convinced he hastened the death of my mother by the way he treated her. People handle stress in different ways. My brother had always told me that Mom *internalized* her worries and anxieties, and there is plenty of medical evidence that suggested severe stress could cause actual physical health problems. Our house certainly ranked pretty high on the stress scale. So I blamed my dad for mother's death as well. He did it. Plain and simple. Her cancer was just a late arriving byproduct of all the junk he'd done to her over the years, his final sadistic "gift" to a thoroughly defeated and dejected woman. For Mom, the desire to earn love from an unloving man was the opiate that caused her to check out of life too early.

Socrates might have died from and overdose of *hemlock*, but my mother died from an overdose of *wedlock*.

It was nice to now be in charge of my own destiny, which of course made Hamartia unavoidable. So here I was. The fresh air on the downward trail was invigorating, reviving in me a renewed sense that this was perhaps the *only* place suitable for me: isolated, quiet, foreboding, and yet intriguing. The old gem collector had dredged up some distant and unpleasant memories, but it was time to move forward…*literally* forward: physically as well as mentally. The only good thing about my hometown memories was that they reminded me of the boy that once tended to look for the humor in life, the "bright side" if you will. I couldn't let my dad steal that from me. Especially not now that I was rid of him forever. Perhaps I made my hometown exit just before the toilet seats would have begun talking to *me*.

Casting my eyes on the immediate surroundings helped jar me from my reverie. The inside of the mountain had an odd symmetry to it. In some ways it seemed processed or planned. And my memories of entering the misty grey "otherworld" left my darker side to wonder if it was also *possessed*. The sides of the trail continued to predictably alternate between sections of obsidian and granite, continued to feel as if the walls could be concealing secret observation spaces just behind its mirror like sections, continued to cast back your reflection which seemed to be out of sync with your actual movement at times. I had developed an odd love-hate relationship with the walls. On one hand, they provided the illusion that you were not alone, and human beings, being social animals, usually found a degree of comfort in company. But the walls *also* made you wonder if the reflections were really that of you, or something more sinister. *Let's don't start thinking like that again…processed or planned maybe, but not possessed.*

The green luminous algae continued to rim the sides of the trail, casting ominous shadows into the dark recesses of the sheer drop off on the right side of the path. I couldn't decide if the synchronicity of the surroundings were comforting or unsettling, inspirational or menacing. As I descended down the trail, I had taken up the habit of grabbing small stones and tossing them over the edge, using them like subterranean sonar to help gage the depth of the drop off. Unfortunately, pings were few and far between, and there was never any certainty as to whether the pebbles actually hit the bottom or were merely glancing off the sides of the forever-descending slope. The spurious notion came to me that perhaps there was *no* end to this descending abyss. My somber sense of humor considered the irony of someone like me, merely looking for adventure, finding the very doorway to a hellish underworld instead. Funny, yet oddly disturbing at the same time. It didn't help that occasional drafts of warm air had begun to occasionally spill over the trail edge from somewhere far below.

I continued to wonder if there were other people in this place. And in the same wisp of thought, I questioned whether I wanted to meet them. My social track record within this mountain was not so good. 0 for one so far. Either way, the only choice was to keep moving deeper into the abyss. Several days of travel revealed absolutely nothing new. Occasionally it seemed that garbled voices would gently float up the trail from below, but rounding each bend in the path failed to reveal a human source for the sounds. The surroundings were cookie cutter images of themselves, the redundant scenery threatening to mesmerize its victims into trance-like states. I once again began to wonder just where this path was leading…if it even *had* an end.

Just as I was pondering the gravity and meaning of a descending trail with no final termination point, the stony path wrapped around a sharp corner and gradually spilled out into a flat section of ground that was extremely wide compared to the constricted confines of my journey thus far. The cavernous space to my right side had finally disappeared, having come to an equal elevation with the trail. Out of boredom, I had stopped throwing rocks over the edge quite some time ago, so it was a bit of a shock to finally see the end of the dead man's drop that had always forced me to keep my mind and footing sharp. The level ground relieved a bit of unconscious vertigo tension and the open space around me also brought an end to the mild claustrophobia that that had been silently hovering just on the periphery of my awareness.

This underground valley was about double the size of a football field and several smaller caves dotted the right side of the far wall. The glowing algae now carpeted only various patches of the valley floor, giving the whole place the spotty appearance of a neglected farm field. The luminosity of the algae also created a shadowy visual terrain that formed a checkerboard conglomeration of light and dark sections of ground. The walls themselves also looked different because they had somehow lost all their sections of granite. Only the shiny black obsidian remained.

Consequently, the all-consuming reflective quality of the rock made the subterranean valley look even larger than it really was. Smoke and mirrors. Fraud and deception. Still, the past monotony of visibly redundant terrain during the last several days made the change of scenery a welcome relief.

I was surprised to find a spontaneous anxiousness in my steps and was equally surprised to recognize the *reason* for the quickened pace. Even though I fancied myself a loner, my mind had carelessly lunged forward to thoughts of possible companionship. Perhaps this place functioned like the base camp of a snowy mountain pass, a spot where visitors gathered, resting and recouping while sharing the ups and downs of their travels. *On the other hand, maybe I'd been in this mountain a little too long.* The caves in the walls seemed the obvious choice for discovering other travelers, but my interest in finding them was *equally* balanced by a fear of what they might be like. Before I'd finished pondering my social choices, the decision was actually made for me.

Without warning, a woman came running out of one of the caves. She stopped briefly and looked around, though not in my direction. Then, as quickly as she had appeared, she jogged further down the wall of caves and retreated into a different grotto several dozen feet from where she had first emerged. Certain she didn't see me, I moved in her direction. Though the view was brief, one couldn't miss the beauty of the moment: long black hair, lithe body, agile movements, and graceful physique. *Okay…I had been in the mountain too long.* Still, it was worth checking out. Female companionship had nearly *always* been my personal favorite choice. Over the years, the realization had come to me that I lacked the male bonding gene which was buried deeply in *most* men's DNA, making it easier for them to spend more time with their buddies than their girlfriends. That wasn't me. Ever since my experiences with dear old dad, bonding with other men was not easy. Company with the fairer sex always seemed preferable. I inched my way quietly across the underground valley towards the woman with flowing hair.

Due to the checkerboard terrain, the light surrounding me alternated between two different hues. Traveling over patches of green algae enveloped me with dull shimmers of pale green light, while traversing sections of barren earth dulled nearly all of the ambient light in my immediate vicinity. It was an odd feeling. Since the luminosity of the algae only carried light for several feet in any direction; it seemed that you could hide yourself right out in the open as long as you were in one of the patches of darkness. This initially gave me a feeling of safety, until I realized that *other* entities could be playing cat and mouse and could *likewise* be undetectable in the gloomy shadows. *Why did my mind always wander to morbid thoughts?* I couldn't quite dispel the notion of previously obsidian-bound watchers now being released into the landscape surrounding me, easily hiding in sinister inky obscurity. Continuing to rewind *that* possibility in my mind brought about the realization that my own movement had been stalled for quite awhile in a murky plot of darkness.

Now, moving into the light seemed risky, more like exiting a secure foxhole and foolishly exposing yourself to enemy sniper fire. *Curse my vivid imagination.* Still, no threatening sounds were detectable, no phantoms *visibly* lurking nearby. Sooner or later the paralysis would have to be broken. *Here we go.* Moving my right leg forward into a patch of dim light got things started again. No voyeuristic apparitions rushed in to claim their gullible prize, so each successive step gradually became slightly easier. Traversing the distance through alternating sections of light and dark eventually brought me closer to the cave entrances.

It was then that an additional player entered the scene. Thankfully, he appeared after I had just stepped into another barren patch of murky blackness. I'd really rather meet these people on my *own* terms, if at all, and then only after some careful observation. That being the case, my apparent veiled anonymity was a welcome thought. It looked like he had emerged from the same cave as the woman. He then looked up one side of the caves and down the other. A surprisingly jealous thought came to me that he was perhaps looking for the woman. Male competition for the female of the species was as old as time. Since I'd not even met the woman, it was curious to me that a potential rival suitor actually aroused anger in me.

Though he first took a few steps towards the direction where the woman disappeared, he for some reason changed his course and went *up* the trail outside the caves instead. At first I was elated that perhaps there was no connection between him and the girl, however, my enthusiasm was tempered by the fact that his change in direction would eventually bring him closer to my stealthy hide-away. Irrationally jealous of this possible adversary to my future love interest, my eyes were closely watching the man…and not without some malice.

As his movement brought him nearer to my position, my body involuntarily recoiled into a crouch. Muscles also flexed in preparation for a potentially unpleasant encounter. But very soon it became clear that apprehension was unnecessary. Still bathed in a shroud of dark gloominess, my form was apparently still invisible to him as he proceeded to travel right past the point where our paths could have nearly intersected. My breath exhaled in a slow controlled expression of released tension. Still, my self-preservation instinct told me that the first order of business was to watch the man and determine the threat level he posed. The beautiful maiden would have to wait. Alas.

The man himself was chiseled, with well-defined muscles barely concealed under fairly tight clothing. There was a certain smoothness in the way he carried himself that exuded self-confidence and charisma. Also cockiness perhaps. He walked the trail outside the caves with long strides and spryness in his steps that betrayed a powerful reserve of strength lying just beneath the surface of his formidable exterior. At one point, the stranger reached down to pick up three stones from the ground and swiftly walked with complete balance down a ridged outcropping of stone as he juggled the newly acquired stones flawlessly. The focused portion of my mind involuntarily reminded my irrational senses of an important and obvious fact: *be cautious with this one*. This was no stupid muscle-bound gym rat, but rather a well-oiled machine who had undoubtedly invested many an hour in self-absorbed fitness routines of both body *and* mind. Those kinds of people, the beautiful and talented people, were often dedicated, driven, and sometimes devious. It was certainly not a good idea to instigate any contact until I could evaluate him a bit further.

At a certain point he made a right hand turn and headed towards the direction from where I had first entered this huge open space of checkerboard dark and light. I carefully followed at a safe distance, flanking him so as not to appear in his line of sight. It wasn't that hard. It simply meant moving speedily through the shimmering plots of algae and then dissolving into the next dark patch of ground. He was oblivious to my presence. As mentioned before, my family life back home had transformed me into an effective master of stealth and hiding. After awhile, it became obvious that he was heading back towards the trail that brought me into this clearing in the first place. And not stopping there, he proceeded directly up the path. It was now painfully clear that my own journey was about to include some backtracking if there was to be any further information gathered on this muscleman.

My surveillance and tailing continued for several days, but inevitably there were the thoughts that perhaps it was a mistake to waste my time going back over old terrain. Nothing new here. Been there – done that. It also occurred to me that we would soon be in the vicinity of the old jewel zombie. Needless to say, there were no fond memories of *that* encounter. But curiosity always seemed to win the day. Maybe this man knew some sort of side trail that I had missed along the way. That might be *one* thing making it worth backpedaling over old turf. Perhaps there was a path that led outside this mountain. That last thought surprised me because I had long ago determined to follow this path deeper into the mountain, whatever the cost. The fleeting notion of escape was confusing and foreign to my current line of thinking. The momentary puzzling contemplation that it might be a good idea to *leave* this place reminded me of the struggles for my attention when I was trapped in the otherworldly land of mystic greyness so many weeks ago. No…I would be content to backtrack until it proved to fully reveal nothing new and until I had some kind of read on the man I was following.

After several hundred yards of further travel, it became obvious that I had *not* missed any secret side trail or hidden vista. But it *did* become painfully clear that we were nearing the cave of the old gem collector. You could see his cave from a fair distance away because of the gem infused light that spilled out onto the cavern trail from the recesses of the zombie's lair. *Great…now what?* Plodding forward seemed the only way to fulfill my curiosity, but common sense continued to spew out the mantra of caution. I was more than ready to listen to that refrain. If these two men were to team up against me, my future was not going to be bright. After all, I'd barely survived the encounter with the old man when he was by himself.

As we approached the mouth of the cave, it occurred to me that my last encounter had ended with the old man lost in his revelry, oblivious even to my presence right in front of him. He could not see me nor could I touch him. He had been content to bask in the sickly hypnosis of his jewel collection. And as for me, if I *could* have "touched" him, there would be no more gem collector to visit. What did my secret travel partner expect to gain by coming here? Certainly there would be no camaraderie between him and a self-absorbed gem hoarder. Well, it was time to find out. My unwitting companion unceremoniously approached and entered the mouth of the cave. As for me: running past the cave and positioning myself with a line-of-sight towards the inside of jewel-central seemed the best course of action. My fellow traveler would have his back to me, and it wouldn't matter if the old man were facing me since he couldn't see me anyway.

I set up my stakeout behind a clump of rocks just outside the cave entrance and dangerously close to the severe drop-off on the side of the trail. Standing once again right on the rim of certain oblivion plunged me back into the vertigo I had just recently lost at the bottom of the trail. But at least the position behind the rocks would serve to hide me from both my surveillance subjects. Kneeling down in the tight spot brought my right foot closest to the edge as my left foot was crammed up against the back of the rock outcropping. The only problem with that position is that it meant my right foot was planted not so firmly on the slippery green algae that spilled over the edge of the trail. Feeling myself gradually sliding towards the abyss several times made it more than worth the risk to reach towards the edge and uproot the slick algae in order to have a more firm footing. Thankfully the sound of my anxious digging did not seem to reveal my presence. It was now time to watch.

What happened next was astonishing to say the least. Upon mutual recognition, *a surprising fact to begin with*, the two men smiled, quickened their pace, and gave each other a brotherly embrace. My mouth actually dropped open slightly in disbelief. Here was the venomous old coot who nearly beat me to death, now hugging someone like he was a frail and dear old grandfather. Trying to piece together what was happening left me bewildered – until I saw muscle man reach into his satchel. His rugged hand pulled out three beautiful gems, not as good as the prized jewels occupying the revered places on the old man's pedestals, but still stunning in their own right. The ancient codger quickly grabbed the jewels and greedily passed them back and forth between his two grotesquely wrinkled hands. Well, at least the mystery had been solved: The ancient and disturbed fellow could readily see Mr. Suave because of the gems he offered to him. This visitor was *definitely* invited into his world; he was now his best buddy.

Trying to fully grasp the situation was confusing. The act of giving these precious gems away seemed out of character for the man I'd been tailing. He had seemed cocky, not the type of benevolent person who freely gives gifts to others. It struck me that perhaps misplaced jealousy had clouded my opinion of this poor chap. But that contemplation was short-lived considering what happened next. As the old man turned his back on his visitor, the supposed generous guest quickly grabbed six jewels from a pile closest to him. My stomach churned in expectation of what would most certainly follow. I was beaten for taking only *one* gem – *this guy just took a whole handful!* At least this trip would now prove interesting considering the high drama that was about to unfold. My blood pressure rose a few points and my senses became hyper-focused as I watched in anticipation. But as I braced for Armageddon, the *inaction* of the old fellow gradually dispelled any feelings of impending apocalyptic violence and allowed me to finally exhale.

It was becoming clear. The pieces of the puzzle were starting to fall together - The man I'd been tailing was an operator. He knew how to present one face *outwardly* to his victim in order to hide what he really was on the *inside*; a world-class hypocrite. The older man could see him only because of the gems. *Mutual interest.* That was, after all, why he eventually saw *me* when I tried to pilfer just one of his prized possessions so many days ago. I had been invisible to him until I entered into his narrow and caustic circle of myopic interest. My unknowing traveling partner was smart. The three gems were simply the bait that allowed this shyster to fleece his target. He was able to double his investment in mere seconds. And in a moment of embarrassment, the realization came to me that taking one of the prized *pedestal* gems had been my downfall. The more savvy and devious person standing before me knew what could be taken and not missed by the victim due to the prey having an immediate fixation on the housewarming gift from his generous visitor. Brilliant.

The smoothness with which he transferred the stolen jewels from the pile into his satchel further betrayed the devious nature of this pretender. It was like watching an incredible slight-of-hand magician. He'd undoubtedly done this *many* times before. The obvious realization came to me that he had probably been to this very cave numerous times and fleeced the man appropriately on each occasion – *all the while still building up trust*. It was pleasant for me to see the old man get what was coming to him. But it was also surprising to encounter some brief feelings of sorrow towards the whole situation. Yes the old man deserved to get taken to the cleaners, and worse for that matter. But the nagging notion of unfairness still stubbornly hung in the air, though it was quickly dispelled after thoughts of my beating began to resurface through the short-lived and unwanted haze of compassion.

After my glimpse into the true character of this charlatan, there eventually came a realization of why he was doubly disturbing to me. It wasn't *just* the fact that he was a potential rival for the lovely girl back at the caves; in many ways this hypocrite also unnervingly reminded me of my father: bigger than life, manipulative, confident, familiar shape and physique, and apparently a similar outlook on life: use people for your own purposes, and use them till they're of no use to you anymore. Nice. Dad was very much about "appearances". My brother once told me that when we were babies, dad was interested in us mainly as supporting evidence of his virility and power: *look at the manly brood he had created*. We were trotted out as cute novelties because we ultimately brought attention to my father. But later, as we became more trouble to him, with more demands, the abuse started so he could keep us in our place. I was too young to see or remember the *easier* side of our childhood, but both my mother and brother testified to it. When we were really young we escaped the abuse for a while. Then the abuse of my brother started first since he was older. He witnessed dad with a lighter touch on me for a while and that must have been tough on him. And of course, mom saw the whole picture; it was one of the many reasons she eventually had to cut and run. Lousy memories. They always come back when you least expect them.

Sinking further behind my rock hide-away, I simply waited for the bandit to return back to the trail and descend toward the caves where I first saw him. It didn't take long. Having got what he came for, he confidently sauntered out of the cave, veered left, and disappeared down the path. I followed, but at a considerable distance. I was determined to *continue* to keep my distance from this fellow as long as it was in my control. As it turned out, the trip back was uneventful, and despite some more battles with unwanted memories, it was somewhat satisfying to know that at least one inhabitant of the caves below had been revealed for what he was. The hypocrite had been outed. But curiosity made me wonder how many people from the clearing new his true nature? Probably not many…this guy was good.

When we once again reached the base of the trail, the now familiar patches of dark and light were no longer as awe inspiring and mysterious as they first were. The caves seemed to promise less opportunity to meet anyone who would be worth knowing. My excitement had been tainted since the first and only person I'd met here so far turned out to be someone less than admirable to say the least. There was still the girl of course. That might be the one bright spot in an otherwise dark sea of disappointment, but even that remained to be seen. And as of right now, she was *nowhere* to be seen.

Settling down in one of the dark patches of ground shrouded me once again in a blanket of welcome secrecy. I watched the hypocrite for a couple more days and witnessed several new players coming onto the scene. One older lady seemed horribly distraught over something, though my distance from her and the hypocrite never allowed me to figure out exactly what her problem was. The charming deceiver listened to her intently, with furrowed brow and deep lines of concern showing on his face. His eyes seemed to radiate waves of compassion as he listened intently to her plight, whatever it might have been. He provided light touches from time to time to the elderly lady's arms and shoulders, apparently trying to compassionately console her grief and express his heart-felt concern. It was probably just another masterful performance. Perhaps there would be an inheritance one day for him down the road if he played his cards right with the aging woman: Gems from the jewel hermit, gifts from the lady?

My suspicions of deceitfully feigned compassion proved correct shortly after the deceiver finished his counseling session and moved away from the mourning woman. At this point another new player entered the scene, a younger woman who emerged from one of the caves. This wasn't my raven-haired love interest. This one appeared to be about twenty-five years old, had short pixie-like red hair, freckles, and was considerably shorter. Again, their conversation was muted since I chose to keep a substantial distance buried in shadows; but their gestures were unmistakable. They spoke conspiratorially and in close quarters, casting quick glances towards the suffering old woman. Most disturbing was the fact that it soon became obvious that their laughter was unmistakably directed toward the old woman and her plight, *whatever* that was. Even some of their body movements were directed towards ridiculing the grief of the poor suffering senior, balled up fists rubbing their eyes to mockingly remove fake tears. Nice touch. This was the kind of behavior one would expect from juveniles at a junior high summer camp.

The man's chameleon-like transformations bewildered me. It seemed that he could seamlessly morph into separate personalities depending on who was standing before him at any given moment. To the old gem collector, he was a good buddy. To the suffering woman, he was the deeply concerned oldest son. It remained to be seen who he was to the elf-like redhead - fellow juvenile delinquent perhaps? And what about my dark haired love interest…lovers? Jealousy reared its ugly head once again. The depth of his deception actually brought a cloud of anxiety over me. If he ever *did* see me, what would be his performance on *my* behalf? What would he sense in me that he could exploit? And if he saw straight through me and suspected I saw straight through him, what would his reaction be? He hadn't perpetrated any violence in the short time I'd observed him, but the sociopathic blackness of his devious soul was readily apparent. Best to keep a wide berth.

As for the young girl, she seemed captivated by the hypocrite, floating all around him as if she were a spritely fairy transfixed by the light of a glowing campfire. Her features were petite, and would have been cute except for the fact that her smile was empty, her lips often pinched into thin angry lines. She would also crinkle her nose in disgust as the conversation turned to some aspect of the pathetic old woman in tears. These two were quite a pair. Not a pretty picture. Rage was beginning to rise in me. It often did over the years. It seemed that genetics saddled me with some anger issues, but the *last* thing I wanted to do was to turn out like my father. I was certainly above that. If I were to give-in to my anger, it would in some way give a sort of wordless approval to the way my father lived. No, I was better than him. That was the one high horse I never intended to dismount. Pride conquered rage for the moment.

After awhile, the conversation grew more intimate. Unlike his chaste performance with the elderly lady, the hypocrite's touches to *this* girl lingered, as he subtly caressed her small hands and bare arms. The spider was working his magic on the unwitting fly that had fallen into his web of deceit. Of course, perhaps I was giving the young waif way to much credit; it was possible that she knew *exactly* what she was getting into. I simply hadn't had enough time to completely size her up yet. But it was easy to see that things were escalating between the two as his strokes to hands and arms were now shifting to her face and hair. I'm sure there must be a rulebook on relationships somewhere, but it didn't take a college degree to realize that lightly brushing fingertips across cheek and temple ranked substantially higher on the "intimacy" scale than mere cozy pats on the back from concerned friends. The personal space bubble between the two was shrinking.

Then, not unlike the performance in the jewel-hoarder's cave, there was another Houdini-like slight-of-hand movement made by our newly formed Casanova of the caves. In one quick gesture, he distracted the vixen with one hand while swiftly grabbing a jewel out of his satchel with the other. It all happened so fast, the only reason I caught it was because of my superior angle of view from slightly behind the couple. The pixie-girl could *never* have seen the swift lunge into his bag. The rest of the trick was not detectable to the naked eye. Not to mine anyway. Somehow he transferred the gem from his right hand to his left, showed both hands empty palms up, and then magically made a beautiful crimson-colored jewel appear, seemingly out of thin air. For the briefest of moments, there was a spark of admiration towards this smooth deceiver. But of course, I had already seen the dark side of this fellow, had already passed judgment on this suave swindler.

As for her part, the red-haired nymph responded with all the excitement of a giddy schoolgirl on prom night. She raised both hands to her blushing cheeks, bending both knees downward as she ogled the shining jewel. As she nervously shifted her weight from foot to foot in anticipation, Casanova wrapped his left arm behind her back, around her thin waist, and pulled her forward. At the same time the jewel vanished from his free hand. Once again, I had *no* idea how he pulled that off. She let out a small gasp of amazement, and then her attractive suitor magically brought the jewel out of the breast pocket of her shirt.

The smile on her face turned devious and yet still somewhat playful as she leaned into the chest of the man standing before her, reaching out and grasping the jewel with her delicate fingers. The whole scene was a bit unsettling; it had the feeling of ritual rather than relationship. Her smile broadened but did not radiate any more joy than before; tight lips only stretched thinner and wider. Truth be told, it wasn't so obvious as to who was playing whom. My suspicion was that this had probably happened before…perhaps many times. Was she legitimately entranced or secretly tiring of the game yet thoroughly imprisoned in habit? Either way, the spider knew its victim was thoroughly cocooned and helpless, either by his hypnotic charm or of her complicit free will. Maybe a little of both. I suppose it didn't matter which. After gathering her slender legs up into his free arm, he pivoted gracefully and the two disappeared into the nearest cave.

Now, left alone in my solitary dark hovel of confined space, a sense of dread began to flow through my mind like a sickly polluted stream filled with the debris of twisted and rancid thoughts. Other than the old mourning woman, whom I knew absolutely *nothing* about, it was beginning to seem that all the inhabitants of this mountain were twisted in some way. Their souls seemed incompatible with what anyone else would describe as normal compassion for others. The prospect of finding any camaraderie amidst these warped narcissists was rapidly fading, and filling the void left by this newly lost hope was only more anxiety about being in this morbid place, surrounded by grossly self-absorbed people.

As this depressing realization set-in, it brought with it an unnerving feeling, as if I were becoming one with my dark hiding place between the algae patches. Joints and sinew were being joined with dirt and rock. Massive lightheadedness made my head spin and my hands involuntarily reached out to the ground to steady myself. Then a vision unfolded before me: hope was evaporating out of my soul like early morning mist rising off a lake. My good humor was beginning to disappear, replaced by a river of thoughts that refused to flow through my mind without leaving the detritus of desolation and despair. My relatively positive outlook was slowly melting into the earth below, leaving the remnants of my bodily shell empty and brittle against the mounting pressure of disappointment and uncontrollable subconscious dread. A picture floated ominously into my mind: my frame, made of sugar glass, being shattered into powder by a mere mild gust of wind. My very essence carried away on the breeze as my consciousness melded into the black void of nothingness. I was ceasing to exist. But of course, just before total blackout - that's when, out of the corner of my eye, I saw the raven-haired beauty walking straight toward me.

Chapter 7 – The Seductress

She was beautiful; dark hair flowing behind her as her nimble figure moved forward with all the gracefulness of a small ship quietly cutting through still waters. There was a hypnotic dreaminess in her movements as she weightlessly drifted in my direction. Her eyes were deeply dark and sensual, focused on mine, and seemed to transfix my soul with unspoken promises of soft caresses. But that was pretty much where it ended. The beautiful visage and sinuous shape of the woman was indeed intoxicating, but short-lived. Unfortunately, my dream-girl was rapidly vanishing, swirling backward as if sucked into the vortex of hurricane-like dark clouds growing and circling just behind her. I'd been here before. There were familiar flashes of light as the menacing vapor engulfed her figure and an ominous electric energy filled the air, reminiscent of rapidly rising winter storms that descend upon dry desert streambeds. But this was no weather system. It was rather a reappearance of the gray netherworld that breached the space between reality and oblivion. It had been quite some time since my last encounter with the mystic world of haze and shadows but it was now back and in full force. As the tangible world slipped away, it felt as if I was being drawn into an ashen snow globe, particles of insoluble thoughts and small shards of murmured sentences floating by just beyond the grasp of my comprehension. Fractured noises resembling some kind of unintelligible speech spun through the air churning up a caldron of confusion, confusion leading to a foreboding sense of dread. The girl had now completely vanished and I was firmly planted back in this gloomy dimension of the unknown.

The ground beneath me appeared to be the same black obsidian as found in the walls that had channeled my path through the mountain up to this point. The airspace above me was a kaleidoscopic conglomeration of dark gray hues mixed with subtle hints of deep purple and crimson reds. Like my last encounter with this mystery world, cloudy synapses fired their electric current back and forth in irregular patterns that gave one the impression of existing within some giant malevolent living organism. But along with all the familiar elements, a new phenomenon had joined the fray, one I had not experienced here before. The new sensation was that of an odd pulsation snaking its way through the air, striking my body like vibrations reverberating off a speaker cone. It gave me the unsettling impression of being sonically poked and prodded at various intervals by some strange unseen auditory hand reaching out from the dark. *Better than a real hand I suppose.*

There was the recurring awareness of both good and sinister apparitions surrounding me, but *this* time the hostile forces seemed to far outnumber their benevolent cohabitants. Their eternal feud continued; a verbally fought battle with words I could not understand. I only sensed that the more maniacal voices were winning this particular skirmish. I didn't know if that was good or bad. Last time I was in this dimension, I frankly had more affinity for the dangerous voices than the benign one's. But my senses had also been dulled during this particular excursion into the realm of shadows. During earlier visits, my mind was reasonably sharp and able to process much of what was going on around me, though I certainly didn't understand it all. But now, there was a fearful sense of intoxication clouding my thoughts, clear focus all but alluding me as I merely drifted forward – wherever *forward* would lead…if there even *was* a "forward" in this dimension. Sometimes I found myself standing still, completely unaware of how long I'd been in that position. Other times, after realizing I had ceased moving, there was still a substantial change of scenery surrounding me, as if I'd traversed miles of terrain, or more appropriately, as if the scenery was changing and moving around me, continuing to envelope me, scanning the remnants of my hazy consciousness. I was a listless cartoon character floating through pages and pages of landscape that were being drawn in by the hand of an unseen force or forces.

This "scanning" feeling was not only new but unsettling, the reverberant pulses that permeated the atmosphere around me were also penetrating *through* me, sonically mapping the contours of my very inner essence. The oscillating thrum of sonic pounding felt like some sort of invasive soul-scan as the vibrations insistently searched my spirit for any cancerous elements of a moral kind. I wasn't sure if sinful revelations would be pleasing or repulsive to whatever was behind the probing sonic-exam. Either way, the imposing soul-sonar felt intrusive, a violation of my personal space as the pulsations saturated every corner of my psyche. It was also disorienting. My heartbeat began to sync itself with the undulating drumbeats of sound and the result was a disturbing feeling of dreaded connection with the dark grayness surrounding me. The fearful thought occurred to me that if the pulsations were to stop, perhaps my newly synced heart would stop with them as well. The mere thought of that possibility brought on a psychosomatic dizzy spell that bordered on a panic attack.

Nervous sweat broke out on my forehead and a slimy nausea began to slide its way deep into my stomach. This was not going well. Somehow, puking my guts out on what could be semi-sacred ground of some sort seemed like it would be highly offensive to whatever spiritual beings inhabited this plain of existence; so I managed to narrowly parlay my urge to purge into a relatively minor coughing fit. On top of all the sensory overload that was already threatening to overwhelm me, there seemed to be one last disturbing addition to the unholy brew swimming around me. At first the smell was so faint that it was nearly unrecognizable – a mere unpleasant odor buried deeply inside all the other sensory debris floating around, in, and through me. The only thing that finally brought the smell into clear focus was the briefest glimpse of two disembodied red eyes floating distantly in the dark recesses of the gray gloom. *That* sight brought on the most lucid state of mind I'd had thus far into my returning journey through the mystic shadow world. Adrenaline is your friend. Sometimes it can keep you alive. The memories came flooding back. Certainly those glowing eyes were not *dis*embodied. Instead, they would be firmly attached to the body of the same hulking and hideous creature that drove me into this mountain so long ago. The familiar smell had reminded me all too well. How could this be? Had that thing really tracked me for all this time?

Already simmering fear now began to boil inside me, starting in the lower intestines and rising like a wave up to my temples, which were now pounding in equal rhythm to the sonic pulsations that permeated the surrounding air. I instinctively rotated my field of vision in various directions, looking for possible escape routes. But the fiery eyes would randomly appear in different locations, creating the unsettling feeling that there just might be more than one menacing apparition staring out from the murky haze. Several times, the distance between me and the floating eyes seemed to shrink, but there was never a clear outline of the face and body that surely accompanied the crimson orbs that penetrated the darkness like dim laser beams. Finally, instead of looking away from the creature, I forced myself to maintain eye contact in case my peripheral vision could detect any *additional* sets of predatory eyes. I needed to at least figure out what I was up against – one or many. Not the most sophisticated plan, but the smartest strategy I could think of on short notice. The only problem was that the surrounding gray mist consisted of various thicknesses, sometimes veil thin, and other times saturating the air like thick London fog. The result was that the distant glowing eyes tended to fade in and out of the cloudy atmosphere that surrounded them. This unfortunately created the disturbing illusion of movement either towards or away from me. Hard to tell which was true. My peripheral vision was *not* picking up any indication of multiple ghouls, which, with my morbid sense of imagination, made me wonder if the creatures were working in tandem like a wolf pack, one scout holding the attention of the prey while the others skirted around behind the victim for the real kill. *Now there's a lovely thought…back to the nature channel again.*

About the time I was pondering the possible sinister and deadly bait-and-switch attack strategy of my pursuers, something directly behind me reached out and touched the right side of my neck. Though not prone to magic tricks, I really do think I instantly developed the ability to levitate at that moment. Okay, so…maybe not, but I did leave the ground, pivoting around in mid air, and landing defensively, bracing myself for the worst. What I saw left me more than a little confused and bewildered. The touch upon my neck had been as cold as ice, sending a tendril of frost down the entire right side of my body. But what now presented itself before me was far from terrifying. In fact it was visibly soothing and inviting. I was immediately transfixed. It was the raven-haired girl from the caves. I had no idea how she got here, but a slight sense of relief brought the terror level down a notch.

Her figure was draped in a thin material that was just thick enough to leave only some things to the imagination. And frankly, my imagination was running amuck. Her movements were as graceful as when I first saw her in this realm of shadow as I was blacking out. Though I couldn't detect any breeze, the silken material she was wearing undulated back and forth, rippling and swaying hypnotically in a phantom wind current that could evidently only play upon her and no one else. Slowly lifting her right hand, she beckoned me forward with that "come hither" look that I had fallen for so many times in my past. Women had been an issue for me. I liked them. A lot. I'm sure Freud would have blamed it on some ridiculous claim concerning the absence of my mother, but I don't think so. I was just an average guy who enjoyed the company of the fairer sex. Perhaps I enjoyed it a bit too much.

It was odd to me that the slender and delicate hand that now motioned for me to follow, was the same one that brought such a chill into my bones only moments earlier. The thought, however, was fleeting as I felt myself drawn into the deep languid pools of her dark eyes. I was mesmerized for quite awhile until the familiarity of staring into a set of eyes finally caused me to remember *another* set of more sinister eyes behind me. The spell was broken and I immediately spun around to check for those crimson slashes staring from somewhere out in the dark abyss. To my surprise the creature had neither moved closer or farther away. Perhaps it too was in awe of the black haired beauty…beauty and the beast as it were. Whatever the case, raw red penetrating and unblinking eyes seemed content to watch from afar. My thoughts drifted back to the woman.

Perhaps this mystery goddess had come to save me. Back in the tangible world, as I was blacking out, the last thing I remember was her, making her way over to help me. Of course my vivid imagination suggested that perhaps she was simply another predator making her way towards her prey. That last thought made absolutely no sense and I pushed it to the back of my mind. I turned back to face her and was once again spellbound by her beauty, but was equally eager to put some distance between me and the bloody red eyes voyeuristically watching us from the shadows. If that *was* the beast that drove me into the entrance of this mountain, then *no* amount of distance would be too great for my taste. An involuntary shudder passed through my body as the suppressed memory of the desperate race to the cave opening and the beast's foul spittle landing on my neck replayed itself in terrible Technicolor. So, following her lead, we moved away from prying eyes.

As we drifted through the misty world of translucent haze, it became obvious that, *she* at least, was very much at home in this world. That thought was both troubling and intriguing at the same time. Her movements were a ballet of oneness with her surroundings, every pirouette and plié in perfect harmony with the strange symphony of sonic pulsing and invisible breathy wind flowing through this place. I, on the other hand, still felt mostly awkward and out of place. This place was intriguing but terrifying at the same time. Part of me wanted out while another part of me wanted to dive forevermore into this strange terrain of mystery. I simply didn't have enough information to take the full plunge. Though I was a risk taker by nature, caution was still a worthy arbitrator between wonton adventure and suicidal escapades. The presence of the brute in the shadows was more than a little unsettling, but the promise of union with my newfound love kept me close to her side: the fish contemplating the hook, the animal walking towards the trap.

Her fluid and sensual movement put me nearly in a trance-like state, my desires and emotions interwoven with her seductive essence in a tapestry of lust and need. At one point, desire overtook caution and my hand reached out to grasp her soft bare shoulder. The electric shock of bitter coldness caused me to quickly snatch my hand back, and as contradictory as it sounds, the chill was so severe, it felt as though my hand had been burned. As for her: at my touch, ecstasy seemed to course through her entire body. But as I released my grip, deep sadness flooded in just as quickly, pushing out the momentary pleasure she had so eagerly welcomed. Then, in a rapid third change of emotion, her countenance changed to one of anger. She raised both hands as if to lash out at me for denying her my touch. Her eyes squeezed into narrow slits, which seemed to spark with the same electric energy as the gray cloudy synapses floating above our heads. Her dark hair became even more stirred by the unseen wind, her features seemingly becoming more angular. *"Hell hath no fury like a woman scorned" as the saying goes.*

Though I braced myself for an imminent assault, the attack never came and she fluidly morphed back into the seductress role once again, though the glimmer of sadness and anger in her *eyes* took slightly longer to vanish. I was once again thinking of the saying about the eyes being the windows into the soul. Maybe. The residue of her dark emotions gradually dissolved from her eyes like water draining through sand. This woman was a mystery for sure. Her sudden transformations engendered within me a deep sense of pity mixed with equal parts curiosity and caution. Beauty had a dark side. But her pure animal attraction was irresistible. This siren's call was intoxicating, numbing her victim's sensibilities. I was still mesmerized. And I was determined to break the code that was hindering our ability to embrace.

Perhaps it was only *fleshly* contact that instigated the frigid response between us. I rolled down my shirtsleeves and wrapped my hands inside the cuffs. She watched silently but intently. Then I extended my right arm and gingerly placed my cuffed hand on the side of her exposed left arm. The initial contact was tolerable for a few seconds, a few seconds in which her expression changed only slightly – a smile that was more depressing than joyful. I tried the same gesture with my other hand and tried to maintain contact for longer, but eventually the cold seeped through the thin material, again making it too uncomfortable to maintain the connection. Well, it was at least *some* progress. I began to draw my eyes back to her face; anxious to see how much her countenance had improved considering my obvious success. What I saw chilled me to the bone even though I was not touching her in any way.

What I saw only lasted for mere seconds and left me wondering if I had just experienced a brief hallucination. The recesses that once contained such beautiful dark eyes were now glowing cavities filled with some sort of translucent boiling liquid. Her lips were drawn back in a wicked contortion, like thick rubber bands pulled back too tightly over menacing teeth. The skin on her face was drained of all color as she brought her face closer to mine. She cocked her head to the left and her mouth formed itself into a predatory snarl, the kind an animal gives when feeding on a dead carcass and is approached by a looting raider attempting to steal their kill. Even her seductive clothing had morphed into moth-eaten rags, filthy with dark splotches and streaks as her figure stooped over like a woman four times her age. My mind wildly tried to process this whole transformation, but as soon as it appeared, it vanished and the goddess had returned, wispy silken covering once again undulating in the phantom breeze.

At this point, I was beginning to question my sanity. *Not the first time of late.* I had no idea what had just happened. Premonition? Warning? Early senility? Whatever the case, my anxiety level had once again peaked and the seesaw battle of emotions was exhausting. I took a couple of nervous steps back from beauty. She cocked her head to the left just as she had done in her misshapen form, but beauty stayed beauty: enticing, alluring, and radiating charm and sensuality. I've often been mystified by women's behavior, but this was something considerably different. I took another couple of steps backwards. Her smile faded to a pout. Confused and emotionally drained, I just wanted some breathing room. Two more steps backwards. Her pout changed to a frown. I began longing for the tangible world to reassert itself as it eventually had done in my previous trips to this dark dimension. I needed to escape from this diabolical shadow land.

As I continued to move away from my raven-haired temptress, the foul smell returned, much stronger this time. There is only so much stress someone can handle and I had already reached my tipping point for the day. Reluctantly, I pivoted around and stared straight into the horrible glowing eyes, which were now close enough to betray the hulking frame that went with them. The ghoul was thirty feet away at most and still bathed in shadows…but barely. I got the impression that beauty and the beast might just be acting as a team; to what end I didn't know: but it was obvious that the big ugly one wanted me to return to the small pretty one. I was pretty sure that if you looked in the dictionary under the phrase "between a rock and a hard place", you would now find my picture, standing there blankly staring forward in sheer terror. My choices as I could understand them were limited: forward towards the beast – unthinkable…backwards toward the woman – unsettling to say the least. So I chose the less than brave third option. I ran to my left as fast as I could. My inner arbitrator of risk versus reward had made his decision. Not glamorous, but perhaps life saving.

This scenario had played out before: me running for my life and the monster giving chase. I had beaten the odds that first time. But one wonders how many times you can spin the roulette wheel of chance and come out on the winning side. Not many I imagined. At least this time my legs were fresh and my injuries were well healed. That was good, because I would need every advantage possible. The first advantage had already been taken advantage *of*. I don't think either party expected the reaction of flight, at least not so soon; transfixed by beauty and immobilized by the fear of beast were the twin shackles that worked in concert to hold me in stasis. I imagine they expected me to stay that way for a while. But self-preservation ruled the day, so I bolted as fast as I could. The slick obsidian beneath my feet made the first few steps rather comical, but once traction was gained my natural athleticism kicked into high gear.

Behind me was the sound of heavy breathing and rapid pounding feet giving relentless chase. I was well in front so far, the animal behind making a bellowing sound that would send a chill down the spine of even the bravest Navy Seal soldier. The ground beneath me was suddenly a little rougher than before, a few spots of loose gravel to negotiate. I risked a look back: beauty was nowhere to be seen, but the beast was well into the hunt. The pursuer let out another booming shriek and the terrain switched to mostly golf ball sized rocks which made for much more treacherous footing. My speed dwindled. The next blood-curdling howl brought about an even rougher running surface; one composed mostly of larger stones where twisting an ankle was an extremely likely possibility if I didn't further slow my pace.

My early advantage was rapidly becoming null and void as I realized that the creature behind me was somehow able to manipulate the environment, something it couldn't do in our first encounter *outside* the shadow land. But I guess this was *his* real world just as much as the tangible world was *mine*. He was in control of my surroundings. One more deafening growl and a chasm opened up about eighty feet in front of me. I watched helplessly as the ravine grew wider and wider by the second, the far wall receding woefully far into the distance. A jump to the opposite edge of this newly formed canyon was now totally out of the question for anybody without a big red "S" on their chest. Feet pumping furiously, I had already made my decision. There was no turning back. At great risk of bodily harm, I increased my speed and threw myself with total abandon over the edge of the crater. But unlike my escape from the beast during our first encounter, *this* leap would *not* end well. It was only while suspended in mid-air that I realized my fatal mistake. The bottom of this gorge was filled with tall obsidian spikes, all approximately three inches in diameter, and all rising to a finely honed and devastatingly sharp point. *The creature would get the last laugh after all…well played.* Holding my hands out in front of my falling body turned out to be a sorry last gasp exercise in futility as the spines pierced me through and through; most vital organs ruptured beyond repair.

Pain

Darkness

Screaming

It took me awhile to realize that it was *me* who was screaming. I frantically clutched and clawed my chest, one of the areas where an obsidian spike had caused the most pain as it skewered me all the way through to the backside of my body. Human shish kebab. Extremely disoriented, I tried to mentally recount the last several seconds of events.

I specifically remember the slick wetness of the blood draining from my body, the bloody metallic scent of copper filling my nostrils, my fading vision reduced to a pin-prick of light like an old tube television turned off in a dark room. Fade to black. I was dead; or so I thought. The screaming sort of negated the whole death thing.

I was shocked with the realization that I was still alive. But it was another shock to realize *where* I was – lying on my back in a well-lit patch of luminescent green algae. It was then, of course, mortifying to further realize that several people were standing around staring at me from the trail next to the caves. I reflexively kept clutching my chest but my shirt was dry; slightly soiled, but not a drop of blood anywhere to be seen. In fact there were no puncture marks anywhere on my body. I gradually rose to my feet and reluctantly let my arms rest at my sides, feeling about as awkward as ever. The curious onlookers gradually moved on, none of them looking particularly threatening for the moment, and none of them particularly interested in me anymore. *Boy do I know how to make an introduction.*

Off in the distance, to my left, standing in the mouth of one of the caves was the raven-haired beauty. I sensed she had been watching me, but as soon as I spotted her, she dissolved into the recesses of the cave. Still a mystery woman, but one I wished *not* to pursue for the moment, or perhaps any other moment for that matter. Which place was *her* real world? Both? She seemed equally graceful in each, but potentially terrifying in one. Thankfully, the creature chasing me had stayed in his world…for now. As for me? I still couldn't figure out how I made the transition from one world to the next without all my vital organs leaking like a sieve. I looked up to find the red-haired pixie girl walking by. She stopped for a moment sizing me up, then, with her nose slightly higher in the air, moved down the trail away from me. I couldn't help feeling like I had failed some unspoken test of hers. No wonder I guess; I looked like a mess and perhaps a bit crazy as I caught myself involuntarily giving myself another pat-down search for puncture wounds. I must have looked like one of those homeless schizophrenic guys desperately scratching himself in order to remove the phantom bugs crawling just underneath his skin. Finally, satisfied that the wind would not be able to whistle straight through me, I set about making plans for what to do next.

The short red-haired girl had joined the suave hypocrite many yards down the trail, both of them stealing furtive glances in my direction.

Sounds of soft, subdued laughter drifted in my direction. It was obvious that the two of them were comparing their notes concerning my awkward entrance into their world. *Ridiculing* analysis no doubt. It reminded me of the way they had mockingly assessed the poor old mourning woman drowning in emotional distress not that many days ago. Having witnessed my mother receive so much abuse from my father, I knew I could *never* lift a hand against a woman. The petite pixie would have nothing to worry about from me. Only bullies and abusers pick on weak people. Mind you, I had witnessed enough of her debased character to despise her and her elitist feelings of superiority over others. But still, she was a female, and weaker than I. As for her charming coconspirator on the other hand, well…my thoughts towards him were not so nonviolent.

You would think the recent realization that I was somehow spared from certain death only moments ago would awaken in me a nirvana of serene peace. But the longer I was in this mountain, the harder it was becoming to control my emotions. Any potential trip to nirvana was short-circuited by a seething desire to cause great bodily harm to the chameleon-like charlatan who called this debased world his home. *More hushed laughs…more sophomoric giggles.* The vivid thought of my fist breaking bone and cartilage, of blood dripping down the face of the pretender gave me a chill of delight. So much so, that my body convulsed with the slightest of tremors. Whoever invented the term "hot head" had it right; I could almost feel the heat emanating off my forehead in waves.

Nearly all the fights I got into after leaving my hometown revolved around my attempts to counteract bullying in *whatever* form I found it. The pixie and the pretender were, in some ways, one and the same. Both used their natural looks and abilities to elevate their own perception of themselves while at the same time devaluing anyone who was not so gifted as they. To be sure, I had not witnessed any acts of physical violence perpetrated by either of these two characters. No, perhaps they were too sophisticated for that. But their intimidation was of a more sinister kind: cool and calculated, all the while undoubtedly ready to declare their own innocence since no actual *physical* contact was used against any of their victims. But emotional bullying was in some ways the same as physical bullying, and certainly both betrayed a wicked loveless heart. I guess I was somewhat familiar with a loveless heart, but at least my lack of love for others was most often due to personal wrongs suffered – not due to some sense of highbrow superiority. I took several premeditated steps towards my targets, wanting desperately to wipe the smiles off each of their condescending faces. In unison, their gaze broke from each other and firmly fixated in my direction. This was going to get interesting.

Chapter 8 – The Jackals

Bullies. I hate them. But Hamartia was hardly the *first* time I had been exposed to people looking for the opportunity to ridicule me and break me down. After my desperate trip through the snow and back to my trailer so many years ago, I finally realized that living within *any* kind of proximity to my father was foolish. So shortly after my near-death blizzard experience, at the ripe old age of eighteen, I moved about 170 miles due south of my old hometown. Perhaps that wouldn't seem very far for most folks, but for me, it seemed like a million miles away. After all, when I was a kid, I had never been further than five or ten miles outside our town borders. There were a couple of reasons for this. First, we weren't exactly the close knit loving family who took summer vacations and traveled to exotic locations. And secondly, with the strict house rules imposed by father, my brother and I dared not chance the possibility of coming home past curfew. So my early life experiences were confined within the boundaries of a single medium-sized town.

Moving to a place where I didn't know a single soul was rather intimidating at first, but then again, out of necessity, I had grown up faster than most kids my age. I was used to being on my own, so it wasn't too far outside my comfort zone. My experience working in a diner back home actually helped me land a job fairly quickly, which was a plus. It certainly wasn't very glamorous: janitorial work in a greasy-spoon café from 7:00 PM to 2:00 AM. But it meant that my car, which had been salvaged from the snow banks back home, would no longer have to serve double-duty as both transportation *and* apartment. As a matter of fact, after saving the lion's share of my first couple paychecks, I was able to convince the landlord of a broken down duplex to let me rent one of the units with very little security deposit. Of course I'm not sure why he needed a security deposit at *all* unless he was fearful that someone might run-off with the peeling paint and dirty linoleum floor tiles. I suppose the broken toilet seat and the shredded window curtains might have been a major score as well. Suffice it to say: the Taj Mahal it was not. It did however come with its own pets. Turning on the lights during the night always revealed the cute little fellows scurrying back underneath the cupboards, which had multiple gaps between the cabinet bases and the filthy cracked flooring. Hard to believe that this was actually an upgrade from the trailer I left behind. But as the saying goes: *"beggars can't be choosers"*.

My job actually served double duty: it provided both money *and* some free food, though the food had to be a rather stealthy arrangement. The restaurant closed at 8:00 PM every night and the owner had me come in an hour before in order to get started on my various duties. This meant that for the first hour, I was able to scrounge through the food scraps left on plates in the back of the kitchen. I couldn't quite bring myself to rummage through the already discarded garbage bags in the trash bins. Not that I was proud; just that the thought was kind of gross. Offering to bag up the last of the trash from the kitchen gave me the clandestine opportunity to grab that half an egg or piece of toast left orphaned on various plates. I knew that I might get fired if I was caught, so I was careful to scrape edible pieces of food onto a single plate, bag up the rest, and then carry both the bag and the plate out the back door to the trash. The path to the trash bin required opening not just the back door but a dilapidated and squeaky screen door as well, so there would be plenty of time to react and cover my tracks if I heard someone coming outside after me. The timing was critical: leave through the back door when the cook was filling multiple orders and all the waitresses were busy with customers…then make haste with my dinner, dump the trash, and get back inside with the naturally expected alibi of taking out the garbage. Foolproof. And rather filling actually. I was continually amazed at how much good food was simply thrown away every day just from our one little diner. It made me wonder what poor people in other countries would think if they were able to see the sheer tonnage of food scraps thrown away every day in hundreds of thousands of restaurants and supermarkets across America. No doubt they would be shocked and certainly appalled.

It was actually during one of my covert food runs where I first ran into the Jackals. The Jackals were a group of guys in their late teens and early twenties who paraded around like a low-rent version of the Hells Angels. Instead of Harley motorcycles - bicycles were their drug of choice –

maybe not nearly as cool or threatening, but these guys were still dangerous because sometimes thug-wannabes were as bad or *worse* than their despicable idols since they felt they had something to prove. Dealing out excessive violence and brutality was somehow a badge of honor, and in their perverted world, it supposedly showed just how tough they were. In my book, it simply made them a pathetic band of low-lifes that had no real honor or courage.

The evening was fairly routine: bag up the trash, separate some of the choicest morsels for a quick meal, and head out the squeaky doors to the trash bins. What was *not* so routine was that as I was standing next to the trash bins, a single Jackal came riding around the right side of the building unannounced, veering left, and spraying a plume of gravel from the back of his tire. He came to rest pointed straight in my direction, the dust from the gravel gently drifting sideways from where he had stopped. He eyed me as I quickly pulled my hand away from my mouth. *No dinner tonight.* He wore blue jeans, black high-top sneakers, and a leather jacket with the emblem of a jackal on the left breast. As I lowered the garbage into the trash and scraped my uneaten meal on top of the plastic bag, two more Jackals rounded the corner skidding to a stop like a synchronized swimming routine, fine dust particles once again wafting sideways off of their back tires. The three of them just sat on their bikes and stared in my direction, muttering things to each other that were inaudible to me.

I'd been around bullies enough to see it in their eyes: they were predators looking for their random prey. This encounter wasn't planned because they seemed surprised to see me. But that didn't matter; they now had their unsuspecting quarry in view and it was time for some cruel fun. I was the new kid in town after all. *Fresh meat.* It's rather pathetic, but it seems that many people find pleasure sticking their nose into other people's business. But worse than that: they take some sadistic joy from hurting people for no reason. Never understood it. Not even remotely. The excuse often used concerning some kind of abuse in their early formative years always rang hollow in my ears since I was well versed in that kind of life and had not jumped to the dark side because of it. No, these people must have had some sort of horrific genetic abnormality that enabled them to prey on the innocents…*with no empathy whatsoever.* The Jackals had the same sociopathic look that I had seen in many other aggressors and they radiated a sense of danger even from a distance.

After quickly dumping my dinner and closing the lid on the trash bin, I tried to make my way back towards the back door. I suppose that was their cue. The worthless losers began rapidly moving forward like a wolf pack preparing to gut their prey. I managed to make it to the door just before they did, and as I slipped in the back, one of the goons kicked the screen door shut, catching my heal and causing me to tumble awkwardly forward into the back of the kitchen. The plate that formerly held my dinner crashed to the floor, shattering into multiple pieces and I heard laughter as the gang rode away on their mighty two-wheeled steads. Hearing the commotion, the cook came back into the recesses of the kitchen and looked down at me pathetically lying on the floor, blood dripping from my ankle onto the floor. I quickly got to my feet and he, seeing that I was apparently fine, went unceremoniously back to the grill.

I suppose like anyone else, I had plenty wrong with me; but I was definitely no coward. I had often put myself in harms way if I felt there was some injustice being perpetrated by the strong against the weak. Perhaps it was a throwback to the days where I *couldn't* fight back against my father. We'll let the shrinks figure that one out. But I did sometimes wonder if I had a death wish, since often the confrontations I chose led to a relatively severe beating and *I* was usually the one left with most of the bruises. That gradually began to change over the years, as learning to fight became more of a necessity. I got pretty good at it actually. But I was not stupid. In this case: three guys against one, in a secluded spot, behind a building – not good odds. Even risk takers had to consider risk verses reward. I would *gladly* have taken on one, maybe two of them. As a matter of fact, looking down to my bleeding ankle, I was already hoping for the opportunity to catch one of them when the odds had evened out. Bullies don't like even odds. They usually waited for the odds to be *so* stacked in their favor, that winning was the only possible outcome. For now, I simply had a mess to clean up in the kitchen. *Next time chumps.*

The rest of the evening went by uneventfully, the Jackals undoubtedly finding someone else to make sport of. After finishing the last of my chores, I piled into my old beat-up bulbous vehicle that *almost* posed convincingly as a car, and made for home. The duplex had two gravel driveways, each one down opposite sides of the building. From the street, my unit was on the left as was my driveway, and because of the late hour, I eased the car down the side of the house and quietly parked near the back. Walking in the front left door, I flipped on the light switch; content to watch my hard-shelled little pets scurry for cover.

Most pet owners had their animals rush to meet them at the door, but mine were more of the reclusive kind. I tried not to take it personally. Having by now fully adjusted to my graveyard schedule, I threw wallet and keys on the kitchen counter and made my way to the bedroom. Sleep wasn't far behind as I soon drifted off, my body resting up for one more meaningless day.

Waking up at 11:00AM was pretty much the routine since the torn curtains let in too much sun to sleep longer. This day was no exception. Making my way to the kitchen, I fumbled through the upper cabinets trying to locate a sealed box of cereal. *Sealed* was the operative word here, because one time, one of my pets had generously decided to share breakfast with me and had started eating before I sat down at the table. Only after pouring out the last of a box of Frosted Cheerios did I see my dining guest fall out of the box and into my bowl, already satiated with his own sugar high. The pathetic fructose-filled beastie was on his back, legs moving slowly back and forth like it was doing the backstroke. *Nothing quite like starting the day that way.* This day however, no dining companions showed up, so I poured out my cereal and fumbled through the mini-fridge for whatever might be left of my slightly outdated milk. For me, expiration dates were more of a *suggestion*, as opposed to a hard and fast rule. Twisting off the cap and smelling the contents brought only a mildly disturbing odor. There was still some life left in this bottle so I was in business: *ah...the breakfast of champions.*

Coming out the front door and down the few steps leading to the yard brought me face first with one of my neighbors whom I had never met. He was a young boy about ten years old, small and haggard, his clothes draping over his body like a tent – sleeves too long and pants too baggy. My sudden appearance seemed to startle him and he began to sheepishly mutter apologies for playing in my half of the front yard. His speech betrayed the fact that he was a special needs child of some sort, his face awkwardly twisting into various contortions as he struggled with a speech impediment. His body movements were also stiff revealing a degree of physical impairment as well. Wanting to dispel his anxieties, I quickly knelt down to his level and assured him that I didn't see any sort of fence dividing our lawn; further assuring him *that* meant that *both* of us could walk to any side we pleased. I even said, "look" as I took several steps to the left, setting my foot on *his* side of the yard. This revelation brought a huge smile to his face and his stature seemed to grow an extra inch or so.

Over the next couple of weeks I got to know the kid pretty well. It became obvious that he had figured out my schedule, what time I got up, when I left for work, and perhaps even when I usually got home from work, though that would have been well past his bed time. I found out his name was Jimmy, and for some reason, right from day-one, this kid had immediately decided that the stranger living next-door was now a potential playmate. Eager to not disappoint, I had gone to my car and dug out an old football from the back seat, and that turned out to be the beginning of what would be our daily routine: usually meeting on the lawn after breakfast, me trying to chase away the remnants of sleep, he waiting anxiously to throw the football back and forth around the yard with his new buddy.

I was amazed and humbled by his determination to learn this new skill. When you think about it, a football is rather an odd shape, and not the easiest thing to throw *or* catch if you're a beginner. And given his physical disabilities, he was having more of a challenge than most. But whatever the difficulty involved, Jimmy was smitten by this magic dimpled leather play toy with the white laces. His attempts to catch the strange oblong sphere were often awkward to say the least. I tried to patiently teach him to catch the ball with his hands in front, but even though the ball was thrown softly, I would grimace as the ball often slapped directly into his chin, cheek, or forehead, and only *then* would his hands and arms clumsily surround the ball. Undaunted, he would always shake it off, smile, and return for more. *What a trooper.*

Our time together reminded me of the simple truth; that happiness is not based on elaborate adventures and unceasing accomplishments – it was most often found in the seemingly mundane experience of living in the moment, content to be where life placed you, merely happy to act and react with another human being. Most people's lives seemed crowded with multiple "things" and grabbing those "things" and holding on to them tightly, *whatever* they were, seemed to choke out the original feeling of enjoyment you had when you acquired them in the first place. People seemed to do this not just with personal possessions but with various life experiences as well. But compiling the trophy heads of memories on your sacred wall of experiences or accomplishments was living in the past, with those remembrances simply collecting dust, mere shadowy medallions of things that were in the past. The problem is that life can't be lived in the past. I was still trying to learn that lesson myself.

Jimmy was truly happy. He lived in the moment. Perhaps he didn't have the intellectual capacity to look further down life's potential paths and covet all the things that would eventually just leave one looking for more. *Good for him.* But for whatever the reason, it was plain that this young boy had a gift; the gift of contentment, all wrapped up in and disguised by a body that most people would either mock or pity. I had a different reaction to this child. *I envied him.* Where as most people were running *towards* the elusive future "trophy life", I was on the other end of the spectrum - still running *away* from my dismal and abusive past life. Neither scenario lives in the present. Neither life ever experiences true contentment. And here was little Jimmy, happy in his small yard, taking one throw after another on the chin, and smiling widely all the time. I'm sure passersby would think it kind of me to associate with Jimmy, but truth be told, I wasn't so sure that it wasn't *me* who gleaned the most out of our encounters. Time with him seemed like time spent in the presence of real unadulterated love, a feeling that up to this point in my life was totally foreign to me.

Eventually Jimmy's mother would have to break up our front yard fun with a call to lunch. "Mum", as Jimmy called her, was a sweet girl who looked too young to have a son. Her real name was Abigail, or Abby for short. I never asked if there was a dad in the picture, after all, what possible good answer could come out of that question? *Oh yea, he left us for another woman, or, no…he's dead…thank you for asking.* It was obvious that they lived alone and that was yet another area of common ground between us. Loners by choice or by necessity. Didn't matter which. Since my work hours meant eating a late breakfast, their lunch hour was always way too early for me. And besides, I couldn't be sure that bringing another hungry mouth to their table wouldn't topple their modest household budget. You could tell she appreciated my connection to her son, but I never wanted to give even the remotest impression that I needed any kind of payback for our relationship. This connection was the closest thing I'd had resembling family in years.

Trouble began brewing a few days later during a typical late work night. I remember it all too well. It was one o'clock in the morning, an hour before I would lock up the diner and head for home. On my way out back to the trash bins, I suddenly remembered that I had forgot to empty the two wastebaskets kept in the front of the restaurant behind the barstool counter. So propping the door open with a trash bag, I made my way back into the diner. Once I picked up the baskets, I saw a couple small piles of debris that I had missed earlier; just some straw wrappers, a paper napkin, and a couple of discarded food receipts. So I swept those up into one of he containers and made for the back once more, resuming the usual routine of disposing all the garbage in the bins. So far so good. But reentering the building, I had the odd sensation that I wasn't alone. I don't know if I had subconsciously noticed that something was out of place, or heard the slightest unfamiliar noise. But whatever it was, it brought a heightened sense of focus to an otherwise lackluster evening of work. Walking through the kitchen and into the patron's area of the diner confirmed my suspicions about unwanted company.

Two Jackals had made themselves comfortable in one of the red leather-tufted booths near the middle of the restaurant. They must have slipped into the building when the back door was left propped open. My unsophisticated alarm system had failed, because had I simply left the squeaky screen door shut instead of propped open, the noise would have alerted me sooner. Of course, I'm not sure that would have made a difference. The Jackals were on some underhanded mission and wouldn't scare off that easy. As it turned out: their mission for the evening was *me*. In the back of my mind there was always the suspicion that this confrontation was coming sooner or later, ever since they hassled me at the back of the diner that day. Still, sometimes even when you know something is inevitable, it nevertheless surprises you a bit when it actually happens. That was okay; I welcomed the chance to face these hoodlums. Two against one were decent odds for me.

I had heard the stories of these guys beating up kids and stealing their lunch money. *Not very original.* But it got worse than that: they once beat two young boys so badly they had to be hospitalized. Seems that these two poor kids had committed the heinous crime of simply getting lost and walking down the wrong street after school: the "Jackals street", whatever that meant. And there were much darker stories regarding what they did if their victim was a girl. The Jackals ruled not just by intimidation, but by following through with the violent acts they promised. *I hate people who prey on the weak.* I had been in this spot many times before. In these situations, the outcome was always in question, but I had no plans of walking away with my tail between my legs. Maybe I *did* have some sort of death wish after all.

At first, they made it clear that since I was the new kid in town, I should pay them proper respect by fixing them a late night snack. We *were* in a diner after all. My refusal didn't exactly make them happy. I knew instinctively where this evening was going to end up. This was a shakedown pure and simple. It was about raw power and control mixed with equal parts intimidation and certain bodily harm. A caustic cocktail indeed. These were the town dogs lifting their legs to pee on yet another tree in their neighborhood. That last thought made me smile: the image of two mangy dogs wearing leather jackets proudly relieving themselves, vainly posturing to someone who couldn't care less and was not intimidated. For some reason, the smile on my face brought a frown to theirs. Calmly assessing the situation, I wanted to cut to the chase. Their position in the booth made me extremely happy. They had both elected to sit on the same side of the table so they could face me when I came back through the kitchen. *A serious tactical error.* Now there was no real way for them *both* to fight effectively at the same time since one of them was tucked next to the wall, his buddy blocking him in, and the tabletop serving as a lap belt. *Good thinking boys.*

I slowly moved towards them and that actually seemed to surprise them. Undoubtedly they were *way* more used to people running away from them. Perhaps they now thought my placid movement in their direction represented a humble submission to their superior power. In reality, the stories of their brutality towards the innocent had already placed them firmly on my radar and now my anger towards them for intruding into my place of employment was barely containable. *Did I mention I hate bullies?* Taking the seat opposite them and calmly staring them down made them just the slightest bit nervous or uneasy, I'm not sure which. I sensed it, but they of course were too stupid to make any rational assessment of the situation. Overconfidence does that. When they fully realized that I was not intimidated and was not going to serve as their waiter for the evening, they began a long list of expletives laced within a general story of what they were going to do to me. I'm no physician, but I think they even included a few things that I believe were anatomically impossible. *Oh well, perhaps these guys had some advanced medical degrees that I was unaware of.* At a certain point I'd heard enough and my patience was worn paper-thin. The thug nearest the aisle eventually finished his diatribe; confident he had said his piece and confident that he had proverbially beat his chest in a convincingly beastly fashion. He then calmly draped his right arm across the back of the booth and around his buddy. *His last tactical mistake.*

Quick as a snake I threw my body into the aisle, grabbed his left ankle, tightly holding it to my chest, and did a crocodile roll. Since he was wedged into the booth, this served to twist his ankle at an alarming angle and also drag him face first into the floor. Then as I stood up, I dropped my entire weight, knee first, onto the back of his right calf. He shrieked in pain, both legs now disabled at least for the immediate future and his ankle most likely severely sprained if not broken. To finish the job I rammed my left elbow down onto his left ear. *Lights out.* Fights from my past had taught me that speed was of the essence when fighting multiple enemies. Most of this happened so fast, the other thug, stupidly trapped inside the booth, failed to react in any kind of timely fashion. That would be *his* problem, because now the odds were certainly more even. I even wondered if he might make a run for it because bullies were often cowards down deep. Not waiting to find out, I scurried down the aisle away from the front door in order to steady myself for the next encounter if there was to be one.

Of course, even with the evidence lying in a twisted heap right before his very eyes, the second Jackal weighed the odds and made the *wrong* decision. He started bull rushing straight towards me. I suspected that these guys really hadn't done much fighting; perhaps using intimidation and larger numbers left them soft in the self-defense category. I on the other hand had spent *most* of my life fighting in one way or another, either just to protect myself or protect others from these same kinds of bullies. Charging straight towards your victim at full speed seems like a good idea, but it almost always backfires. It gives your opponent the opportunity to use your own momentum against you. That was *exactly* what I intended to do. In this case it would prove doubly deadly because I had strategically placed myself close to the back wall. Bullies often forget that fighting is not all about brawn; *brains* have to be brought into the equation as well. As he reached full speed and was nearly on me, I quickly sidestepped, grabbed his right wrist, wrenched it painfully upward and behind his back, and then simply continued his momentum straight into the back wall. Most people don't fare so well when they come face first and high speed into an immovable object. This guy was no exception. After his intimate collision with lath and plaster, he dropped like a sack of potatoes - broken nose for sure, and broken wrist probable.

After these encounters, it was always hard to curb the rage. Gloating over a victory was never the inspiration to fight. At least not for me. No, my desire to engage in violence against those who mistreated others was somehow *overly* important to me. I'm not a psychologist so I don't always understand it. But it did betray a sort of inner rage that was fueled by some hidden dark part of my spirit. Right now, murderous thoughts floated in the gloomy recesses of my mind, circling like vultures over wasteland carcasses. *How much better the world would be without these two.* I don't think I could ever act on those sinister feelings, but the fact that I had them in the first place scared me. Eventually I just sat on the cold floor, watching the villain's chests gradually rise and fall with the shallow breathing of unconsciousness.

After a short while, I stood up with a plan. I certainly didn't want to get the police involved because I couldn't risk losing my job. So the only alternative was to move the bodies somewhere else where they could sleep it off. Thankfully there was a city park directly across the street from the diner. Picking them up one by one elicited the expected groans from those with multiple injuries, but I actually tried to be careful and not hurt them any further. The rest of the story was not very exciting: locking up the diner, dragging them over to the park, desperately trying not to throw their bikes in the trash in favor of bringing them to the park as well. And that's where I left the thugs: both of them on one park bench. I realize it was a dirty trick, but I couldn't resist lying one right on top of the other in a seemingly rapturous embrace. A little juvenile I agree, but I couldn't help myself. When they woke up, they would find their bikes parked right next to them and they could work their way home to lick their wounds. I'm no fool. I realized that I was lucky this time. They had not even laid a hand on me. Many fights from my early days did not end so gracefully. But this time, I could enjoy the fact that it was a *complete* victory and also one from which I didn't have to nurse any injuries. The drive home gave my anger time to slowly drain away, though I'm not sure it ever left me entirely. Ever.

The next day was certainly not as eventful and Jimmy and I settled comfortably into our daily routine of playing catch with the dangerous facial orb. It was good therapy for me and always seemed to make the already happy Jimmy even happier. But there was now the nagging notion that change was blowing in the wind as they say. The perception was that of seeing just a mere glimpse of storm clouds off in the distant horizon. But knowing that they were coming your way. Something felt more dangerous in the wind and in the rustling of the leaves in the trees. It didn't take me long to realize what it was. It had been subconsciously rumbling around in the back of my mind, unspoken since last night. The

Jackals were probably not the type to just roll up their storefront and move out of town. They would be on the hunt looking for me. And that's when the full lightening bolt of fear hit me. I wasn't concerned for myself. But what if they were somehow able to connect me with Jimmy and Abby? The thought caused a wave of nausea and panic to overtake me and I shot to my feet, pacing back and forth. Jimmy was immediately concerned, asking what was wrong. But after being assured that everything was okay his bright smile returned.

Harm coming to this family in *any* way was unacceptable. They were family. Yet here we were, unprotected and visible to all right in the front yard. Our duplex basically had no backyard because it backed up into a sheer hillside, so that meant hanging out behind the house was not an option. I didn't feel comfortable burdening Abby or Jimmy with the details of what had happened, and in reality I didn't want them living in fear, so it was going to be my job to make sure nobody found out where I lived. My mind raced furiously, trying to remember whom if anyone knew my address. To my knowledge, only the owner of the diner could know since he had my job application somewhere in his files. As far as I could remember, that was the only connective tissue that could lead to my whereabouts. I convinced myself that I would just have to be careful. And that began by purchasing a car cover for my rather "unique" vehicle. Truth be told, covering up that hideous car probably single-handedly raised the property values in the neighborhood.

Being careful worked. For a couple of weeks. It turned out that my suspicions were correct; the Jackals were on high alert and looking for me. I had expected them to return to the diner late one night with all their forces, and I had planned accordingly. *More about that later.* But surprisingly, they never came. I imagine they were concerned that I might have gone to the cops and that the diner might be under surveillance. They were wrong. During that fateful night, one of the two thugs that had showed up in the restaurant had been blathering on and on about the gang, trying to scare me with gory details. But one fact that came out during his little speech, and stuck with me, was that the gang consisted of only six members. This had confirmed one of the things I thought might be true of the Jackals: small time…small numbers…big mouths. But still nothing to trifle with.

Their search basically consisted of bicycling through the neighborhoods looking for a guy who fit my description, a description undoubtedly given to them by the bloodied and now recovering dynamic duo. As unsophisticated as it was, it eventually and regrettably worked. This was a pretty small town after all. Not really *that* many neighborhoods to check if you were obsessively committed to finding your prey. They were. It happened one morning. I was always careful to watch the street when we played in the front yard, but unfortunately, this particular day I let my guard down at just the wrong time. Jimmy and I were tossing and chasing the ball around and when I looked up, there was one lone Jackal pedaling by the house looking right in our direction. Quickly turning my face towards the house was my only defense against possible detection…*if my cover was not blown already*. I had the sinking feeling I was too late. After a while, I risked another glance at the street and saw that the hunter's once leisurely pace had been replaced by an all out sprint, pedaling back in the direction from whence he came. *Not good.*

So after that day it wasn't a matter of *if* but *when*. They knew my address. They could study my routine. Eventually the Jackals would make their move. Of course, just when you think you have figured things out, life throws you a curveball. I knew these guys were going to come for me, but what they did defied any rational thought process of normal human beings. Having had so many encounters with bullies, perhaps I should have seen it coming. One morning I woke up to the sounds of moaning and screaming coming from the front yard. An ominous sense of dread spilled through me, saturating my entire spirit. Fumbling with my clothes, I quickly dressed and ran out the front door only to be sickened by what I saw. Abby was on her knees with Jimmy's bloody face in her lap. The small boy was moaning and rocking back and forth as his mother cradled him and sobbed uncontrollably. *Guilt by association.* In their sickened and perverted sense of justice, the Jackals had attacked Jimmy in order to punish me.

I was eventually able to piece the picture together as Abby slowly gave me what information she could muster through rivers of sobs and tears. She had just finished washing dishes from breakfast when she heard Jimmy cry out from the front yard. Running outside, she was horrified to see six guys in leather jackets beating on her poor son who undoubtedly had no idea what was going on. She punched and clawed at those on top of her only child only to be slapped with a backhand by one bully and pushed roughly to the ground by another so they could get in their last few blows. Then they all took off on bikes leaving their victims in a heap on the front lawn. I remember trying to control my breathing while at the same time making involuntary guttural noises of pain and frustration. My sense of shame was nearly overwhelming as I dropped to my knees and put both arms around the two of them. I couldn't have missed the brutes by much. I had no idea where they had gone, but I certainly knew exactly who they were. And painfully, I knew why they did what they did. They had hurt Jimmy to send a message to me. My heart raced so fast, my pulse pounding so hard it felt like my head would explode. Maniacal rage was boiling hot inside my soul pushing me into a near frenzy, but I had to hold on to my last precious ounce of composure for the sake of Abby and Jimmy.

The Jackals had sent their entire gang, six putrid human beings, all to terrorize one innocent child. *Real tough guys.* I ran back to my car and ripped off the cover letting it float to the side of the driveway. Then, returning to the wounded couple, I scooped up Jimmy and led Abby by the hand to the car. Those monsters were going to pay, one way or the other. After gently lowering Jimmy into the back seat, mom joined him and I ran around to the other side of the car, flinging open the driver's side door. Jimmy's cries had dwindled down to a whimper. He was going to make it, but I wondered if he would ever be the same carefree child he once was. He had now been ushered into the cruel heartless adult world, a world that in his condition he could *never* possibly understand. I stood on the gas pedal and rocketed out of the driveway wildly spewing gravel in multiple directions. The hospital was not far away but the county police station was even closer.

Since Jimmy was not in any immediate medical danger, I swung into the police station first. Abby and I spilled out the story in vivid detail but there were a few specific bits of information that I had already decided to keep to myself. One of which was *who* exactly did this. I'd witnessed small town justice before and it often worked slowly because of excessive due process. My plan was not to wait for that nonsense. This was going to be dealt with sooner rather than later. This stop just assured that a complaint was filed and put on record for my later use. They eventually ushered us into a back room, one where they usually interrogated potential criminals, and we finished our story and the necessary paper work. As it turned out, one of the policemen used to be a paramedic and he was able to tend to the wounds: Jimmy's being a broken nose, a cracked rib, and multiple contusions; Abby's, physical injuries were of a far lesser concern - some scratches and bruises. But her mental and emotional injuries were yet to be seen in the long run.

After leaving the police station, I took Abby and Jimmy back to their side of the dilapidated duplex and made sure they were safely locked away. Part of my plan, ever since I knew the Jackals had found me and were coming after me, was to preemptively gather as much information on all the gang members as I could. It wasn't really very hard since nearly everyone in town had some kind of story about the gang's evil exploits. My dear sweet Abby, on the other hand, was sheltered enough on her side of town to not realize who the attackers were. That fact helped me with the police since the Jackals identity was the ace in the hole for my plans. But plenty of other townsfolk new *exactly* who the Jackals were and they provided reams of information about the hoodlums. The beauty of a small town: it wasn't long before I knew all their names, addresses, hangouts, and there main "secret" meeting place out near the county line. *Secret…what a joke: hard to keep secrets in a small town.* I now had a clear focus as to what to *do* with the information. It wasn't going to be pretty for the Jackal boys.

It was time to get down to business. This would have to be done quickly if my plan was going to work. I couldn't risk any one of the six Jackals going underground before the job was done. I figured I would have about 24 hours at the most to complete things. My first two visits were to the thugs that had tried to shake me down at the diner. To that end, I had purchased a long ratty overcoat at the local thrift shop and a small bag of charcoal from the hardware store. A simple disguise, but one that would initially get me close to each of the gang members. The tattered coat made me look like a homeless guy, with charcoal applied to the face in splotches completing the picture. The one whose ankle I snapped in my first attack that night was named Dan. He liked to hang out at a local burger joint trying to pick up underage girls. *Nice guy.* I approached the restaurant my head down, my hair a mess, and with a fresh beer partially poured onto the front of my jacket.

The underage market must have been slim this evening, because Dan was standing outside all by himself. As I walked by, I staggered slightly into his shoulder as if drunk, then proceeded down the sidewalk. Predictably he started calling after me, offended that I had soiled his nice leather jacket. Then a simple half run set the bait as he clumsily chased me around the corner of the restaurant. When he hobbled around the bend I was facing him and calmly asked in a very non-inebriated and threatening voice why he was limping? The recognition shown immediately in his eyes, and all confidence drained from his tough guy image. But it was too late. My foot came down on his partially healed ankle, which put him in enormous pain and in a perfect position for the knock out blow to his right temple. *One down….five to go*

The other thug from the diner was as predictable as a Swiss watch. His name was Bret, and he spent most nights barhopping in the downtown district trying to lift a few wallets from drunken patrons. *Ah…Mother Teresa would be proud.* It took me a few tries in different bars, but I soon found him in a place called Dottie's Distillery. My shabby disguise would make me an unwanted guest in any establishment, so, not wanting to draw attention to myself, I simply waited for him outside the bar; it was close to last call anyway, so the wait wouldn't be too long. Sure enough, before long, he exited the building and started walking up the sidewalk. I fell in step behind him. When he sensed someone invading his personal space, he whirled around. I distinctly remember that his nose was still swollen from our last encounter, and rather than reinvent the wheel, I threw a crunching blow right to the same spot. He howled in pain and a couple more well directed blows finished him off. I then proceeded to drag him into a dark ally where I left him lying in a puddle of his own blood. My parting gift to him was wiping my bloodied hand on his nice leather jacket, right across the Jackal emblem.

In my mind, I had been relatively kind to the first two Jackals, figuring that they were banged up pretty bad from the diner and probably did little more than keep watch as the other four beat on Jimmy. As for the remaining Jackals, well, they were going to have some pretty serious long-term recoveries ahead of them. I did manage to find all of them within my 24-hour window. The next three encounters went pretty smoothly with me getting the drop on each one of them and then trying desperately to leave them alive. I managed to do just that, but it was harder than you might imagine. The third gorilla from this terrible trifecta recognized me before my attack and started to fabricate various unkind things about Abby. *What is it about guys who can talk such disgusting things about a woman and think that makes him tough?* My rage was already at a fever pitch, so he wasn't doing himself any favors. He was going to wake up in a hospital and realize there was substantial dental work to done in his near future. So far, he was the toughest to leave behind still alive.

The last Jackal turned out to be the hardest battle by far. I'm not sure if one of the others managed to get a phone call through to him, but he

103

actually seemed ready for me as I pulled up to his house. My intelligence gathering had revealed that he was the leader of the Jackals: one big mean ugly guy in his mid twenties with hands that were as hard as bricks. I found that out the hard way. His name was Ryker and he was the oldest of the bunch, square in the shoulders, with muscular arms, but flabby at the waist. My strategy was to keep my distance and count on speed and intuition to win the battle. I parked the car and stepped out onto the street. He had been waiting for me. Ryker wasted no time; he stepped out from behind his screen door and began with a fairly complete though inaccurate account of my family heritage, most of it involving farm animals mating with various ethnic groups. *Funny how nearly all bullies were typically racist as well…and I'm pretty sure he flunked his high school health class given his bizarre descriptions of breeding and reproduction.* He finished with some more anatomical exaggerations that seemed to bend if not break the laws of physics and then beckoned me forward with a smug smile in his face.

That was fine by me; I was more than ready to get this over with. Cautiously I advanced on his position. I felt that if I could best this bum, it would be a serious blow to the reputation of the Jackals; perhaps it would even be the beginning of the end for these losers. Usually, once bullies were defeated, it emboldened others to stand up to them. These guys needed to be taken down a notch and I hoped I was the one who could at least start their downward spiral. But either way, this guy was going down, or I was going to die trying. My mind was already made up the minute I saw Jimmy and Abby lying bloody in the front yard. Ryker was undoubtedly the ringmaster of the other goons and would have ordered and played the biggest part in Jimmy's beating. Looking at the size of this brute made my heart sink as I pictured him throwing punches at a poor defenseless kid; I couldn't imagine the horror little Jimmy must have felt.

As I neared his position at his front door he quickly reached inside his house and pulled out a solid two and a half foot long spruce two by four and lunged towards me swinging wildly. The first swing caught me by surprise, grazing the top of my head as I narrowly ducked under the swing. Though stung by the shot, I thankfully had enough sense left to leap backward because the next downward slashing blow would have nearly taken off my head. Bludgeoning weapons were risky: connect fully with one and the battle is likely over right then and there. But when you *miss*, your weight is shifted to one side or the other leaving you vulnerable for a counterstrike. That was the opportunity for my first connecting punch, which was placed solidly into his left kidney. I know I'd hurt him, but with a swift recovery he gave me a backhand to the face that left me seeing stars. This gave me some rather discouraging information: this guy was strong as an ox but could also think on his feet. *Not a good combination for me.*

The battle of cat and mouse went on for a while; him often coming dangerously close to connecting with his mighty swings, me trying to study his movements without "becoming one" with the big stick. Finally the moment came. After one of his wild swings I sprang forward and dealt a crushing kick to the front of his right knee bending it backwards to the point of tearing several ligaments. The excruciating pain caused him to drop the two by four. Feeling that the moment was right I continued with the next blow to his face but was surprised to discover that he still had had enough presence of mind to block it, even though he was in excruciating pain. That's when it got ugly for me. After blocking my punch he grabbed my wrist and pulled me to the ground as he rolled on top of me. He then began choking me with both hands, a disturbingly evil glint glowing in his eyes. At first it was all I could do just to grab his wrists and keep as much pressure off my neck as possible. But he was winning the war of attrition, his sick smile widening. I was dangerously close to blacking out.

In a last moment epiphany I suddenly remembered the dropped two by four and risked taking one hand off the brute's wrists in order to grope for the weapon. Thankfully finding it fairly quickly, I used the remainder of my waning strength to pound the right side of his leg, hoping to find the shattered knee. On the fifth blow I'd found my target, connecting a solid heavy blow to the side of his already damaged kneecap. This caused him to shriek in pain and loosen his grip. As he reached back with his left hand to grab the board, he lifted his head a bit. I was then able to pull his right hand off my throat and get enough room for a solid head-butt to the bridge of his nose. The crunch of cartilage and the stream of blood reinvigorated me. *Perhaps this was not going to be my last day on earth after all.* Now that he was severely hurt in two different areas, I was able to push the behemoth off of me and rise to my feet. What followed was a frenzied and maniacal rain of fists into all the vital places I could think of. It took me awhile to realize that at some point I was beating a body that had long ago gone limp. He was a bloody mess and my clothes were covered in equal parts sweat and blood spray. For a moment I thought that I might have killed him. And at that moment it hadn't bothered me in the least. It was only a couple of minutes later that I recoiled at the thought and checked for a pulse. He was still connected to this world, though I suspected he would be the longest Jackal out of commission. *Good.*

I reached down again and searched the body. It was time to finish my plan. As luck would have it I found what I was looking for in his left back pocket; his smart phone. Then I picked up the bloody two by four and made my way back to the car, my neck in pain and already beginning to show deep purple and sickly yellow bruise marks. Their main hang out was in an old abandoned one-room farmhouse out near the edge of town. That hideaway was a vital part in the next step of my plan. On the way there I pulled behind a gas station and slipped into the restroom to clean up. The sink ran crimson with bloody water as I washed up as thoroughly as I could. Then I ditched the ratty overcoat in a trash bin, stopped at the pump filling a two-gallon gas can, and made for the Jackals hideaway. Along the way I made sure to press the speed dials on the phone one by one, connecting for as long as the recipients would keep the line open with me saying not a word. Of course considering their injuries, most did not even pick up.

When I got to the farmhouse I took the gasoline out of the car and poured it around the wood connecting the base of the house with the dirt. It only took one match. The house was soon completely engulfed in flames and since we were on the edge of town, away from any firehouse, I risked a little private viewing of my pyrotechnic masterpiece. It was actually quite beautiful, the yellow flames set against the backdrop of a reddish-orange sky; but beautiful mostly for what it represented – *the Jackals were not untouchable.* Not wanting to tempt fate for too long, when it was obvious that the hideaway was going to completely burn to the ground, I hopped back into the car and made my way towards home, repeating my speed dial routine once again. That should leave the police with some interesting cell tower evidence. The dawn was not far away as I parked in front of Ryker's house. He was no longer lying in his front yard, so either he had dragged his sorry butt back into the house or one of the other Jackals had shown up to help him. The most likely scenario was that he was already at the hospital. Before arriving at Ryker's house, I had made a call, trying my best to approximate the voice of a man who had been beaten badly. My impersonation wouldn't win any Academy awards, but it got the job done.

The gist of the call to the police was how sorry I was that the Jackals had beaten up poor Jimmy and that I couldn't take the guilt anymore so I burned down our gang headquarters right off of Cedar Road, near the county line. I also included the details of beating up the other gang members but sustaining a severe beating of my own. That last detail wouldn't hold up, but it might confuse the cops for a while. When they asked for my name I croaked out "Ryker...Ryker Henderson." Let's see: assault and battery on a minor and a young woman, destruction of property, and arson. That would throw a wrench in the Jackals plans for quite awhile. And most importantly, they would *dare* not lay a finger on Jimmy and Abby ever again since the police were now on the case. Of course there were plenty of holes in the story, but whether or not convictions resulted was not the point. Payback and future safety for my newfound family was the goal. *Not bad for a single days work.* I wiped Ryker's phone for prints, threw it into the bushes right next to his front door, and drove away.

The hardest part emotionally was yet to come. Early morning sunrise was gradually overtaking the night, bathing the countryside in a soft yellow hue and banishing the darkness back to its dismal chambers on the other side of the world. Not wishing to wake anyone at this early hour, I parked in the street by our duplex and quietly made my way to the door. For stealth, I guided my steps to the dead grass on the side of the lawn instead of the loose gravel of the driveway. It didn't take long to gather up my belongings. I was the antithesis of a hoarder, living modestly with very little in the way of worldly possessions. Before long, the car was loaded, and I then sat down at the kitchen table to write a short note to my soon to be lost family. I only gave the broadest outline of what I'd done and gave them advice about what *to* do and what *not* to do from this point on. It was only fair that they knew who their attackers were. And it was also only fair that I move away so that any attempts at retribution would not spill over into their innocent lives. I also left them a present: one of the Jackal's coats. I had taken Dan's coat after re-breaking his ankle. I'm not sure why I picked him, but I think it was his prowling around for underage girls that sealed the deal. I let Abby know that it would be a good idea to take it to the police and tell them that one of the thugs had left it on the front yard after the beating. *A lie, I know, but it's hard to live all of life within the lines of black and white morality.* The earlier police report we filed on the day of the beating would mix quite nicely with this new bit of evidence.

Now, I knew what had to be done next, but it was nearly unbearable for me. My hand was shaking slightly as I finished scribbling the note. Once finished, I shut off the lights and closed the door so my creepy pets could once again have full run of the place. Then I inched up the steps to their door and wedged the note inside the rusty screen door. My final gesture was one that, in some ways, hurt the most: I placed the football on the front porch, laces up just like Jimmy liked it, and then quietly stepped back down the stairs. The trip out of town was quiet, a sleepy town just now beginning to wake up to another day. As for me, when I came to the highway, I made a completely arbitrary left turn taking me east. To where, I had *no* idea. My mind was clouded by the heavy and costly decision I had just made. I knew it was the right one because I could never risk jeopardizing the safety of my two friends. But it was still incredibly hard for me. The only way for me to stay in this town *and* ensure the safety of everyone would be to kill all six Jackals. I couldn't quite take that step and live with myself afterwards, though I'd be lying if I said I didn't consider it. As I drove out of town I tried to be a tough guy, but eventually a single tear drifted lazily down my cheek. Family now gone forever. Again.

Chapter 9 – The Beginning of the End

What had once presented itself as pure adventure and exploration had turned out to be more like captivity and enslavement. This mountain seemed to be a monument to failed dreams and unfulfilled expectations. In Hamartia I found no friends, only people that disgusted me for various reasons. The quest for fulfillment in this earthen graveyard was always baiting you to proceed further, while at the same time escorting you into one depressing situation after another. And yet here I was. No ability to go back and only the rapidly disintegrating hope that something was still worthy of discovery inside this deceptive mountain. As for now: righting one particular wrong was foremost in my mind. My footsteps were taking me directly towards two less than desirable human beings - two people who seemed to actually find humor in the suffering of others. The red-haired elfin young woman had made eye contact with me and was moving a couple of hesitant steps away from my advance. That was fine, because she was not my target. The debonair hypocrite on the other hand was holding his ground. *Good.* I had no patience with people who made sport of others and mocked the suffering of others. The man was my target and perhaps the waiflike pixie would watch and learn a valuable lesson on proper respect for others today.

Pacing myself, I locked eyes with the hypocrite and made no secret of the fact that I was unwaveringly going to continue in his direction. I'm also sure I telegraphed the fact that this was not to be a friendly "get to know each other" moment. As for my new nemesis, he seemed to grasp the situation fast enough, but was not ready to give way to an unfamiliar foe. *His mistake.* As far as I could tell, he had deceived all who came into contact with him, putting on various faces that suited his selfish interests at any given moment. Even though others might not see his underhanded purposes, it didn't change the fact that he secretly pushed others around just like any other bully. He was just more subtle and devious about it. I remembered from previous observations that this guy could very well be a problem in a fight. That was okay; it seemed that most of my life was one big fight after another. So be it. I marched forward.

The touch to my shoulder surprised me because I hadn't perceived anyone following me. I whirled around only to find the raven-haired girl standing right behind me. Déjà vu to say the least, but this time there was no flowing garments and no phantom wind blowing through her hair – just beauty standing there looking at me with a wry smile. She was one of the very few things that could have distracted me from my immediate progression towards the twin mockers. Okay…maybe the *only* thing. Her allure still overwhelmed me, though my fascination was tinged with a fairly large presence of caution after witnessing her alter ego in the gray shadow land. But she seemed so different here in the real world. There was warmth to her touch in this reality, her eyes captivating and penetrating with a hypnotic promise of real human connection; a connection that I simply couldn't resist. I've often wondered what would have happened if I'd avoided her once and for all that day. But I suppose that's all irrelevant now; I ultimately did *not* resist her charms and for many weeks after, I was almost solely in her company.

At first it felt like new life was breathed into my dying spirit. I didn't know much about spirituality, but if there *was* a spiritual realm, then surely the connection between lovers was the one connection that came closest to transcending this barren world. But in this case, it didn't take long to realize that every intimate encounter with her left me feeling diminished in some way - each moment of passion seeming to forfeit a crucial piece of me. I think these feelings came from an intuitive knowledge that her affections were tainted in some way, and that I was taking advantage of that fact…she likewise. Moments of togetherness, which *should* have made me, feel loved and accepted, always left me feeling hollow and guilt ridden. Eventually the guilt was replaced by darker emotions, ones of obsession and depression. Those two emotions were strange bedfellows, as were we, both of us obsessively drawn to something that only brought despair; but there I was: poisoned by her every embrace, yet powerless to give her up for fear of not feeling alive at all. That was perhaps the main root of my fear: to not be able to feel *anything* except the callous texture of indifference towards all that surrounded me. So accepting the dying embers of what was a cruel substitute for love was my choice by default.

That's how it went for quite awhile, my connection to beauty gradually draining the life out of an already desperately depleted soul. I knew I was perpetrating a crime against my own body while at the same time destroying what little sanity I still had left. Despair was slowly infiltrating my mind, body, and soul forming a trifecta of hopelessness. This despondency reached a fever pitch on the day I realized that I was not her only suitor. She tried to hide the betrayal of course, but I eventually put all the pieces together. There seems to be no greater disloyalty than cheating the one you say you love by giving your love to another - it's a dagger to the heart that penetrates living tissue up to the hilt and then breaks off the blade leaving it imbedded as a permanent reminder of the brutal treason. It leaves the betrayed one with a desperate feeling of inadequacy that most often scars them for life. Most people *never* fully recover from the treachery.

My inner-reaction to her moral treason scared me – I began to have violent thoughts that were dangerously close to spilling out into real actions. Having witnessed so much abuse against my mother, I had long ago vowed never to raise a hand against any woman, no matter *what* the offence might be. But her infidelity left me teetering on the brink of abandoning my convictions. Still, all the anger had to go somewhere; so I simply thrust it deeper into myself. I'm not sure if psychologists are correct when they say depression is simply anger turned inward, but that was certainly how it worked for me at least. I was trapped. The only thing for me to do that fulfilled *all* the duties of my internal moral compass was to leave beauty behind, no matter how much that devastated the remnants of my spirit. And devastate it did. I was rapidly tiring of leaving the things I love, even if this *particular* love was a mirage found within a wasteland of broken humanity.

I remember walking around despondently for several days, not really paying much attention to my direction or surroundings. As it turned out I had been gradually heading away from the trail that had first spilled into this encampment, moving towards what I initially thought to be the dead end wall of this box cavern. Surprisingly though, as I neared the far wall, I discovered that the trail had *not* ended within this settlement of malcontents – it actually picked up again at the far left side of the huge cavern. The choice to leave was not that hard. What was I giving up? The wayward people? The counterfeit love I could never embrace again? I was wrong about her warm touch in this world. It was actually as cold as ice in any kind of real emotional way. I took one last look back toward the caves. And watched various figures ambling around in what was undoubtedly some useless and empty endeavor. I wondered if they knew they were trapped here. No matter. As for me, I would not link my destiny to this place or these people. Less than enthusiastic, I once again joined the trail that I thought had ended. Downward.

I no longer held to the spurious notion that there was *anything* of worth to be found in this mountain. But, unable to go back, I resigned myself to the futile effort of moving deeper down the path into the unknown. As I descended, the surroundings seemed to grow more barren and ugly, the glowing green algae was now mixed with a brownish hue that dulled the ambient light considerably. The cave walls had also changed; they had become craggy, the black obsidian fragmented like broken glass and reflecting things in multiple facets like a kaleidoscopic house of mirrors. My reflection stared back at me, shattered and misshapen, which was probably a good representation of my life at that moment: a lost soul simply wandering forward for no immediate reason and with no guiding purpose. The sheer drop off on the side of the trail had also returned, the only difference being that it was now on my left side instead of my right. The relatively narrow path brought back a feeling of claustrophobia, as did the ceiling, which hung down slightly lower than it had on the upper trail.

There was another new addition to my surroundings. Thin hanging vines draping down from the cave ceiling gently swayed back and forth as an invisible wind current from somewhere deep in the crevasse gently stirred them back and forth. The undulating movement of the vines combined with the fractured reflective walls made a dizzy carousel of movement that made me feel woozy. To maintain my equilibrium while walking, I found that it was best to just stare at the trail directly in front of me. That helped to avoid feelings of lightheadedness. I really did not feel like succumbing to vertigo, fainting, and falling over the edge of the trail. That would probably *not* be the best way to test the depth of the drop. So carefully down I went, measuring my steps, ready to drop to my knees if the dizziness threatened to overtake me.

The faintest hint of voices would sometimes gently float up from somewhere deeper in the chasm, but they were never distinguishable as coherent language; just some unholy utterances dredged up from the bottom of this dismal and decaying mountain. Oddly enough, they reminded me of the voices I had heard in the smoky dimension of grayness. But that couldn't be; I was firmly planted in *this* world, and wide-awake. I tried to ignore the faint nonsensical words and instead concentrate on not becoming paranoid or delusional. With one foot in front of the other, and my eyes firmly planted on the terrain in front of me, I made my way down the path. This myopic concentration on the trail continued for many days but at least the pathway seemed a much better focal point than the fractured obsidian walls.

Many months ago, on the *upper* trail, I vainly imagined that the walls just might conceal menacing apparitions gazing out from their secret hideaway chambers. But now, the splintered walls with their twisted reflections of my surroundings gave the impression that those watchers had broken free from their bonds, the walls shattered and left as a memorial to their newfound freedom from a stone prison. It didn't help that at various intervals there were now substantial chunks missing from the inky walls, the vacant gaps receding back into the wall for unknown depths. Curiosity ran rampant, but the thought of sticking my arm into one of these fissures made my stomach turn. Too many childhood horror movies made me imagine a full arm going in but a far shorter and bloodied arm returning. *Still had my vivid imagination.* Trying my best to ignore all the bogus sensory warning bells, I pressed forward.

As fate would have it, I met two other individuals over the next few weeks. Like myself, both had come equally deep into the mountain and presumably both had traversed through the same camp that I had left not so long ago, though I never asked them about it. Perhaps they too saw the moral bankruptcy festering in that fraternity of fools who saw nothing better in life than to use and abuse those around them. Leaving had been a good choice. It was comforting to know that others had made the same wise decision as me. I met the first man when rounding a sharp corner of the trail. My eyes, focused down onto the trail as they most often were, failed to give me adequate warning of a body firmly planted in the middle of the pathway. I had been lost in reverie, thinking about my dismal journey thus far when I bumped straight into him, giving me quite a start. Adrenaline immediately coursed through my body as I backed away from the man. In my experience, most encounters in this mountain ended poorly. I expected nothing less from this meeting.

As for his part, he didn't even seem startled. As a matter of fact, it was as if he expected someone to be coming down this trail. That was probably no great feat since I wasn't exactly trying to be stealthy. Though not exactly pompous, he did exude an air of analytical intellect as he simply gave a nod in my direction and continued jotting something down in an old leather-bound journal. I took several more steps backward and quietly studied the man. He looked to be in his sixties with shoulder-length gray hair that was swept back behind his ears. The open collared dress shirt underneath a cardigan sweater gave him a professorial look, the pleated pants and leather slip-on shoes completing the picture. He seemed to be studying the cracked obsidian walls and making some kind of scientific notes in his journal. Eventually, he placed his pencil in the binding and casually closed his book. Then he began staring in my direction. He must have sensed my nervousness because at one point it seemed that he deliberately gave me a look that easily conveyed his lack of malice towards me. I had nothing to fear. Of course that reasoning was tested when he pointed back up the trail from where I had come. I pivoted to glance in the direction he was motioning, but before I knew what was happening, I felt an eight-inch blade positioned just below my Adam's apple. Needless to say I froze, slowly measuring my breathing. Then, after mere seconds, the blade was removed and as I turned to face the man he was quietly placing the blade back into its hidden sheath. The gesture had proved his point: if he had wanted me dead, I would already be bleeding out onto the dusty trail right this moment.

Though a little shaken by the ease in which he had gotten the drop on me, I was still glad he didn't have it out for me. My journey had already produced plenty of other enemies within this mountain. I didn't need another. I was also glad that my head was still attached to my neck, as it should be. *Thank God for the small things in life.* As he reopened his leather journal, he returned to his study of the obsidian walls, making copious notes of some sort. Mineral composition? Refractory capacities? I wasn't sure his purpose but I risked a closer look, reading over his right shoulder. The meticulous scribbling seemed to be mostly mathematical equations sprinkled with bits of undecipherable prose. Undoubtedly, the portions of text were something that brought some sort of clarity to the numeric calculations. It was "all Greek to me" as they say. I hated math in school. In my mind I gave him the name "professor"; it just seemed to fit.

His appearance deep in this mountain was just one more strange anomaly in a long list of abnormalities found in this place. He communicated only with gestures and facial expressions. It was odd that he would not speak to me in any way, but I intuitively responded in kind. Something told me that speaking to him would produce nothing in return, so silence ruled the day. As I glanced further down the trail, I made eye contact with the second new person I found deeper in the mountain. He was coming up the trail directly towards us. I wondered if the professor knew about the new guest almost upon us, but then I remembered how perceptive he had been with *my* approach not that much earlier. *He knew.* This new character ambled towards us with a slight limp in his steps. He seemed to be out of touch with his surroundings, his head swaying back and forth at arbitrary intervals looking *for* or *at* something that was only in his own mind. I'd seen the look before in the drug addicts who populated my school. In a small town, there was nothing much to do for the youth, so drugs were a popular choice for many.

When I was a kid, I always kept my distance from any substance abuse. I'd already seen how alcohol provoked my father to extreme anger, and I could only imagine what the effects might have been on our family if he had used something more extreme like narcotics. This wobbly fellow on the trail seemed harmless enough, but if drugs were in the picture, you could never tell for sure. Of course, it was possible that he simply had some sort of debilitating mental illness. As he approached, I could see that he wore multiple layers of tattered clothes on the upper half of his body; two button up shirts with an open sweater over a dirty undershirt. A loose belt cinched up tight held his baggy trousers in place. As is the case with many addicts or homeless folks, he had serious issues with personal hygiene. His face was unshaven and discolored from the layers of dirt that clung to his skin. There were also several open sores on his arms and neck where it looked like he had either fallen or had simply scratched his nails along the surface of his skin. Perhaps in his unstable condition he had endured a few tumbles straight into the sharp obsidian walls. Either way, it was not a pretty picture. I lowered my defenses a bit; this guy was deathly frail and not a threat to anybody. My caution was replaced by pity. Whatever had happened to this man had made him a mere shell of whatever he once was.

For his part, the professor finally turned to face the man, studying him, and flipping his journal back to some earlier pages. He was jotting some notes as he studied our unsteady friend. Then, after a while, he pulled a small bag out of his pocket. Apparently the two knew each other. Up until now, the shaky visitor had been completely unfocused…until he saw the small bag in the professor's outstretched hand. At that point, his entire focus shifted. His *only* interest was the shiny two-inch square cellophane bag filled with some sort of brownish green material. The contents of the packet looked a lot like the algae from the trail but with a more grainy texture and a slightly darker color. Perhaps this was a chemical combination of the professors' making. The guy seemed to be a genius after all. The pharmaceutical mastermind held up the bag, gently turning it forward and backward, and then placed it at his own feet. He then sat down and continued writing in his journal, studying the man, and making more notes. The shaky man began to whimper and shift his feet nervously back and forth as if slowly dancing with himself but eagerly looking to partner up with the bag lying at the professors' feet.

This had all the earmarks of a drug buy, but the odd connection between these two men had me baffled. The professor had obviously made up the concoction that the addict so eagerly craved. But the fact that he was dispassionately studying the man and presumably taking notes on his behavior was more than a little disturbing. This was like some sterile observation of a lab rat in a medical experiment. I couldn't imagine what the addict had to offer in exchange for the substance he was craving. And his "dealer" seemed perfectly content to simply study the man's misery and bodily moments, continuing to jot down annotations in his journal. As for me, I desperately wanted to help the poor man, but this was well beyond my level of ability, especially so deep in the mountain with no access to medical supplies. I didn't like witnessing the suffering of others…been there, done that…to see it in others only reminded me of my own dark days of helplessness. I kept trying to think of ways to aid the jittery addict, but my reverie was broken when the professor snatched up the bag and threw it directly at his test subject. The bag bounced off his chest and landed a few feet in front of him. The distance did not last long as he quickly dropped to his knees and scrambled forward on all fours to claim his prize.

The professor rapidly scrawling notes, the addict frantically clawing at the bag but being careful not to spill the contents, the *observer* pausing only long enough to quickly stare at his subject, the *observed* shamelessly and greedily opening his prized treasure: what was happening in this crazy scenario? I never figured it out until later. For now, the addict brought out an old plastic cup and dumped the grainy material inside. Then he grabbed a small canteen of water from his waistband and completed the mixture, gently swirling the concoction back and forth in his cup until the gritty powder was completely dissolved. Then, in joyous rapture, he slowly lifted the cup to his mouth and drank the contents. It was odd how fast the drug took affect. Within a few seconds, you could visibly see his muscles relax, jitteriness vanished in favor of serene calm, and his eyes seemed to glaze over as he looked upward towards some fixed mirage on the cave ceiling that only *he* could see. Of course the other partner in this disturbing scenario was still coldly jotting down observations in the leather journal.

After awhile I lost interest in the two new folks I'd just met. Once again the mountain offered nobody who would prove to be a friend with common interests. The addict was totally out of it and the unemotional analysis of the professor was disturbing, bordering on sociopathic in fact. How could someone, not just *stand by*, but also actually *contribute to* the pain of others? Sure, the drugs made our grimy compatriot happy for the moment, but at what cost? The one thing I knew about drugs is that they may make you euphoric for awhile, but the crash and the addiction that come afterward can be horrifying, and given enough time, even deadly. Meanwhile, the two kept their own silent vigils: one forever motionless, staring up towards a phantom vision in the sky, the other circling his test-subject like a vulture examining his prey and filling up a notebook with unnecessary facts. Perhaps his great intellect had driven him mad. It seems to me that knowledge for the sake of knowledge means nothing if it is not tied to the responsibility of making the world a better place to live. Perhaps the cold pursuit of facts and figures, data and obsessive analysis, can create a mathematical and maniacal mind that can no longer perceive the needs of those around them. Then again, maybe he was stone cold crazy. Which came first: the chicken, or the egg? I don't know. My choices for the moment were to sit down, lean in towards the cool wall of the trail, and get some rest.

I'm not sure how long I was out, a few hours maybe? The noisiness of my drugged-out friend woke me up. It seems like it was time for another fix. The jitteriness and anxiety had returned. Even through the grime on his face you could see that his color was not good. In a nutshell, *that's* the problem with drugs: *great* for the fleeting moment, *bad* for the long haul. High highs were always followed by low lows. And, in terribly deceptive fashion, the highs eventually got *lower* and the lows eventually kept getting *deeper*. Certainly an unfair trade off that the victim never sees coming. But that's the despicable deal you strike with any drug. Too bad you couldn't take a picture of yourself and send it back through time to warn you as you were contemplating starting any sort of substance abuse.

Alas, our technology only goes so far. Meanwhile, mister note-taker had gone back to studying the obsidian walls while I had been asleep. He kept throwing annoyed glances towards his patient whose withdrawal symptoms were increasing by the minute. I wiped my sleepy eyes, trying to rejoin the world of the living. The professor was growing more and more irritated as it became obvious the addict was pushing for another fix. *Hey, whose fault is that? Who probably got him addicted in the first place?* I eventually stood up slowly, still a bit groggy, and contemplated how I might help the poor fellow. But my bleary-eyed senses came fully awake when the professor began to react violently towards the one distracting him from his research.

At first it was just some verbal attacks. That was surprising by itself since I had never heard him speak. But then it turned more ugly as he approached his subject and began slapping him hard with his open palms. I lunged forward to get between the two but a vicious backhand knocked me all the way back against the wall. My head slammed into the fractured obsidian fairly hard and I was seeing stars as wooziness dulled my vision for several seconds. When I regained my composure, the professor had backed off from the addict but his rage was still apparent as he began fishing through his pants pocket. Out came another cellophane bag, just like the first. He held it over the deep drop off, teasingly tossing it up in the air and catching it just before it would have flittered into the deep void off the side of the trail. Then he offered it to the addict who moved forward only to receive a palm in the air signifying him to stop. This went on for a few more times. The sadistic behavior gave me a chill - I was being given an eyeful into a cruel soul.

Finally, the professor dropped the bag on the ground and the addict moved forward again. At the same time, the professor slowly bent down and gradually moved his hand down to snatch up the bag just a fraction of a second before the addict could reach it. The poor soul began whimpering and shaking; the object of his desire had been so close. He was calmly walked back to his starting position by the crazy chemist. *Message sent...move faster next time.* Sickly, he brought out his journal and began taking some notes on what had just happened. A slight wave of nausea stirred in my gut. When the note-taking time was finished, he calmly put away the journal and dropped the bag on the ground again. The addict moved forward, faster this time, but not fast enough. He was once again walked back to his starting place. *One more time.* I can still see the third drop in vivid detail: the bag falling onto the floor of the trail, the addict moving quickly, determined to get there in time, and the professor beginning his stoop. But this time the ending was *horribly* different. Just before the addict got to his prize, the professor stood up straight, throwing both hands behind the running man. His left hand grabbed the belt and his right hand grabbed the collar and with a mighty toss, he hurled the addict like a rag-doll right over the edge of the chasm. The distance of the toss showed an incredible, and perhaps even super-human strength.

I was frozen like a marble statue, motionless, stunned beyond belief as the poor man seemed to float in the air for a moment just before disappearing into oblivion. His last desperate gesture had been to try and rotate his body around in a futile attempt to reach back for the edge of the trail. But that only served to give me one final glimpse of his pain filled face contorted by abject horror. You could see it in his eyes: the moment when he realized: *this is it…my life is over.* I felt the bile in my throat start rising and I turned my head just enough so that I wouldn't vomit on my clothes. Multiple quick shallow breaths barely staved off the purging, but starring blankly down at the dusty trail couldn't erase the horrible sight I'd just witnessed. The whole scenario had been burned into my corneas and continued to replay itself on the dusty surface of the trail like a demented movie trailer. Closing my eyes merely made the back of my eyelids the new screen upon which the scene gruesomely echoed. After a few more moments, I cast my glance back towards the maniacal medicine man. To my surprise, he was calmly sitting on a rock facing my direction, a vacant stare painting his face. *Business as usual…all in a days work.*

His stoic look would actually be part and parcel of his next sociopathic gesture. With his lifeless eyes never breaking contact with mine, he unemotionally reached into his jacket and pulled out his journal. His glance only wavered when he looked down to write something in his notes. *Apparently, I was his new subject.* Then, as if that thought wasn't frightening enough, he threw a two-inch square bag of cellophane at my feet. Sweat trickled down the back of my neck. My right eye had developed a slight nervous twitch. I slowly reached toward the bag and then cautiously tossed it back to him. My arms felt like rubber. The weak throw landed several feet in front of him. This was an important moment. I had no idea what he would do next. He stared at me for an uncomfortable length of time, and then rose to his feet. *Here we go….hopefully there were no frequent flyer miles coming up in my near future.* He approached the bag, looked directly at me for several more seconds, and shrugged his shoulders at me in a "whatever" gesture. Then dropping to one knee, he retrieved the small package and put it back in his pocket. A wicked smile played across his face. He was not in any kind of hurry. He went back to his study of the obsidian wall just up the trail from me.

There was no debate in my mind as to what to do next. The only question would be *how* to do it, because it would involve maneuvering around this lunatic. When his back was to me, I made a move to climb back up the trail in the direction from which I came. It didn't escape his notice. Seemingly aware of things that were happening, even behind his back, he took a few steps that blocked my retreat. And it only *took* a few steps on his part, because after witnessing the poor addict vanish headfirst into the abyss, I was not about to get close to the professor if I had anything to say about it. He seemed to perceive exactly what my thought process was and simply stopped in the middle of the trail putting a single finger up, wagging it back and forth, signifying that the direction I'd chosen was off limits. No words were necessary. I got the message loud and clear.

I didn't like my possible choices, because now they were actually whittled down to only one: Somehow get down the trail further, with or without his notice. Staying here was certainly not an option. The outcomes of my solitary choice were few as well: possibly die in the chase if he was faster than me…possibly be caught and dragged back to the starting line (*let the games begin*)…possibly make a successful run into the unknown lower levels *if* I could best his speed. For some reason, perhaps common sense, the third outcome seemed unlikely. *First of all*, if he were as fast as he was strong, then this would be a pitifully short race. *Secondly*, I had no idea of the topography that awaited me on the downward trail. I still had some not so distant memories of chasing the jewel zombie and nearly falling into the abyss a few times. *Thirdly*, it was quite possible that the professor knew the trail below very well and could anticipate as well as negotiate the necessary changes in course much faster than I. *Finally*, in this deadly mountain, I had no idea what dangers might be lurking further down the path. Lacking even an ounce of confidence, I imagined the dismal but likely scenario: *me running full speed around a bend in the trail, my uncontrolled momentum accidentally carrying me right over the edge.* At that point I would look back only to see the professor quickly jotting notes in his journal as he watched me plummet to my death. *I hate my imagination.*

Of course, none of my morbid musings or personal objections concerning my next action made a bit of difference since staying *here* would eventually be the end of me. I wondered how many lives this merciless killer had taken? The thought occurred to me that perhaps there was a good reason why people congregated safely in the village above. Maybe nobody coming down this trail from the upper village ever lived to tell about it. Or more likely, perhaps *one* lucky soul *did* manage to somehow make it back and warn the others to stay put. *Simple message: village – good, trail – bad. Not exactly Shakespeare.* The sick image of hundreds of bodies lying at the bottom of the chasm just below the professor's encampment came all to clearly into my mind. I steeled myself and began to slowly move away from the obsidian wall and towards the center of the trail. Even though his back was to me, he somehow once again intuitively sensed my movement and possibly my intention. Immediately the professor pivoted to face me, his smug facial expression replaced by a frown. His new test-patient had now disappointed him. Trying to escape from his morbid experiments was apparently an incredible insult. His very posture radiated a sense of betrayal and irritation. His research must have been terribly important to him. How dare the mouse attempt to escape from the cage. The vines hanging from the cave ceiling waved restlessly back and forth, as if mimicking a crowd that was impatiently awaiting the ensuing gladiator battle.

Now facing each other, I took a casual step backward. *But oh how I flatter myself.* Really, it was more like a nervous slide of my right foot skimming slowly backward across the gravel on the dusty trail. His frown was now accompanied by a blank stare and his eyes seemed to dilate, sinking back into oily pools of black liquid. Perhaps this was the same face my addict friend saw before plummeting into the gorge below. *Not a great last memory…but at least a memory that would not have lasted long.* The professor's skin had also taken on a darker ashen color and somehow his facial features had become more angular, as if his head and neck were being squeezed from each side by some demonic vice grip. At his feet a shallow pool of gray mist gradually seeped up from the trail below him, eventually billowing up and stopping only a few inches below his knees. The murky haze was familiar…mostly gray and black hues, but flecked with crimson reds and deep purples. I'm no shaman, but it was becoming clear that this man wasn't just evil; he seemed to be *possessed* by evil through and through - his body a mere shell for the vile spirit that lurked inside the corridors of his body. The swirling vines above us seemed to pick up their pace. I felt innumerable goose bumps on my arms and legs, my limbs tingling as if the blood was drained from them and was only now returning slowly. I could actually feel my right leg quivering. *Oh that will be great for the required running that was surely in my near future.*

I was too nervous to look behind me. I wasn't about to give him the opportunity to charge forward and get the drop on me. Especially since *"getting the drop on me"* would perhaps mean *"me getting dropped"*...straight into the abyss. But in the end, running became unnecessary, at least for the moment. My salvation was to be found from an extremely unlikely source directly up the trail, behind the professor. Looking over the professor's left shoulder, about thirty yards back, the hideous creature that had dogged me at various times in this godforsaken mountain was awkwardly, but stealthily, moving downward towards the professor. It is weird to say that I was "glad" to see the ghoul, and of course it was at least partially untrue. This thing had nearly killed me twice already, and it was disconcerting that it somehow continued to find me no matter how deep I plunged into this mountain. Still, choices being what they were, it presented the only possible escape from the possessed lunatic standing before me.

Just as the professor had lifted a wagging finger towards me not long ago, I lifted a finger to point past him in the direction of higher ground. Standing up on my toes and craning my neck to the right added some emphasis. At first he continued to stare me down, imaging that the prey was only trying to distract the predator. I raised both my eyebrows for added effect. Eventually, his mottled neck contorted unnaturally, slowly spinning much farther to his left than should have been humanly possible as his torso continued to squarely face me. *Creepy...part professor...part contortionist.* I admit to just a slight hint of smugness beginning to bloom within me because I was eager to see the change in his demeanor once he got a good look at the horror descending towards his position. It's a wonderful thing when life occasionally turns the tables on a situation and shines down a little good fortune in your direction. The professor looked towards the beast for quite awhile, undoubtedly weighing his diminishing options. The man was smart. He would see that the tables had now turned. *Let's see you take out your notebook now.*

The hunter was changing roles and becoming the hunted. Can't say I felt sorry for him. To the contrary - I harbored quite a bit of ill will towards this murderer. At least this would put us on equal footing - both of us fighting a common enemy. The thought definitely brought no sense of camaraderie. And I, for one, certainly had *no* intention of getting into any sort of brawl with the beast. A plan began to take shape pretty quickly in my mind. My best hope now was that the professor certainly couldn't handle both of us at the same time. *Stalemate.* What's more, is that he was positioned closer to the beast than me just by virtue of our position on the trail. For perhaps only the briefest of moments, *his* problems were worse than *mine.* After a long while, his grotesquely twisted neck and face began to rotate back in my direction. But when his misshapen face had turned once again to meet mine, the expected sense of fear was nowhere to be seen. Instead, a devious and sinister grin played across his contorted features.

My newfound hope evaporated as quickly as a faint breeze on an otherwise hot and humid day. A horrible question haunted my mind. What kind of soul would have no fear of the clearly evil entity mere yards from his position? Of course the answer quickly dawned on me: the soul that didn't fear horrific evil was one who was happy to be with a kindred spirit. It seemed that both of these monsters were quite comfortable with each other. *"Two peas in a pod" as the old saying goes.* The distance between the two was shrinking rapidly…soon the creature was standing right behind the professor. The odds were now sickly stacked in the devilish duo's favor. It was highly unlikely that I would have been able to get away from the professor alone. But now that the two had formed some maniacal merger, there was *no* reasonable chance of my survival. To them it was like the schoolyard game of chicken. *Who was going to flinch first?* Pretty soon their distance from me was mere feet. I had no choice. I may now have two hideous creatures on my tail, but my only option was to run. I did.

The biggest shock was not being pounced upon within the first few feet of my flight to freedom. And that was not the *only* unexpected thing that happened. Behind me, I swore I could hear the professor being torn limb from limb by the ugly beast. Grotesque screams, guttural noises, and the sound of tearing wet flesh permeated the surrounding air, echoing off the fractured obsidian walls. The ceiling vines now thrashed back and forth in some sort of frenzied and maniacal death dance. The sights and sounds reverberating throughout the diseased mountain were ones usually reserved for a gruesome horror movie. I imagined the scene playing out behind me but dared not risk a glance back. Did the brooding beast just kill the professor? *Was that possible? And if so…why?* I didn't look back…couldn't look back. I kept running.

Chapter 10 – The Runner

I had spent many a day running in my early life: nearly all of it running from people or circumstances that were threatening me in some way. But running has many contexts: It can be self-serving, self-preserving, or *sometimes* - it can be a noble act of self-sacrifice. The last option reminded me of a story told to me by one of my old schoolteachers. I wasn't a great student by any stretch of the imagination, but I did like school, and I *loved* history. Mrs. Johnson was a big part of that because she was one of my favorite teachers and she always told stories of antiquity with an enthusiasm that betrayed both an interest in her subject and a determination to inspire her students. I also enjoyed the study of history because it reminded me that there was a much bigger world out there than the one I had experienced within the confines of my radically dysfunctional family. At the end of my sophomore year in high school, Mrs. Johnson told the class a story that was one of my particular favorites. It was a testimony to bravery that has stuck in my mind to this day. It helped that she spoke with her usual flare for the dramatic, typically holding the interest of the entire class…even the kids who were supposedly *"too cool"* for a lesson in history. The true story was about a young American soldier and his platoon that were pinned down and overwhelmed by a much larger group of German fighters during World War II.

The story unfolded during the Battle of Normandy shortly after the D-Day invasion in June of 1944. It seems that in the chaos of one particular battle, this soldier's group had gotten separated from the main Allied battalion. Unfortunately, the Americans had grossly underestimated the strength of German forces in a spot not far from Cherbourg France. So when the Germans cut straight through their ranks, this splinter group of American soldiers had to retreat further back into newly-defined hostile enemy territory. As evening was approaching, their options were limited:

ultimately, they had no choice but to dig in and simply hope the enemy didn't detect them. Not the most *comforting* plan, but the only realistic plan at their disposal. The vicious shelling continued all through the night and devastated the platoon. The Germans seemed to be everywhere and the rest of the American battalion eventually had to retreat several miles back up into the French countryside. By morning light, the painful realization set in that our hero and his platoon had been whittled down to only eight able-bodied warriors. And "able-bodied" might be stretching the truth a bit - many were nursing fairly substantial injuries from the brutal battle. Successful evasion from the enemies seemed all but impossible. If they were to leave their newly burrowed trench, they would risk being spotted by the German army and slowly picked off one by one. So they crouched down in the trench, behind enemy lines, outnumbered, quietly hoping they would remain unnoticed as the hostiles moved all around them during the night.

The odds were not good. It would only take one enemy soldier stumbling upon their position and it would all be over; if spotted, the call would go out and overwhelming numbers would soon be swarming the area. That's when the hero of the story comes into view. The trench was near the top of a hill, which gave them a pretty good vantage point to watch for approaching trouble. All the American soldiers were lying low, doing their best to keep calm in an incredibly intense situation. Wounds were tended to and soft nervous banter filled the lonely ditch with false bravado. Thankfully, the darkness of night helped keep them concealed from enemy troops. But somewhere around 9:00 in the morning, things took a turn for the worse. Our hero, Bill, glanced over the embankment and saw a dispatch of fifty German troops headed straight towards their position. Still unaware of the Americans lying in the gully only seventy yards in front of them, the enemy troops continued their slow casual march straight up the hill. There was little doubt in the minds of the Americans that time was now running short. Though the *pace* of the enemy was unhurried, the *trajectory* of the Germans was unmistakable. Before long they would eventually stumble upon the hidden Americans. Minute by minute the circumstances were mounting towards a no-win situation. As for our hero: all his fellow soldiers knew very well that Bill had been a star runner on his high school track team. What they *didn't* know was that he had recently made a commitment to save them all, or die trying. Bill had chosen the run of *self-sacrifice*.

Everything happened quickly. Unannounced, Bill suddenly crawled up and out the back of the trench so as not to betray their position to the Germans. But then, rather than running up and *over* the hill, he ran up and *sideways*, sprinting down the ridge crest of the hill in plain view of the approaching enemy troops. Up and *over* would have given him the *self-serving* sort of run that puts every man for himself. But that type of run would only serve to bring the Germans up the hill faster and directly towards the men hiding in the ditch. Bill's plan was one of misdirection. As expected, it wasn't long before he was spotted by one of the approaching enemy soldiers; then whistles blew and guns were cocked as the German soldiers were stumbling around, trying to process and react to this lone American soldier sprinting along the top of the hillside. Cigarettes dangled loosely from some soldiers' mouths as their faces took on a look of astonishment. Others were beginning to laugh at the whole scenario playing out in front of them. As for the Americans - it all happened so fast that the remaining troops in the trench had no time to react. If they all followed Bill, their position would be revealed and all would be in danger. Instant death for sure. Since two of them had sustained relatively serious injuries, running with Bill was *not* an option. The only thing they could do is watch in disbelief at their comrade ran one of the fastest races of his life.

After awhile, sparse gunshots began to ring out, echoing over the otherwise beautiful French countryside. Back in that day, a seventy-yard shot with a normal German service rifle was far from a sure thing, and Bill at least had the element of surprise in his favor. Some Germans continued to laugh or yell jeering taunts towards the direction of this crazy runner. Others were beginning to give chase. Shots would eventually work…chasing would not. Bill owned the fastest time in his state for the 100-yard dash and he was also fairly short, giving the enemy only a small and quick moving target. For many moments it was working well. Most rounds were landing far behind his position, but a couple of them were getting dangerously close. The enemy soldiers were learning to adjust their aim. One shot finally hit the dirt directly in front of him, bits of earth and gravel forming shrapnel that peppered his right shin. At that point, Bill knew it was time to finally crest the top of the hill and make the Germans give chase instead of giving them the free turkey shoot he had initiated. But the simple beauty of his plan had already set in motion the salvation of his friends. By the time he changed his direction, Bill had created a big enough angle that his pursuers would have no recourse but to drastically switch their direction and pass well beyond view of the other trapped Americans. Quick thinking on his feet. Quick thinking *with* his feet.

The astonished trench-bound American soldiers waited quietly, hunkered down in the ditch with their faces pressed against the dirt and their breathing slowly regulated. Fingers twitched nervously on the triggers of their M-1 rifles. Enemy troops advanced. But just as Bill had planned, the Germans moved forward at an angle that was up and *away* from the trapped Americans. The pursuing soldiers hurried forward panting, their packs, canteens, and army gear rattling away like wind chimes in a windstorm as they gave chase. As the Germans crested the hill, more shots began to ring out. One of the young Americans, one whom Bill had befriended and looked out for during the earlier battle, eventually risked a bit of exposure as he climbed out the back of the trench and crawled up the embankment to spy over the top of the hill. The backside of the slope emptied into a very narrow valley, and just beyond the valley was a fairly thick forest of trees and medium size vegetation. The young American watched as frustrated German soldiers tried to strike a balance between giving chase and firing their weapons at this elusive fleeing Allied soldier. The last thing the spying American soldier saw was Bill sprinting into the underbrush with German rifle rounds spitting up dirt and severing tree branches around Bill's point of entry into the forest. Now out of view, presumably Bill kept running with the added advantage of cover from enemy gunfire. The pursuing Germans continued to give chase and eventually reached the forests' edge, moving into the trees cautiously to continue their search.

Back in the trench it was mostly silent, the gravity of Bill's sacrifice hanging thick in the air. Many of the following hours passed in a continued silence as well, but the quiet was tinged with an unspoken reverence and bewilderment towards the brave soldier that put the needs of others before his own. Eventually, in a night raid that began some twelve hours after Bill's brave run, the recently removed Allied forces returned and reengaged the German army, retaking the area surrounding the trench. The pinned-down American soldiers were now free…but they were reluctant to move at first. Perhaps that might have seemed odd to others, but something seemed irreverent about merely exiting the ditch and going on their merry way considering the heavy cost of their freedom. Before leaving their recently dug hiding place, the formerly trapped Americans looked at each other with misty eyes, the youngest finally saying what they all were thinking: *"Remember Bill."* The statement was choked with emotion and it was a simple but obvious testimonial to what was already saturating all of their hearts. One by one, each soldier repeated the newly coined mantra: *"Remember Bill…remember Bill…remember Bill…"*. Grown men…strong warrior men, all cried that day, their redeemed tears watering a dirty foxhole in a distant foreign land.

Bill had chosen a self-sacrificing run, one that had saved his entire group. Even up to the end of the war, there was never any sign of Bill. No body was ever discovered. There was no surprise appearance at one of the many Allied army camps that dotted the countryside after the invasion. Nothing. The conclusion should have been evident to all, but the survivors refused to assign words to the obvious. They knew they had an un-payable debt due their friend. Bill would be forever kept alive in their memories. As a matter of fact, for decades afterward, the trench survivors got together every year for a commemorative barbeque in honor of their near death experience. And every year there was always *one* chair left vacant at the table. The table setting however was complete in front of the honored empty seat: plate, silverware, napkin, and glass all carefully laid out with an ornate card placed in the center of the empty dinner plate. The inscription was always the same:

Still waiting for you to finish your race and join us. This spot is for you Bill. Thanks.

Drinks were raised and stories were retold around the table every year, but the unspoken respect for Bill remained palpable. The friend that had saved all their lives was going to be honored, if not publically, then simply by his friends who were first hand witnesses of a true American hero.

As a kid, when I heard this story, I couldn't help but think: *The power of self-sacrifice transcends our normal mortal experience. When*, and perhaps more importantly, *why* does someone put the needs of others before their own? The very act seems to be a distant echo sent deep into our souls, an echo that has been initiated from some outside source that resonates a greater morality than our surface earthly existence betrays: that there just might be more important things than this earthly life itself…something more honorable…something more fulfilling… something *worth* the ultimate sacrifice. In the end, self-sacrifice seemed to be the very embodiment of unadulterated love. Somewhere down deep, everyone intrinsically knows that love is the answer to what ails humanity. But as far as I was concerned, the world seemed to promote only a counterfeit concept of love, one laced with conditions, restrictions, and mutually gratifying expectations between two parties…more *contractual* than sacrificial. And in its worst worldly form, it is often simply based on unbridled lust. The big problem, as I saw it, is that contractual love or animalistic lust never seemed to be able to sustain itself for very long. But self-sacrificial love somehow seemed to come from a much deeper wellspring: one that bubbles up from something greater and more pure than ourselves. *That* kind of selfless love merely acts directly from its own essence and doesn't have to begrudgingly manufacture within itself something foreign to its very substance. This unearthly devotional virtue merely acts upon its own nature, and the end product is pure unimpeachable love for others. This kind of love acts and reacts simply because it *is* love and can do nothing more than be true to itself, with no strings attached. This was the elusive love I had sought most of my life but could never lay hold of.

I suppose it was this idea of self-sacrificial love that helped me make the decision to leave Abby and Jimmy behind. But I never fancied myself as having completely attained that level of supreme love towards others. In fact, there were so many selfish moments where I secretly wished that I could return to my friends; even though I knew that would not be the best and safest choice for Abby and her son. So shallow was my commitment that twice I rented a car and drove by the old duplex. It was a long trip and I couldn't decide if my visits showed noble altruism or temporary insanity. Perhaps a little bit of both? I knew there was potential risk involved, so I made sure it was safe by renting a car that had darkly tinted windows, and I never left the vehicle until I had gotten back out of town. The first trip back was disappointing because neither Abby nor Jimmy were to be seen outside the house. Thankfully, no Jackals were seen either. At first it was simply enough just to see the old house and superficially connect with the more pleasant memories of my past. Perhaps I should have left it there, because the second trip back was gut wrenching – that time they both *were* out in the open where I could see them; two of the most beautiful people I'd ever met, out in front of the old deteriorating rental house. After driving by, I parked far enough away so as not to draw any attention.

Abby was sitting on the front porch steps, her golden hair stirred gently by a quiet breeze. The hem of her long summer dress billowed softly from side to side as well and her arms stretched forward allowing her small folded hands to rest upon her knees. To complete the picture, her face was turned at a gentle angle that superimposed her beautiful silhouette against a descending orange sun. I've never seen an angel before, but after that day I wasn't so sure. She often glanced lovingly at her son and just as often closed her eyes and raised her face towards the dying warmth of the receding sun. She seemed to be the very picture of contentment. As for Jimmy, well, that was perhaps the hardest part for me, the hardest tug at my heart: he was lumbering around in the front yard, tossing the football in the air to himself as he ran back and forth trying to catch it in his usual clumsy manner. Man I loved that kid. My thoughts returned to the brutal day when the Jackals had done their best to rob him of his childlike innocence. Thankfully, their attempts had failed. Jimmy seemed no worse for wear, his pure naivety was still fully intact: a simple soul able to enjoy the simple pleasures with total abandon and justified indulgence. As always, I envied him, and admired the purity of an unspoiled soul.

As for my own soul? It wasn't clear to me if this trip was good for me or detrimental. It was after all a grim reminder of self-imposed deprivation; here I was: a young man, desperately looking for a family, and the *one* family I now knew was off limits by my own choice. Well, really by necessity as far as I could see it. And yet just seeing that the two of them were doing well gave me a sense of satisfaction somewhere deep in my spirit. Eventually though, *too* many memories of our times together came flooding back to me and the tide threatened to take away either my resolve to remain anonymous or my determination to stay sane in an insane world. To give way to either wave of emotional current was unacceptable and thus I was ultimately left with a hollowness of heart that was nearly unbearable. It was time to leave…again. Though I suspected that this was the last time I was going to see my two friends, I still knew that it was best for them not to get entangled in my problems ever again.

What followed was basically uneventful. Not sure how else to describe it. I often felt like a dust mote; something small and insignificant that was being pushed through life by the unseen winds of chance and cosmic randomness. I held down jobs, but nothing that brought on the self-satisfaction of a cherished career. I managed to involve myself in various recreational activities, though none involved much passion or personal fulfillment. More importantly, in terms of emotional connections, I had a few relationships with descent girls over the years. But they all fell way short of the self-sacrificial love that I was searching for. To be fair, it fell short on both sides of the equation. I knew that I probably brought way too much baggage to the relationship table. And as for their part? Well, I could never quite shake the feeling that the girls were merely looking for someone to take care of them while at the same time selfishly guarding their own independence and freedom. After witnessing my fathers' treatment of my mother, I'm no misogynist, so I wasn't about to blame women for all my problems. But it did seem to me that self-sacrificing love involved *giving up* your freedom and independence, not clinging to it. And that was needed from *both* parties involved. This actually seemed like a healthy step to me: intentional mutual abandonment of the self that would then help usher in an all-consuming love. At my best, I felt I was ready for that kind of commitment, but on the part of the girls there always seemed to be an undelaying subtext of hidden backup plans if I failed to meet with their approval in some way. I was too insecure to survive under that kind of a relationship. Then again maybe all this is simply the age-old mystery that has plagued mankind for millennia – to get and give love you must loose yourself fully to someone else. I suppose there are very few who have had the courage to make such a commitment.

So after failing to achieve career, recreational, or romantic goals I switched to more nebulous ambitions. I searched for some sort of broader meaning in life, but was always either thwarted by my past memories or shackled by my disturbed outlook and pessimism about the future. It seemed to me that to have a happy life, you needed to have a happy *past* life, which was what formulated the possibility for even pursuing a future hope. And so the vicious circle of bad past memories and dismal future expectations led to an infinite loop of crushed dreams and dead-end disappointment. Treading water seemed an appropriate description of my life. When you are treading water you are not really moving anywhere, but there is a lot of energy expended in the process. Perhaps that could be fine and even necessary for a season, but to live an entire life like that seemed unreasonable.

I remember one year when I was a kid and desperately wanted to swim in the deep end with my friends at the public pool. But in order to do that, there was one obligatory test required. The lifeguard made anybody under the age of twelve tread water for three minutes right in front of the lifeguard stand in order to qualify for admittance to the deeper waters. So I enthusiastically started the task and watched the minutes slowly advance on the big clock by the far side of the pool enclosure. By minute two, I was starting to feel the burn. Also at minute two a particularly pretty teenage girl approached the lifeguard and struck up a conversation. Minute three came and went with no acknowledgement from the guard. In fact, minute four and five also ticked off the clock and my stamina was fading fast. Giggles and laughter from the girl along with some twirling of the hair with her index finger had completely transfixed the infatuated young city employee with the red trunks.

My trips to the public pool were few and far between and I wasn't about to spoil the opportunity to swim with my friends from school, so I stubbornly refused to speak up or give up. But by minute six I could not fight the pain anymore and reached out for the edge of the pool. That must have been some sort of visual wake-up-call because suddenly the lifeguard allowed me to reenter his world. I expected to be allowed my new freedom after enduring the grueling test, but his only response was to chastise me for quitting early. His scolding was so fervent that I began to believe that I really did violate some cosmic law of pool safety. For a moment I wondered if the top-secret water police would be called and I would be hauled off to a prison for aquatic offenders hidden somewhere deep in the bowels of the city park. But thankfully, after multiple protests that my time had already finished, he eventually backed down and allowed me to join my friends. Truth be told, I most likely gained my freedom just because I was annoying him and interrupting his time with the pretty teen girl. Either way: no maritime prison for me.

I suppose that's kind of an odd memory to reminisce about, but I often think back to the feeling of exhaustion and stress from that childhood swimming test. And regrettably, it became somewhat of a metaphor for a stagnant life surrounded by turmoil. A life spent treading water. *My* life, unfortunately. It seemed to me that advancing in years *should* bring about a more leisurely form of existence: career settled, romance settled, maturity bringing in a modicum of personal peace. But my life was exhibiting none of that. And it didn't help when I noticed others around me experiencing the kind of tranquil existence that was continuing to elude me. Truth was; I lived my life on the run. Unless I'm flattering myself, the self-sacrificing run from Abby and Jimmy was a noble gesture on my part. But it led to running as a way of life for me: running from job to job, from relationship to relationship, from town to town. This certainly seemed abnormal to me, but at the same time, I felt powerless to break the cycle: My feet kept me incessantly moving while at the same time eternally keeping me locked into my own private vacuum of futility, destinations and experiences simply scene changes draped around the same empty and meaningless life.

Throwing myself into charity work with underprivileged kids somewhat stemmed the tide of depression and fulfilled, at least in part, my desire to find a broader meaning in life. But even *that* had its downside. Many of the abused kids found their way into "the system"; a system that was unfortunately a little bit like Russian roulette – it worked for some while further destroying others. The state usually deals with these young ones through welfare, foster care, or in the worst cases – the juvenile justice system. But marginalized children were victims through and through in my book. When I looked into their eyes, I often found that it was *me* who was staring back. And for every success story, there were many more accounts of kids just treading water in the system…running from life just like I had done. It was painful to watch. The really young ones were often luckier than the older ones. Foster parents often adopted the babies, or if not, the kids eventually went to adoptive homes if the foster family couldn't support another child. As it turned out, adoption was really the Holy Grail for child abuse victims: loving families who desperately wanted kids got to have a part in removing children from abusive families who failed to see the blessings of parenthood.

Over the years, I noticed that the earlier the child was taken out of an abusive home, the better it was for the youngster. Perhaps that sounds overly obvious, but the system had a built in preference for reuniting families…*whatever the cost*. That sounds like a noble goal, but most of the time it merely put the child back into an abusive situation. The courts and laws of our country favored birth parents, and sometimes favored them at the expense of the abused child. But there were rays of hope sprinkled throughout the system. The early placement of kids in foster homes or adoptive homes mostly happened with the children who tested positive for drugs at birth. Those children obviously had a toxic situation in their birth homes and needed to be protected immediately. Ironically, if there was no permanent damage from the pre natal drug exposure, these babies tended to be the lucky ones. They found loving parents through the process of adoption. But the ones who were physically, mentally, or sexually abused were often lost in the cracks, not coming to the attention of the state until most of the damage was already done. *Permanent* damage in many cases. These kids had it the worst by far. These were my kindred spirits, searching for meaning from a life that had devastated them simply by birthing them into an abusive household. Luck of the draw. *Bad* luck of the draw.

The kids suffering permanent damage by long term exposure to abuse were usually the ones that landed in the juvenile justice system. I'm not sure what the best solution is for these kids, but I'm pretty sure we could do something better than locking up all the youth with the worst problems in the same place. That simply created a dangerous festering cauldron of hatred and malignant peer pressure that pretty much sealed the fate of thousands of teens across our country. These kids were forever cemented into behaviors and habits that pretty much *guaranteed* future failure. I know my background gave me some strong views on these issues, but it did seem to me that a civilization was only going to be as good as the next generation it raised. That was a scary thought.

So for a time in my life, I tried to champion the cause of the abused child. It made sense that someone needed to help those who were helpless. Given my background, it was also not a surprise that I would be attracted to this particular cause. But eventually, witnessing the darker side of the system caused me to reenter my life on the run. And it was one particular example of failed justice that forever soured me from expecting good from the system ever again. It came on the heels of my experience where two half brothers were placed back with a birth mother who managed to get them killed by her drug-dealer boyfriend. Having worked with the two boys at the county orphanage for a time, their deaths shook me to the core. After retreating from the system for a few weeks, I eventually returned to my cause of helping kids in need, but I was emotionally frail to say the least. Still, I was bound and determined to test the waters, at least one more time. I had made friends with one family who was in the foster/adopt program for our county. I met them during some charity work at the county orphanage. Jeff and Sarah were their names and they had taken in a two-month-old baby girl whose parents were meth addicts. This of course meant that Allison, the baby girl, was *also* addicted to meth, obviously not by her own choice, but because she had been hardwired into the circulatory system of the mother before birth. Though newborns tended to be fairly resilient, exposure to drugs before their birth can cause many difficulties. Some problems were relatively mild, some moderately extreme. Either way, it often takes a child months, and in some cases years to rid themselves of the detrimental effects of these deadly chemical cocktails. When you think of a child being formed in the womb of a heavy drug user, it's amazing they can live through the process at all. Jeff and Sarah worked with Allison and saw her through the rough time of withdrawal and were eager to become her legal parents.

As for Allison: she was tough and made good progress until she was basically a normal healthy baby within months after her birth. The birth parents however continued their addictions to meth and other drugs while the county tenaciously guarded their visitation rights, even for *years* after Allison was placed with Jeff and Sarah. The state moves extremely slowly when considering terminating the rights of birth parents. In fact the county guaranteed the birth parents child visitation rights even though they were unwilling to give up their dangerous lifestyle. Drug tests would routinely came back positive, the father was often in and out of jail, and the mother was basically disinterested in Allison, although she occasionally made minimal efforts merely for show in front of the social worker. On top of all this, often times the birth parents never showed up for the scheduled visits that were conducted at a neutral site and monitored by the social workers. *Try explaining to a two or three year old why her parents didn't feel like taking the time to see her this week.* These were some seriously bad people. But the wheels of justice were stuck firmly in the mud of legal wrangling and misguided loyalties. It always seemed to me that, when it came to abuse, the birth parents had *already* forfeited their rights to care for a child.

The disaster for Allison began when a new social worker was assigned to the case. She did not fully understand all the details of the situation and allowed a judge to return custody of Allison to her birth parents. It seems that she was worried about a technicality in the paperwork, but somehow, as her concerns came to the forefront, it ushered in temporary insanity to *all* who were considering the evidence of the case. The little girl was already three years old when she was removed from the household of Jeff and Sarah. I remember watching little Allison as she was taken away in tears from the only loving family she ever knew, all her belongings packed into the car with her. The scene was beyond pathetic. It was like you were transferring a piece of property from one place to another instead of the real truth: a newly formed family was now completely obliterated. And I felt deep shame because I couldn't even try to console Jeff and Sarah because I myself was so devastated, suffering from equal parts dismay and denial. Surely this was just a mistake that would soon be rectified and little Allison would once again be back in her *real* home. But as it turned out – that never happened. As soon as the birth parents had the child in their custody, they skipped town and were never heard from again. The court eventually realized that the clerical error should not have had *any* bearing on the case and so they rescinded the court ordered reunification and searched for Allison and the birth parents. But unfortunately, by then it was too late. Jeff and Sarah even hired a private detective to pursue the fleeing couple, but nothing ever came of it.

I've never been good with situations that were impossible to fix. Bullies could be faced down. Certain isolated and individual injustices could be taken care of, either lawfully, or behind the scenes if necessary. But this situation defied closure. Feelings of helplessness and anger absolutely overwhelmed me. No matter what I did, I couldn't make this particular situation right again. Jeff and Sarah were good people, but they were never the same after that day. And I felt that any connection I tried to maintain with them would only serve to remind them of the worst day in their life: the day they lost their child. As for the system: it had miserably failed yet again. I know that most social workers are good people. In fact most people serving *inside* the system are good people as well. But somehow the *system itself* could sometimes arbitrarily act as if it were some kind of cruel sociopath, dispassionately serving up the most heinous kind of neglect towards those whom it promised to protect. If you polled ten decent people as to what to do in this particular case – ten out of ten would *never* have removed Allison from her new parents. But somehow good laws, written by good people, could be twisted by some unholy wind of cruel fate into the most deplorable outcome imaginable. This kind of injustice often walked the city streets unashamed and uncloaked. What's worse is that it paraded the highways and byways as the harbinger of good will towards mankind. What an awful imposter.

As for me? Well, Allison was the proverbial straw that broke the camel's back. I had to get *out* of the dysfunctional system; so I went on the run again. Unfortunately, this time it was the run of self-preservation…far less noble than the run of self-sacrifice. It was too painful to continually see the failings of justice, especially when its evil hand had stooped down to annihilate a child and her new family. Admittedly, I was weak, and being exposed to the dark side of the system brought back too many remembrances of my own abuse. So back on the run it was: more dismal towns, more meaningless relationships, more mundane and unfulfilling jobs. I wasn't suicidal or ready to give up on *all* future expectations. But the relentless sense of futility was life-draining and was eventually what drove me to pursue Hamartia. Surely there had to be *something* on this earth that could deliver on its promises. I was banking heavily on the mountain to supply what I lacked. I just didn't know that I was investing in a bankrupt quagmire that sucked people in and stripped them of what little was left of their humanity. Tired of treading water, I reached towards the edge of the mountain for relief as a drowning man might reach for any piece of flotsam, trying to keep himself afloat in a stormy sea. But now, instead of treading water, I was slipping beneath the surface and into the murky depths of eternal despair.

Chapter 11 – The Final Confrontation

I knew instinctually that the professor was no longer a part of this world. And his exit must have been of the most repulsive kind. Only in the vilest of nightmares could one ponder the fate of falling into the hands of that hideous beast. My vivid imagination was running amuck as I sprinted down the path, picturing the brutal dismemberment of the professor in my mind. As I ran, the cracked obsidian walls were becoming blurry in my peripheral vision, and it seemed that all color was being drained out of my surroundings. A direct glance at the wall to my immediate right confirmed my sensory intuition – the once deep and rich black color of the walls had been diluted into ugly gray streaks. The streaks themselves emanated outward from every fissure in the rock walls, giving the impression that the mountain was imploding upon itself…feeding on itself first, but then ultimately dragging everything else into a swirling vortex of stony oblivion. The walls of the trail began to intrude upon my personal space, as did the width of the path, which seemed to shrink with every step I took deeper into the mountain. The ceiling was also gradually getting lower with each stride. My dilemma was clear: I was being funneled into a futile race where the finish line would not be teeming with cheers and applause.

I couldn't hear the creature behind me, but I knew it was undoubtedly there. Like its first descent into the cave, the fiend was probably in no hurry to chase its prey. After all, there were no other escape routes available to me, and for all I knew, this path could come to a complete dead end soon. As the ceiling continued to descend, gray mist began to pool in a thin layer around my feet. After a few more minutes of running, it was encircling my calves. Eventually, it was swirling up around my knees and was spilling out into the abyss just to the left of the trail. Wherever the mist touched my body, it brought about a numbing feeling that penetrated straight into my bones. I was gradually loosing feeling in my legs and my speed had slowed down considerably. It was a peculiar feeling, because at one point my feet had ceased from moving, and yet I still seemed to be gliding through the mist; or perhaps I was being *pulled* into it by either momentum or madness. Both?

At one point, the surrounding fog was so thick it began to blur the boundaries between trail and drop-off. Now up to my waist, the mist had effectively split me into two separate parts: my lower body gradually loosing all feeling while my top half still fought to continue my descent down the trail. Of course, with no discernable edge to the trail, I was forced to hug the cadaverous gray streaked wall, its surface mottled with veiny crevices that threatened to draw you permanently into the very substance of this evil mountain. That last thought surprised me, but only a little a bit. The idea had been swirling around in my mind for quite a few days: *this mountain was indeed evil*. Every experience I'd had here, no matter how promising it might have *initially* seemed to be, had turned out badly. Anger, jealousy, and outright fear had been my unwanted traveling companions and this contemptible trio had taken turns taunting me right from the beginning of my trek up the mountain.

My senses were overloaded, but there were other changes going on around me that were rapidly adding to my already dismal state of mind. At one point it seemed that the walls were actually breathing, and their foul inhalation was pulling at the extremities of my body. Then I detected another source of breathing – one that was guttural and not so far back up the trail. What followed next was the familiar smell of the beast; the foul stench assaulting my olfactory senses and nearly making me gag. I'd been in this dilemma before. History was rudely repeating itself. Ever since entering Hamartia, the passage of time had been hard to track; but one thing was becoming painfully clear: after so many months, perhaps even years inside this mountain, I was no better off than when the beast first tracked and pursued me to the mouth of the upper cave entrance. Once again, the nature channel was fully reasserting itself in my mind, the cave walls doing nothing to interfere with the strong visual broadcast signal emanating from some unholy source within the mountain itself. *Terror in Technicolor.*

Eventually the fog encircled my neck and the once inhaling walls now seemed to exhale, pushing me towards the hidden drop off which was at this point completely shrouded and undetectable in an increasingly thick layer of ghostly haze. Most of my body was now numb. What little mobility I still possessed only gave me the limited strength to turn my head back for a glance up towards the descending trail. As expected, the demonic brute was casually and contentedly descending towards my position. The final push from the exhaling walls left me suspended in mid air as the fog encircled me completely and helped to pull me fully into the seething abyss. Vines from the ceiling also pelted me with lashes that only reinforced the direction of my deadly plunge into the chasm. I remembered the earlier feelings of tug-of-war played out within the gray netherworld of alternate reality. This time however there were not two *opposing* forces vying for acquisition of my body, but only one *singular* force. As to which force it might be, benevolent or malignant, I could not say. I only sensed that the battle was settled and the victor was now claiming his prize.

Into the expanse I fell. Every second of the fall carried with it the awful expectation of the brutal landing that surely awaited me. Seconds passed. Mist swirled. Colors darkened around me. Each second of the fall exponentially magnified my rising sense of panic as the realization began to take full root in my mind: *no one* could survive a drop from these heights. I remembered and gained a new sense of empathy for the poor drug addicted man who had already met the similar fate that now awaited me. Just like his: my luck had fully run out. Then…we'll, then an interesting thing happened. My descent gradually started to slow and my extremities began to gain feeling once more as the mist, seemingly from the feet up, began to dissipate. When the fog finally drained upwards past my eyes, I clearly saw solid footing about twenty yards beneath me. My free-fall continued to slow until I gently landed on solid ground. But during the last part of my descent, I clearly saw a man holding his hand up with his palm facing me. The angle of his palm directly aligned with the trajectory of my declining and ever slowing drop.

Unfortunately, my combination of bewilderment and relief were short-lived because the pursuing creature landed only about thirty feet behind me. Though its landing was far rougher than mine, my hurried backward glance revealed that it was *more* than healthy enough to tear me limb from limb. Its rapid lunge towards my position only served to reinforce that thought. When the beast was mere feet from me, the man who had so carefully tracked my descent with his outstretched hand shouted a single word. "*Stop!*" That was it. That's all it took. With that one word, the hulking behemoth stopped dead in its tracks. And that's not all. This once formidable ghoul now abruptly shriveled up in fear. Actually, *abject horror* would more aptly describe the creatures' newfound demeanor. This massive brute now cowered as if it were a small terrified child. The scene was so disconcerting that I risked a glance towards the man. He was unassuming, plainly dressed in a single one-piece garment…a robe of some sort. There was a single crimson sash tied at his waist and some dark leather sandals that completed his entire wardrobe. Not very scary as I could tell. But the beast must have had some hidden knowledge about this man who was lingering at the bottom of this god-forsaken mountain.

Then the mysterious stranger uttered two more words: *"be gone"*. Not exactly a terrifying speech, but to my surprise, it worked. And it worked *immediately*. No discussion, no arguments. His words, short as they were, dripped with authority and bold confidence. The beast *instantly* scurried away, hurriedly and even frantically retreating back into the horrible mist from which it came. I turned back towards the man. When our eyes met, he finally said something directly to me: *"sit"*. Okay, evidently he was a man of few words. And I couldn't tell if the statement was an invitation or a command. But either way, there was a kindness in his voice and I was emotionally and physically exhausted so I gladly took a seat on a rock not too far from the stranger. What followed was a fairly long period of silence as he merely continued to build a fire inside a circle of small stones. I actually welcomed the silence. I needed some time to regroup my senses. He was carefully placing some short thin branches around a fire that appeared to have been newly started. The pyramid of dry twigs crackled and glowed warmly in the otherwise dark surroundings.

"You have questions," he said. His utterance was not a question, but a statement of fact. I guess he was right, but I didn't know what the questions were. Eventually, I lamely started with my first question, which was to ask his name. *"J.C.",* came the response. It figured that the man of few words would have a name shortened to only two letters. Another lengthy period of silence followed. Whatever this place was, it seemed to be calm and quiet, the stillness only broken by the gentle dripping of water from the cave walls onto the cavern floor. Even that sound only served to make the atmosphere more serene and relaxed. It's hard to describe, but there was a sense of tranquility and peace that permeated the air, as if the man standing before me held all the evil from this place at bay simply by his presence. As I collected my thoughts, the questions *did* start to bubble to the surface. If this man could give me some answers regarding this place, then I was more than onboard with

that idea. I thought about the very beginnings of my journey to Hamartia. This place had seemed to have the potential of such great discovery and adventure, but it had consistently baffled me with its deceptive promises. In fact, the calmness that surrounded me now only amplified the realization of how miserable I had been of late. So the question spilled from my lips almost before I knew what I was asking:

"What *is* this place?"

His answer was short and to the point: "it is a place of great evil." Of that much I had come to be sure. But I didn't fully grasp what my connection was to all the circumstances that led me to these great depths. So after a short pause, I figured I should start right from the beginning. I asked my second question:

"Why didn't I see any others when I first ascended the mountain?"

J.C. slowly lifted his gaze from the fire, and the man of few words turned out not to be so. In fact his answer was quite lengthy, though it was not the answer I'd expected:

"Your initial decision and journey towards this place of waywardness was yours and yours alone. But once *accomplished*, you *did* run into several people who had made similar choices. That is the very nature of the journey of an individual soul; it is a journey ultimately made alone." He paused for a moment, and then continued, "This place is deceptive and blinding, but the desperation found within these walls also sends a signal to all those willing to hear it; that they will need to find *me* within the chaos. And by the way, I make sure that everyone has a chance to find me…when the time is right. When they *do* find me, there is always an individual choice to be made. Nobody finds me or rejects me in groups, though those who reject me often *form* groups with others of like-mind." J.C. seemed genuinely saddened by his last statement, but spoke further. "That's a shame because it threatens to solidify their personal decision against receiving true life from me. But at *any* time, someone can turn around and leave the path of sin that has entombed them here. My gift of life is free - it simply awaits the taking. After all, I demonstrated my own love toward mankind, in that while they were yet sinners, I died for them. It doesn't matter what sort of person you are. Personal salvation is free to all because I am no respecter of persons; I am as close to paupers as I am to kings, in fact I'm often closer to those who are poor in spirit: the weak, the abused. They are often the one's willing to listen. I never give up on anyone, no matter *what* their condition. On this journey towards life, no one will be removed from my presence unless they ultimately demand it to be so by their own life choices. For a little while you'll see me, and then you will not see me"

His answer took me off guard. What kind of life was he speaking of? His statements about accepting him or rejecting him echoed curiously in my mind and made me uneasy. What did he mean that I would see him for a little while and then not see him? Though completely in the dark, his words did provide a promising alternative to my dismal existence. But perhaps that was just one more empty promise within the multiple false promises in this mountain of deceit. After a bit, I simply moved on to another question:

"At various times, I have found myself in some sort of mystical gray shadow land that seemed to house two opposing forces. What was all that? Is it real? Is it my imagination?"

Okay, it was really *several* questions wrapped up into one subject, but the foreboding tempest of sinister color and lightening-filled cloudy synapses scared me. Was I losing my mind? Was I destined to be drawn into this ashen netherworld against my will and simply on any whim of the creatures that lived within it? If he truly knew anything about this shadowy place, then I wanted to know. He calmly looked behind me into the pooling mist that now housed the retreating beast and began an answer that was longer than the last one he had just given me.

"That 'shadow land' as you call it is actually part of this world in an indirect way, though it certainly has elements from a spiritual dimension as well. It's probably best described as a spiritual battleground. I know that might be confusing to you, but there are other dimensions in this world that operate in ways you don't know, and in fact *cannot* know in your current earthly bound body and mind. The spiritual entities within this realm simply *reinforce* your choices of free will, they do not force evil *or* good upon anyone. You see, mankind is the only thing in this creation that is *not* under my control…free to choose their own destiny for good or evil. I have made it so in order to bestow upon mankind the dignity of personal freedom. The principalities and powers within this realm work for their respective masters and try to win converts. But only *one* Master truly leads to the way to life. The others lead to death. This mystical grayness as you described it is the very arena where war is waged for the souls of men."

With a chill in my spine I suddenly remembered the ghostly cadaverous hand that had once reached out from the gray mist and grabbed my arm. Fear returned as I recalled being pulled in the direction of the malevolent voices hidden deeper in the ashen cloud. I also remembered the waiflike vapor of white smoke that had encircled my midsection, pulling me in the opposite direction. Frankly, it was all a memory I'd like to forget. After he allowed me to process what he had already said, J.C. continued:

"The darker forces within this realm make promises and appeals to mankind that are treacherous because they draw people away from the salvation I offer. Blustery winds of lies and deceit blow through this terrain like chaff, often pushing away the good forces within this realm that would show people the way to salvation. But the opposite is also true. Beautiful etudes of love, mercy, and truth permeate the misty wasteland, songs of redemption echoing back and forth and wooing people to the Master's side and drawing them out of darkness. Many souls listen to these godly voices and find eternal life with my Father and I. But many other souls are caught up and enticed by their own desires and drawn away into the darkness. For all people, consequences depend on individual choices and there eventually comes a time when only *one* voice will dominate this spiritual realm, drowning out the voice of the other. This is the point of no return where individuals embrace either light or darkness. The tragedy is that, when sin is fully grown and reinforced, when darkness is fully embraced, it brings forth spiritual death. You see, the path to life flows through a narrow gate: Only I am the way and the truth and the life. No one comes to the Father except through me. But because of the stubborn wickedness found in man, the wide gate and broad path leading to destruction is well traveled."

The mere mention of dark forces within the shadow realm brought an immediate disturbing picture to my mind. I blurted out the next question with much more intensity than I had intended: "What was the creature chasing me?"

"That was definitely a demon - part of that spiritual dimension I just spoke of. People who reject my voice are often left open to demonic forces, though these forces have *far* less power than most imagine. They can assert *no* power whatsoever upon those who are fully committed to me. Oh they might pester them in an odd encounter or two, but it is nothing of consequence. As a matter of fact, they can't really influence anyone *outside* my kingdom either, unless the person is *willing*. Unfortunately there is no shortage of those. The problem for those outside my kingdom is that they follow the dictates of their inbred corrupt hearts and find complicit accomplices in the realm of demonic influence. Demonic forces are indeed sworn enemies of the coming kingdom, setting themselves completely against me using pride, pleasure, and panic as their greatest weapons:

Pride focuses on the creature rather than the creator. The freedom of a human spirit is one of the most beautiful things ever created. It has the ability to display great good: love, honor, sacrifice, and charity just to name a few. But freedom infected by pride turns the soul into a self-seeking, shallow, and even abusive entity that only exists to feed its own perceived wants and needs. Demonic forces will always encourage the elevation of self over others through pride, and once that happens the soul is deceived into thinking it needs nothing more than itself. The god of this age has then effectively blinded their spiritual eyes through pride. God cannot save those who deny their need of salvation.

Pleasure is another tool of the enemy, not that pleasure in and of itself is bad; Father, Son, and Spirit are actually the *authors* of pleasure as a matter of fact. It is only when the pursuit of pleasure takes center stage in a life that the tyrannical rule of corrupted desire takes over. Pleasure has then unfortunately been twisted into an idol, and this particular idol is an insidious one to be sure because it only satisfies for a moment and then demands deeper and darker thrills. Eventually it leaves its victims as hollow shells with no capacity to appreciate the earlier innocent pleasures ordained by God. People worshipping at the altar of desire are left in the dark groping for things that will never satisfy. It's tragic, but man has often substituted pleasure in place of honor. People forget how to love one another as they were created to do. Once that happens, then love is exchanged for lust, charity is exchanged for greed, and self-promotion drowns out servanthood. From the beginning this was never meant to be so.

As for panic: demonic forces will usually rattle their sabers in people's minds concerning fear of the unknown, fear of others, or fear of death – those anxieties all create a person that turns *inward* for self-protection when the only possible solution for man is external…through me. The fearful man safely calls all the shots in his life and follows an isolated path of narcissistic self-preservation. He will also selfishly put his needs above all others. Once the spiritual forces of wickedness have turned a person inward, they have achieved their purpose - that kind of person becomes a protector and master of their own guarded destiny, something that is *incompatible* with my kingdom, a kingdom that runs on mutual communion with the Father, Son & Spirit."

As he mentioned a man that could be completely turned inward, the old gem collector came vividly into my mind. That old man was so turned inward; he couldn't even notice anyone else unless they offered something that was beneficial to his own restricted sphere of existence. J.C. seemed to sense my reverie and paused, studying me with eyes that pierced directly into my soul. I didn't notice at first, but as my eyes turned to his, I noticed he was just a bit misty-eyed with emotion, presumably towards me, but that didn't make any sense: he didn't know me. We had just met. I felt a little awkward and hoped that I hadn't said anything to upset him. The longer I was in his presence, the more I wished not to offend this man. There was something in his words and gestures that emanated a love for others. I wondered if that included me? The fleeting hope that this could be true ignited a spark of excitement that the memories of my father soon extinguished. I moved on to another question:

"Why could some people see and hear me while others could not?"

He readily answered: "People were meant to be united with me, but if they reject our connection, they will be forcing themselves to run contrary to their very nature…like a gas-powered vehicle trying to run on diesel fuel. Everyone reacts differently as they try to run their lives apart from me. Some retreat into himself or herself - like the old gem collector - while others keep their senses alert in order to take advantage anyone they might meet."

The mention of the gem collector actually startled me. Was he reading my thoughts? How did he even know about the old hermit? J.C. then proceeded to further confound me by talking about someone *else* I'd encountered in this mountain:

"The one you call Mr. Suave falls into that last category; he sees everyone as a mark, a score ready to be taken down and plundered. Keep in mind;

I offer a place in my kingdom to all who would honestly seek me, but mankind has been about the business of building their own kingdoms and ruling them by force, intimidation, or deceit. Often all three. Because of that, people ultimately see what they want to see and hear what they want to hear. The gem collector is so absorbed in his worship of wealth, nobody is of any importance to him unless they can perpetuate and expand his treasure. Mr. Suave is a user of people who will take and take from someone until there is simply nothing more to take.

At this point, I figured, *whoever* this man was, it was becoming obvious that he knew *me* even though I didn't know *him*. He seemed to have intimate knowledge of my experiences within this mountain. A blush reddened my cheeks as I wondered the extent of his knowledge. My intuition told me that he fully knew about my every action and was even sympathetic towards my time spent in this mountain. So, I went for broke and asked about the one circumstance that perhaps in some ways disturbed me the most during my travels in Hamartia…about the experience that pushed me into the deepest despair when what little trust and love I had was betrayed. With a softer tone, one that probably betrayed a broken heart, I quietly asked:

"What about the raven-haired girl? She was so alluring and yet so frustrating…I felt like a part of me died when I had to leave her."

Now some tears began to moisten *my* eyes. The experience was still something that both saddened and hardened my heart. J.C. seemed to understand my emotion, and gave a reply to what I thought would be an unanswerable question: "What a noble thing to be joined to another. It's a sacrificial yet mutually possessive act for two to become one. Beautiful. But it's amazing to me that one of our best gifts to mankind, the gift that in some ways is the most mystical and most representative of a true *spiritual* union has been degraded and exchanged for lust. But choosing lust rather than true love is like grasping after smoke driven by the wind…the minute you think you have something of it, you open your hands only to find emptiness. Lust is the unfaithful mistress of those desperately expecting to find love. She divides her sexual love between multiple partners, and this is the antithesis of the bond between a man and woman. Exclusivity is an irremovable component of real love. The minute it is compromised, true love dies. So paradoxically, lust is actually *incapable* of love…it is only capable of creating hollowness. What's worse is that the overindulgence in lust hardens the heart into a cold deadness where the original coveted 'act' finally brings no satisfaction. In truth, lust fails *itself* and then robs the possessor of the ability to return to the simplicity of love as it was intended. It is really a sin against your own body, let alone your spirit.

The raven-haired girl you so desperately sought is dangerously close to this point of no return. She has fully corrupted herself and has enticed many souls down the same path. Her coldness comes from an over indulgence in the flesh. Her hollowness saddens me."

When he mentioned her coldness, the frigidity of her touch within the nebulous spiritual realm came foremost into my mind. The words I was hearing were dripping with truth and yet were somehow both encouraging *and* hurtful at the same time: Encouraging, that a better way of life just might exist – hurtful when considering all the years I'd wasted by wallowing in the mire of difficult circumstances and relationships. After allowing me to ponder the first part of his reply, he then finished the answer to my difficult question:

"If she were to only go and sin no more, then we could begin to establish a relationship. But with her, and with many other men and women alike, the search for love has been twisted into a powerful addiction to lust that slowly kills their spirit. And because of the blindness of their heart they are past feeling, and have given themselves over to lewdness, to work all uncleanness with greediness. How sad: the very thing they are chasing can *never* be caught. And the thing itself - lust - is such a poor substitute for what they really need: true love."

This idea of *true* love struck a chord deep within me. It was this true and unadulterated love that I had searched for my entire life. I never found it at home and the many relationships I'd pursued with women always fell short by disintegrating into self-serving lust either from one party or the other. Sometimes from both. His mention of being 'past feeling' also terrified me, because I could feel the tendrils of coldness that were encapsulating my heart in an ever increasing way over the past many years. Was it too late for me? In trying to desperately believe that I was not 'past feeling', I remembered the compassion I felt for the old woman back at the camp. If this man knew so much about the life he promised, why was he not doing something about it? I asked my next question with a degree of indignation in my voice.

"Why was the old woman mourning and others mocking her? How far can we have fallen to participate in that kind of callous ridiculing?" He answered in his usual calm way:

"Ah…few things trouble me more than making light of those who suffer. But oddly enough, the old woman is close to finding my kingdom, for contrary to what some people think, it is those who mourn who are actually blessed. It is those folks who are at least beginning to realize that there is a problem with their life. Oddly enough, sometimes it's better to go the house of mourning rather than the house of feasting: it brings you back to the world I want you to focus on. Not that mourning is a means to an end all by itself; but that it can produce something wonderful - mourners are usually contemplating and coming to terms with the brevity of their life and searching for answers once their false preconceived notions about life have been swept away. In some cases, what they have been wrongfully taught all their lives is finally coming into question. That's a *good* spot to begin an honest search for me. And I am never far away; Behold, I stand at the door and knock. If anyone hears my voice and opens the door, I will come in to him and dine with him, and he with Me. The bottom line is that mourners will be comforted should they choose to fall into my arms.

As for those that mock? Well, they are in a dangerous position and ultimately have no excuse for their unbelief and lack of compassion. I offer truth and life, and any *honest* consideration of my ways will always bring forth results because even the heavens declare the glory of God…what may be known of God is evident to all people…I've put eternity into their hearts so that they know instinctually that God exists and has a moral code for all mankind to follow. But the foolish willfully forget, allowing their hearts to be darkened…they still believe there is life in darkness.

Unfortunately, most mockers have already put to death those spiritual questions regarding their future and my calling. They do not want to return to the pain of being faced with the fact that they could be wrong…about *everything*, so they want to suppress the truth with a lie. But God gives grace to the humble and contrite, while only knowing the proud from afar. My ways are not your ways, and that offends a self-righteous person. They forget to love their neighbor the same as they love themself. They are ignorant of the righteousness of God and try to establish their own. That will never work, but unfortunately, in these last days, there will be many who mock my kingdom and the children I love. This has been foretold for centuries."

After awhile, it became apparent that asking questions of this man was safe. His responses felt like they contained some sort of spiritual cleansing; like it opened, or reopened, a purity only found in the eyes of children. It was time to ask some deeper an even more personal questions. I tried to formulate some sophisticated question about the meaning of life, but the truth be told, I had already given up on such a quest. So the question that came from me next was rather darker than I'd expected. It still was a question I struggled with deep in my crushed spirit. In asking it, I realized that it was I who had become a man of few words:

"Why bother with life…it all only adds up to pain, suffering, abuse, and death?"

I thought the question might have some shock appeal for J.C., but he seemed to expect it – like he'd been asked many times before about the futility and emptiness of life. He took the question head-on:

"Well…it wasn't always so and it will one day *not* be so. At the beginning there was the purist relationship between God and man. But we chose not to overwhelm mankind or create a human character that was compulsively programed for good only, because that would give man no choice as to his free will submission to a greater good. It is also impossible for any man or woman to exhibit *real* love if the object of that love coerces them in any way. Real love is born out of a heart of compassion, not duty or even desire. When someone chooses good over evil, love over hate, the well-being of others over their own – *that* is the best humanity has to offer because they are now acting in our image, for our first choice, *always*, even to those that the world would deem unlovable, is love. We love even when rejected. We love even when mocked. We love even when I was tortured for the sins of those that crucified me. If some choose to reject our kingdom, it is their free-will choice to do so. They willingly turn their back on the God who loves them, but they have forgot that no eye has seen, no ear has heard, and no mind has imagined what God has prepared for those who love him. Mankind is thoroughly loved by me but rarely recognizes it."

At this point he turned his hands upward toward me, first showing me the scars in the palms of his hands, and then showing me the scar tissue from a deep laceration in his side. He then continued his answer to my question with a simple statement:

"To all, I offer a future and a hope. In the meantime you will have tribulation."

I know I should have figured it out *much* sooner, but my state of despair and the coldness of my heart had kept his identity hidden. I also think the deceitfulness of this place had cast a blinding shroud over my eyes. In my childhood, my upbringing had not placed me in a church except for a couple of stolen moments where mom tried to take us to Sunday school at a church down the street. Of course dad would have none of it, and after a couple of visits we were yanked out of the church. It seemed that dad had no time for weak people who needed church to solve their problems. At the time I thought that he might be right. But now, the veil was being lifted and I knew who was standing before me. J.C. indeed. I always thought the person of Jesus was a fairytale. Despite my epiphany, he merely gave a little wry smile and continued:

"Since much of mankind has chosen to leave the presence of God's love, it has created the environment of pain, suffering, abuse, and death that you asked about. These are the naturally occurring side effects when people try to run their lives apart from the Creator. People are designed to function in tandem with God's Spirit, with God's love and provision empowering them to serve others out of joy and not compulsion. And people know a lot about God whether they are willing to admit it or not. God has made it so, for since the creation of the world God's invisible qualities—his eternal power and divine nature—have been clearly seen, being understood from what has been made, so that people are without excuse. Mankind intuitively knows the right things to do because God's moral law has been written into their hearts. But as they try to *follow* that law without the Spirit's power, they fail miserably. The most common side effect of those failures is hypocrisy blended with some degree of sociopathic sinful behavior.

The hypocrisy comes in because people intuitively know they aren't measuring up to God's standards. They know they *should* be measuring up, so they 'fake it' as if they are indeed following the moral law. This sets up a conflict between their mind and their actions that eventually forces them to create excuses for why their behavior contradicts the moral law. What's worse is that often these excuses become codified in their minds so strongly that they form a new and aberrant moral law that God never intended. Here is where rationalizing sin can eventually degenerate into sociopathic actions. Since they have rejected their God-given moral compass, they eventually embrace whatever suits them. Then the evil that is spoken *against* in the true moral law now becomes that which fills the void. That's why people tolerate the mistreatment of others. That's why people turn a blind eye towards immorality. That's why people can murder another human being, all the while being convinced they are acting in the name of God. This new *corrupted* moral law becomes ingrained in entire societies and *that* fully enables its power to infect the generations that follow. Without a spiritual revival and a rekindling of the true moral law, some cultures have been forever devastated, never to reawaken.

The final effect of trying to follow the moral law without the Spirit's power is that a person simply gives up and embraces darkness. If a person continues to reject God, God will honor their free will and give them what they want - God will give them over to the shameful behavior they so desperately want to embrace. Furthermore, just as they did not think it worthwhile to retain the knowledge of God, so God will give them over to a depraved mind, so that they do what ought not to be done. They will become filled with every kind of wickedness, evil, greed and depravity. At that point they will spread various forms of pain, suffering, and abuse throughout society, and at their death, they will be unfortunately separated from a God who had offered them a place in his kingdom."

At the mention of people becoming evil, the Jackals came to mind. Now *there* was a group that was surely evil. When I had researched the gang that had so mercilessly beaten Jimmy, I remembered that a couple of the Jackals were known to be involved in their local church. Not being a church kind of guy, it certainly soured me on the notion of any goodness inside of religions. I risked another pointed question:

"How come so many religious people are such awful human beings? I remember hearing many of them aligning themselves with much of what you say, but their lives are certainly not displaying the love you speak of. Why are there bad people in your church?"

J.C. Sat down by the fire pondering his response, then turned his eyes toward mine and started:

"Well, this is going to be a long answer. Are you comfortable, because this may take awhile? If by *bad* you mean sinners, I would ask you, why on earth *wouldn't* sinners be in church? That's exactly where they belong for there is none righteous, no not even one. Church is a good place to hear the words of God and the words of God can change people's lives when they fall upon honest seekers of truth. The *tougher* question is: who is really honestly seeking? Unfortunately, the sad truth is that most people are *not* seeking, and many churches are mostly about indulging in a convenient religion that surrounds them with comfortable rituals that actually isolate them from the truth about their depravity. It's *so* frustrating to me, but man has always been fond of ritual, forever missing the point that I desire compassion, not sacrifice. There is ultimately nothing you can do for my Father and I anyway. We quite literally spoke this entire universe into existence. What can man offer us? You can only submit to His goodness. And that shouldn't sound cold or impersonal; it's just the reality of the damaged relationship we now share with mankind. There is a great love and reuniting awaiting men and women who join our kingdom now. But as for right now, with the human fallen condition, it is mostly one-sided: mostly from God to man. That's okay for now. We love man simply because we love man, it's really that simple. Contrary to man, who most often surrounds himself with those who can benefit him in various ways, our arms are open wide to *any* who would want to come into our kingdom. There is no partiality with Us. I say, come *all* who are weary and heavy-laden and I will give you rest.

Now, if by bad people you mean truly evil pretenders, well, that is actually quite easily explained: they are *non*-disciples no matter what they may say, filled with knowledge *about* me, but not living the life I ask of them. Remember; people can call themselves anything they want, but that does not make it so. Many a Pharaoh called himself god. Roman emperors did the same. That was always a funny one to me. Because unregenerate man is so evil, and because some sinners are transitioning to the truth, it becomes hard to separate the wheat from the weeds in every church without damaging the *whole* church body. And just know that I will one day sort all this out. Some men's sins are strikingly evident to all while others stay hidden and will only be evident to others at the Day of Judgment. And by the way, some sinners are destined to become mighty saints. I've seen it so many times. It's one of my favorite things to witness.

Man is simply not capable of judging who is who. I'll take care of that in time. Meanwhile, I hope *all* those in a church will soften their hearts and come to the knowledge of the truth. I died for ungodly people, while they were yet sinners, so why would I give up on them now? As for *ultimate* judgment upon those who reject my grace and mercy; don't be deceived, because I am certainly not – I know my sheep and my sheep hear my voice. Unfortunately, there are many wolves in sheep's clothing who have entered my flock. They have rejected me. They are not in *deed* what they are in *word*. They fleece my flock for their own benefit, either for personal gain or for the sake of their pride, which only further insulates them from me. Those that choose to reject God will be allowed to do so, I give them the dignity of their own choice, but sad to say, I cannot withhold from them the consequence.

I know it sounds odd, but ultimately man *chooses* his own judgment. God's hand always stays open to them down to their last gasp, but what are we to do with those who will not accept the grace and mercy offered to them. Alas, those with clenched fists and heart's committed to evil have made themselves totally incompatible with the kingdom of God, but make no mistake; *it was their choice to do so*. Every sinner can change his way. Even the hardened criminal who died beside me on a similar cross came to his senses before it was too late and he is now my child. But his friend hanging not far from him entered the presence of God unforgiven by his own choice, with a heart still full of malice and hatred. He could have been my child too. I wanted it to be so. And this brings up the last point you should consider.

'Bad people in church' is usually the mantra chanted by people who like to point the finger at others in order to justify themselves in whatever *their* indulgence of choice may be. Be assured of this; an *individual* man can only be able to be responsible for his *individual* choices…no one else's. Comparisons between one man and another most often degenerate into prideful self-justifications that men use to allow sin to remain in their lives. In reality, *all* have fallen short of the glory of God. So if you must compare yourself to anyone, compare yourself to me, for I always do that which pleases the Father. Also, remember, I have walked in your shoes, but without sin. I can sympathize with your weakness as your High Priest. I want you to strive to be like me, and the very Spirit of God will help you do that. And always remember: I am patient with failings. If you turn to me in weakness *my* strength will be made perfect. The Bible, my words left to all mankind, is full of examples where my followers failed, but their love and devotion to God kept them *trying*. It's only the lack of trying that ultimately separates man from God because God gives His gifts freely to those who ask. Those who give up were never committed to me in the first place and it saddens me."

I never expected to hear such beautiful logic on a seemingly impossible question. I was nearly speechless. But if this man were indeed truly God, then he could certainly entertain the *tougher* questions. And I had a couple of big ones that had literally plagued me for my entire life. These questions had repeatedly drained the life out of me. They often removed all hope for my future. And they certainly called into question either the existence of God or at least his moral character, which seemed to be filled with indifference towards the suffering of others. In this case it was *personal*: I felt anger beginning to well up inside me. I spat out the next question…it was short and not so sweet:

"Why did my mother suffer and die?"

The question was laced with bitterness, but J.C. calmly proceed with his answer: "Oh yes, precious Olivia. I love that child. Okay, first of all; those kinds of questions would require an understanding of the entire web of human and cosmic history, far beyond the scope of human beings to fathom, far too complicated for a mere mortal mind to comprehend until the end when all things will be made clear. After all, we *do* require a little faith on the part of our followers. For now, just understand, if you can, that man embraces different values than God. Man assigns great importance to people and things that are actually trivial to God. And the opposite is true as well: man often has no esteem for some people and circumstances that actually have *great* heavenly importance. God is weaving a tapestry in which we see from underneath the amalgamation of strings dangling randomly in apparent aimlessness. But from *heaven's* point of view, it is a beautiful portrait with all the threads of human history and human experience lining up perfectly.

It is *impossible* to understand or accept this except through faith. Your mother *did* have a rough life, but she fulfilled an amazing purpose in my kingdom. She *fully* understands that, now that she is on the other side of eternity. I know that's hard to believe, but you will eventually find out that I am the great equalizer. There is not one thing that escapes my notice, not one wrong that will not eventually be made right for my people. There will be a day you'll eventually know fully, just as you have been fully known by me. And in that day you will be *more* than fine with the end result of all my plans. One day you will see the embroidery of God and it will be glorious; every knee shall bow and every tongue will confess the glory of the Lord. You will be astonished. The one glimpse into eternity I can give you for now is that your mother's suffering was the hinge pin that drove her into my arms and her life was a beautiful and precious thread in the tapestry of God. There will *never* be another day of suffering for her. *Ever.*"

Hot tears began streaming down my face. And the tears were still equal parts anger and hopelessness. But somewhere in the mixture there was now the smallest glimmer of hope to be found. I hated it though. Why should I bother to allow another false sense of hope to infiltrate my life, a hope that would certainly be dashed on the rocks of bitter disappointment as my past history always dictated? Why should I allow one more broken promise to further drive more piercing nails into the coffin of my empty soul? The next question came with my anger continuing to build:

"Why was I left to suffer at the hands of my dad?"

"This is cosmic web territory again, but I'll give you just *one* precious silver strand in the weave of eternity: The death of your brother and the collective abuse your father delivered to the both of you, among *other* purposes, set the stage for your dad's salvation."

To say I was stunned would be the understatement of the century. I was repulsed by the thought of my old man walking off scot-free into the arms of a blindly forgiving god. If there were *any* justice in the heavens, then my abusive dad would one day be rotting away in hell. As I seethed in anger, J.C. plodded forward:

"Your tough life journey up to this point is also what ultimately made this conversation between the two of us possible at this very moment in time. Your father has been forgiven, but he carries a huge burden of depression because he still sees himself for what he *was*…even though it is not what he is *now*. He's floundering in deep remorse."

This man had not lived in my shoes. What gave him the right to forgive my father for anything? My mother, brother, and I were the one's wronged. It was *our* choice to forgive or not forgive. And I definitely had *no* forgiveness in my heart for that man. I hoped that what J.C. said was true: I hoped my father *was* depressed, despondent; maybe suicidal was okay with me as well - But not forgiven! J.C. seemed to read my mind on that last thought:

"Your father would agree with you. What he did is unforgivable in his mind and indeed *would* have been unforgivable had he not found room for repentance. It's hard for people to remember that I am compassionate and gracious, *slow* to anger; I want *all* mankind to come to repentance. I know that men are nothing more than dust. That's how I created them in the first place after all. When someone enters my kingdom, I do not hold their past sins against them and I actually have the power to remove all iniquity from a willing soul. My sacrifice on the cross purchased that gift for humanity. It was costly, but very much worth it. My mercy is from everlasting to everlasting and my mercy triumphs over judgment. But now your father is stuck in a nursing home and spends his days praying for you. He also does not know that your brother, his son, is already with me in paradise."

The thought of my dad praying made me laugh. And the laugh was of the most bitter variety, tinged with malice towards both J.C. and my abusive father.

"I know this is tough for you. But it is time for *you* to make *your* choice. I know it is hard to live by faith and not sight; hard to believe in the substance of things hoped for and the evidence of things not seen. But believe me when I say that the present sufferings of this world are not worthy of comparison to an eternal life with me. How can I explain it? Living with me brings eternal warmth and security into your very essence. Do you remember that snowstorm where you wrecked your car? Do you remember the penetrating warmth of the heating lamps after you nearly froze to death trudging through the snow back to your trailer? The euphoria you felt in the warmth of your trailer way back on that snowy day is perhaps a shadowy depiction of what happens within your soul as we unite"

I nodded dispassionately but continued to become more and more unnerved by his apparent knowledge about my *entire* past life. He continued:

"Okay, now imagine that warmth as a feeling, not just of body, but also of mind and spirit as well; a sense of well being that permeates everything about you, all fears relieved, all past failures and troubles smoothed over by an overwhelming saturation in God's love. That's as close as I can explain it for now. Your earthly father shaped you in ways that you'll never understand. The great mystery now is - what will you do with your life experiences up to this point? They've all shaped you, the good *and* the bad.

"Why should it matter", I retorted. "Why don't you just tell me what I *will* do since you seem to know everything?"

His response was quick but patient: "That's not how it works. That would interfere with your free will and place undo burdens on the individual moments that lead up to every action you'll pursue from this point on"

By this point my head was spinning. I couldn't process all the stimuli and apparent divine revelation surrounding me. My only recourse seemed to be to strike out from my inner nature: "You must know that I have the same anger issues that plagued my father. The only difference is that I have good reason for my rage. He was just a sadistic jerk who only thought of himself. I've got permanent issues from all the damage dealt to me, and yet you choose to simply forgive despite all the fallen people found in my father's wake. Why is it that I'm still plagued by him and his abuse even after so many years? Isn't your love supposed to take care of that?"

Undaunted, he continued: "Yes, you are saddled both genetically and experientially with some pretty bad wiring. But *everyone* has some wiring issues in this fallen world. A disciple of mine once called them 'thorns in the flesh'. But my grace is sufficient even in those areas of your life. In fact, it goes deeper than that. People with tougher debilitations will receive a greater reward when they overcome them than those who were fortunately wired with a naturally pleasant personality. Things in this world are not always what they may seem. Sometimes what man intends for evil, or thinks is evil, God *still* uses for good. That's one of the great mysteries of the cosmos. In your case, your wiring has led you to make some very honorable choices, like protecting the weak and the poor. I liked that. I liked that very much. Of course, sometimes the way you went about it would not have been my choice. Still, your anger combined with your sense of justice often reflected a love for those less fortunate. And by the way, *speaking* of the less fortunate; did you know that your own father was abused as a child, grew up with alcoholic parents, and left his house at age fifteen?"

By now, most of his words were falling on deaf ears, but that one last statement caught my attention. It was a story I'd never heard. And fifteen happened to be the *exact* same age that I began my own run from my father. Was this some sort of trick? Trying to play on sympathies that simply didn't exist? I was doubtful of his stories, and more than that, *determined* not to allow any crack in the concrete wall of resentment I'd built up over the years towards my father. J.C. followed up:

"Yes, his home life was an absolute mess. Didn't you ever wonder why you never met your grandparents? Sorry to say, they never gave your dad much of a chance, never told him they loved him, and never really supported him in any way other than the bare necessities. And they beat him. *Boy*, did they beat him. He actually ended up in the hospital three times before the county finally caught up with his folks and then put your dad into the foster care system. Of course, by then the damage was done. It was a long road for him to finally come to me." At this point J.C. offered some very unwanted advice. He looked me straight in the eye and said:

"You need to forgive your father".

As if I wasn't angry before, *this* ridiculous request sent me near the edge of oblivion. He must have seen into my seething heart, but he was relentless in his counsel:

"You must mimic your Father in heaven and be merciful. It is one of the non-negotiables in Our kingdom: For judgment will be merciless to one who has shown no mercy; mercy triumphs over judgment. Trust me - he has already been *completely* devastated. After you left, he tried to commit suicide twice. Once he came dreadfully close to succeeding. Unfortunately, your dad tried to find respite from his parent's emotional and physical abuse in the bottom of a bottle. That never works. His drinking only caused untold misery to others and also to himself. Your brother's death was the tipping point. The horrible emotional aftermath of the tragedy ate away at him for months until he was reduced to a mere shell of his former self. Even though his repentance was painfully authentic, he just could never come to terms with the fact that he accidentally killed your brother after one of his drinking binges."

And *that* revelation shattered what little was left of my emotional stability. I had never known, nor even remotely suspected, that it was my own father who had run down my older brother that fateful night so long ago. And then what followed was an overwhelming sense of shame because I had failed to put it all together: My dad had totaled his own car due to one of his earlier drinking binges. He then stole my brother's car, and must have gone on another bender, which caused him to accidently kill his oldest son. The newly revealed dark irony was too much for me to handle. I lost what little control I had with my emotions. I'm not sure if I'd ever felt angrier any day in my entire life. And this wicked information just came from one who was espousing love as a virtue to be held above all others.

I didn't believe it was possible, but this insidious mountain had managed to contain one last bit of horrible revelation. I now knew the answer to life: There was *no* love in this world…only people looking out for themselves and selfishly plowing forward through the sea of humanity that happened to be in their way. Where 'their way' was directed, I wasn't sure because it seemed to me that we were *all* on our way to *nowhere* and the bookends to this life were pain and suffering on one end and despair and death on the other. My anger rose to the point where it dulled all emotion and made me nearly catatonic.

At that point of hopelessness, I remember simply turning and running towards the menacing gray curtain of mist that was churning directly behind me. This was the same expanse that swallowed up the beast as it ran from J.C. How odd that I would run in the same direction, but I'd made my decision. Whatever fate awaited me was fine, for I was done with this life. For good. The swirling ashen cloud welcomed me and surrounded me with its caressing yet caustic embrace. Numbness once again began to overtake my extremities. I remember thinking back to the last command: *"you need to forgive your father."* It was something I simply couldn't do. *Wouldn't* do. That would literally take an act of God. How deeply unfair. J.C. was asking for the impossible. The haze darkened and churned around me, the now familiar electrical synapses crackled with an intense charge, and then hundreds of ghostly withered hands began to reach out towards me. Somewhere, nestled in the gloom, the creatures' piercing red eyes began floating towards me. So be it. I was done. My disillusionment in this life would, in the end, doom me to whatever fate awaited me in this seething cauldron of hatred and despair. My last thoughts in this mountain were: "why is it that nobody ever helped me?" And then specifically: "Jesus, why won't you help me?" As it turned out: *that* was the right question.

Chapter 12 – Redemption

My next memory was that of the evil cloud of writhing bony hands and ashen smoke giving way to a piercing light. The brightness banished the darkness like a magnet dispels an opposing magnetic pole. The sinister grayness was being pushed away from me in concentric rings, with me at the center of the explosive power of the blinding light. I was the center, but *not* the source. That much was clear. I was completely spent both emotionally and physically. So the power obviously came from another source. And I had a pretty good idea who that source might be. As a matter of fact, the source was standing not far from me, tending to another small fire next to a rocky trail that had been worn smooth by its frequent visitors. The most astonishing thing was that this was the same trail I had traversed so long ago when I had first approached Hamartia. The glorious truth was that we were now *outside* the hideous mountain. In the depths of my despair, I had given up all hope of ever seeing the light of day again. But now, as the supernatural light was dissipating, the brilliant light of the sun was now bathing my skin. Warmth filled me. Body and soul.

My initial euphoria was due to the fact that I had just been saved from certain physical death. But the elation penetrated to a deeper level than that. My soul had also been touched. It felt like deep-seated emotional burdens had suddenly and miraculously been lifted from my life. I remembered asking J.C. for help in my final moments within the spectral gray shroud; but my belief in any possible rescue was tinged with equal parts unbelief as well. It had been a pitiful prayer on my part. But in hindsight, it was a prayer focused in the right direction. Jesus was quietly stirring the embers of the small fire. I thought back to the angry way I'd spoken to him and I was immediately filled with shame. But to my surprise, he turned his gaze toward me and his face only emanated a sense of pure unadulterated love. It's hard to explain but I instantly knew that *this* was the love I had been looking for all my life. I could see it in the softness of his bodily gestures and in the purity of his smile. He then asked me one simple question:

"Would you like to follow my ways and become my disciple?"

The question took me by surprise, but my reaction was even more of a shock. Without any hesitation at all, I blurted out, *"yes"*. It was as if my spirit spoke before my brain had time to even consider the question. Giving over the helm of your life to someone else was something that doesn't come easily. Probably *shouldn't* come easily. And commitment was not something I gave out lightly, especially with older people of my own gender. But my response seemed to be the most natural act I could imagine; the freedom of being outside the mountain and in the redeeming presence of J.C. was simply overwhelming. Jesus began to speak:

"Your real problem is lack of love; first because you were never *shown* love, but secondly because you *chose* never to love as a tactic to avoid further rejection"

It was not a harsh criticism but simply a statement of fact. And it was spoken with such love that it captivated me. It was the truth. My life experiences had made me guarded to say the least. But I could feel the power of those caustic events slowly draining from my spirit. Still, I was curious and somewhat fragile. Nervous even. I had asked for help once from this man, and that worked awfully well. So I risked another request that came in the form of a question: "How can I possibly love my father as you have asked me to do?"

His answer was short but thoughtful: "with man this is impossible, but with God, *all* things are possible." I could feel my heart softening, but love still seemed a long way away for me. When I thought of my past, it seemed *impossible* to love in such a way. Once again, He peered directly into my mind and answered my silent train of thought: "God can do the impossible". He who comes to me is a new creation and I will replace their heart of stone with a heart of flesh, one that can love and accept love." He went on: "You will love because you realize *you* are loved, and you'll come to realize that it's always the right reaction towards your fellow man. Remember your high school story about the World War II soldier named Bill?" I certainly did. That story had a huge impact on me.

But that didn't mean I understood the deep meaning of it completely. Again following my thinking, he picked up where he left off: "Bill *was* and *is* one of mine. And as much as you admire his sacrifice of love, you ought to know that there are thousands of people like him in my kingdom. *You* will also be like him in many ways." That seemed like an incredible promise directed towards a broken down vessel like myself. I'd lived most of my life under the introspective burden that I was not worthy of love, and thus mostly worthless to others. What could I offer to anyone?

After all I'd been through, I dared not doubt the man standing before me, but remnants of my old life still clung to me and cast shadows into my newly found landscape of freedom and joy. Nevertheless, I had a burning desire to please this man who rescued me from complete physical and spiritual annihilation. He once again came to my emotional rescue: "you will never accomplish these things on your own…it would be unfair to even *ask* for such a thing. It's somewhat of a mystery, but have faith my child - my Spirit in you is the hope of glory. And the Spirit will give you wisdom and revelation as to the knowledge of me and my new kingdom. When the time comes you will know what to do. You *will* one-day love your father. For now, there are *others* who need you.

I wasn't sure where he was leading; I honestly couldn't think of *anyone* who needed me. For *anything*. Jesus went on: "You have made a very important connection with two incredibly special people. Your destiny was always meant to be intertwined with theirs." I immediately thought of Abby and Jimmy, and was somehow *certain* in my heart that these were the two of whom he spoke; it was why leaving them had been so brutally hard. He smiled at my epiphany and simply said: "they need you…and you need them. Go to them. This is part of your new start, your new life. Those two precious souls have been with me for a long time, but they are incomplete just as you alone are incomplete."

My mind was spinning with equal parts excitement and fear. Questions began swirling in my mind: *What did all this mean? Why was my destiny linked to theirs? Why was I the recipient of this glorious second chance in life?* When I was young, I had a general faith in some sort of God, because when I looked up to the evening sky, the stars seemed to reveal the logic of a supreme designer at work. I didn't imagine that this designer had any reason to desire a connection with any specific individual, but since most of creation seemed good, perhaps that told us that the creator at least wished us no harm. But now, after spending time with Jesus, I found that this God was *way* more personable and caring than I ever imagined. And his promises were going to ring true; I instinctively knew it in my heart. To that thought, Jesus replied:

"You've looked for God all your life...today your quest is complete - I am He...no one comes to the Father but by me. You've seen me, so you've now seen the Father. I serve the Father and I invite you to serve me. We'll both serve the Father together." For a moment he seemed lost in thought, but then continued: "You know, I was once asked to do this for all the wrong reasons, but it seems more than appropriate now." After that last statement he reached down to pick up a medium-sized stone that had been lying next to the fire. And before my very eyes he transformed the solid rock into a sweet smelling loaf of bread; one big enough for both of us to share. I had no idea what it meant but I couldn't help but feel the importance of this ritual as I took the bread and ate. It was more than delicious. Then he said something that saddened me:

"I must go now. You've seen me for a little while, but now you will not see me. But my Spirit will always be with you."

My grief was suddenly palpable. How could someone who so profoundly changed my life now be leaving my side? But he comforted me: "I will listen to your every cry and be present in your every trial. I will be with you in good times and bad. But for now, there are many more trapped in Hamartia who have lost their way just like you had, and these precious souls need my hand upon their lives just as you did." I didn't understand everything - that he would not be visible but his Spirit would be with me. But by then I didn't need to understand *everything*. I only knew I needed to trust his words. And trust them I did. His parting words to me were clear:

"Remember...God can do the impossible."

And after that comment, he gently turned and proceeded up the trail, back towards the entrance to Hamartia. I watched as he walked stoically upward, surrounded but never touched by the floating mist that evasively evaporated before him. Eventually, after he was quite a ways up the trail, shadowy tendrils of menacing fog spilled back into the space behind him on the trail, making him disappear from my view. And that was the last I ever saw of Jesus. But somehow I knew that his Spirit was with me, just as he had promised.

I never understood the idea of a pardon until that day. A pardon now seemed *so* much different than a plea for immunity. A *pardon* assumed a wrong was committed, while claiming *immunity* was merely an attempt to cover up the transgression. Foreign diplomats often hid behind the flag of immunity to escape punishment that a *normal* person would incur for the same offence. Coming face to face with Jesus forever put my life in stark relief against his perfect life and love. It made me realize that most of my life had consisted of claiming immunity instead admitting that I needed a pardon. In my heart, I knew I was guilty of *so* much in my life; and yet, the King had just offered a pardon for me despite my sins. No…it was even beyond that: He offered me a place of service in his kingdom. I wasn't exactly sure what that meant, but the thought was overwhelming. How long had I run from my admission of guilt? How long had I only served myself? Too long. That was the simple answer. The newfound feeling of freedom brought wings to a formerly flightless soul.

The rest of my story was a beautiful one. Oh, there were some ups and downs to be sure. Part happiness and part heartbreak. But the lesson I learned was that life was about love; God's love for us in the person of His Son. *That* love could conquer anything thrown in its path. And even though allowing yourself to love others often brought with it a certain amount of pain, it also ushered in a truly amazing connection to both God and humanity. His promises were true. And I had the feeling that my story was similar to millions of others who had had an encounter with the living God; whether in person or in Spirit, it didn't matter.

After a time I was reunited with Abby and Jimmy just as he said would happen. They had moved to a different town about one hundred miles away from our shared dilapidated duplex. The old landlord knew the new address since Abby had left it with him in case there were any pieces of mail to be forwarded. I had expected a fight when asking him to share the information, but to my surprise, he simply gave it to me as soon as I asked. I got the distinct feeling that something, no…some*one*, was working behind the scenes to make our reconnection possible. It wasn't hard to figure out who that might be.

I wish I could fully describe the looks on their faces when I drove up unannounced to their new home. I was both apprehensive and anxious that day, hoping they would be as happy to see me, as I would be to see them. Thankfully it wasn't long before I saw that feelings were very mutual. Of course they didn't recognize my car since I had long ago gotten rid of the ugly wreck that I used to drive in the old days. Can't say I missed that car. I'd nearly died in it after all. When I pulled into the driveway, the scene was very much like the last time I saw these two dear souls: Jimmy playing football in the yard…Abby sunning herself on the porch. And Jimmy's reaction was quite literally priceless. To this day it is still etched deep into my memory. As soon as I stepped out of the car, the football he had thrown in the air to himself quietly fell back to the ground as our eyes met. He simply put his arms at his sides and burst into tears. Often times, kids with special needs have a hard time dealing with their emotions. I found that character trait to be very special indeed; that their reactions were so genuine and without hypocrisy. In this case, his joy simply overwhelmed him and tears were the only outlet for his profound love. I was humbled beyond belief: *that someone actually cared that much for me seemed to contradict everything I always thought about myself.* Of course, noticing his tears was all I needed to see to begin my own waterworks.

Abby leapt off the porch and ran to meet me, wrapping her arms around my shoulders and squeezing me for all she was worth. After a precious few moments, moments which seemed to saturate my soul with an incredible elixir of love and acceptance, we both ran to Jimmy and formed a circle of hugs and tears. It really *did* feel like we were destined to be together. I just hadn't envisioned the full meaning of the words of Jesus. *"Your destiny was always meant to be intertwined with theirs"* were the exact words he used. And as I gazed into Abby's eyes, a crazy new thought entered my mind. She was beautiful. And not just in the way the world looks at beauty. Her soul seemed to be of the purest kind, and that made her all the more lovely. Those thoughts continued to germinate for many months after our reunion. My feelings for her and Jimmy led me to an interesting question: What *exactly* did Jesus mean when he said: "Your destiny was always meant to be intertwined with theirs"?

The three of us grew very close over the next few months. Gradually, there was a level of comfort between us that I had never experienced with anyone else in my life. I sensed that they felt it too. The normal social and personal barriers came down easily and it wasn't long before we shared our life stories. Abby was only four years older than me. She had lost both her parents in a car accident when she was only sixteen years old. Placed with some relatives who didn't really seem to want her around, she marked off time until she could move out on her own. As soon as she could, she did. She married very young and her marriage had only lasted for two years. It became quickly apparent to me that her marriage had been of the worst kind.

Not too long after Jimmy's birth her husband began to abuse her both physically and emotionally. *The deadly duo for a woman's spirit.* He had blamed her for what he thought were 'deficiencies' in his son Jimmy, often calling him "a retard" in front of the both of them. I listened to her experiences with a heavy heart. We definitely had a common bond of abuse from older men. Eventually, after two grueling years, he divorced her and took off, taking all the money from their meager savings account and the only car they owned. Abby, being who she is, never filed any charges and never looked for any child support. In addition to his abuse towards her, woman's intuition somehow told her that her husband had been involved in multiple affairs during their short marriage. Instinctively, her primary focus in the marriage had shifted into being a protector for Jimmy, trying to shield him from all the chaos created by her husband. Once he finally left, in true mother bear fashion, she was simply content to have the offender out of her life and away from her son.

At that stage of her life, the local church took her in and helped her get back on her feet. It turns out that she had her *own* encounter with Jesus through the actions of His people in this small country church. Her conversion was far less dramatic than mine, but every bit as real. An elderly couple opened up a spare room in their house and supported the two newly orphaned souls for an entire year. It would have been longer except for the fact that Abby did not wish to be a burden to these kindhearted people. To Abby and Jimmy, the couple was affectionately known simply as Ma and Pa. Their unconditional love and compassion revealed the true Spirit that she had grown to desire for herself, and one evening, in the quietness of the old folks house, both she and Jimmy gave their lives to Jesus for the first time. She stayed busy in the church and in due course landed a job at a small daycare facility. After saving enough money from that job, she was eventually able to move into the duplex where I had first come into her life.

Her sweet but tragic story revealed a person who was industrious and yet filled with love for others. Her story also gave me hope that someone *could* really learn to love despite their past experiences. Her life gave me a picture of the same love Jesus said *I* would be capable of one day. I wasn't sure I believed that fully yet, but Abby was a great example to me. I thought back to her frequent invitations to dinner when we lived in the dilapidated duplex. That had been three years after her divorce. She exhibited the same kindness to me that had been shown to her in the local church fellowship. Now, Abby and I had become the closest of friends. But after many months, my feelings for her began to grow beyond mere admiration of her beautiful soul. To my surprise, I had the crazy notion that our destinies just might be tied together in the most intimate of ways. *Is this what Jesus meant?* Then one day, I was determined to get my answer.

We spent the day at the ocean. It was a two-hour drive to get there, but conversations between best friends always seemed to make time go quickly. Jimmy spent most of his day down at the water's edge, fascinated by the undulating motion of the incoming and receding waves. He always seemed to find wonder in the simple pleasures of life; a lesson for all of us I think. As usual, Abby and I were engaged in pleasant conversation that revolved mostly around our growing common interests and our mutual love for Jimmy. The sun was just beginning to sink into the distant horizon and a soft breeze was stirring, gently caressing Abby's long beautiful hair. Watching the surf and her son enjoying life, she looked genuinely happy and content. That made me smile. The seagulls were floating on the mild offshore breezes, making their final appeal for food to departing beachgoers. The time seemed right, so I called Jimmy back to the beach blanket that we had placed on top of the warm sand. *I had one shot at this and I desperately wanted to get it right.* There was no way to make my request without taking into account *everyone's* feelings. So with a deep breath and a prayer in my heart, I laid all my cards on the table, starting with a talk with Jimmy.

I walked down to the water's edge and explained to him that he needed to be with us for an important conversation. He was more than anxious to oblige and we all huddled next to each other on the blanket not far from the incoming tide. Then, in partly rehearsed and partly improvised awkward sentences, I laid out the fact that I deeply loved them both. Abby smiled warmly and Jimmy got quiet and seemed to realize the gravity of the moment. Turning to Abby, I looked deep into her eyes and told her of my feelings for her. In so many words, I told her that my life would only be complete with her *and* Jimmy by my side. *In hindsight, that was after all what Jesus was leading me towards.* I left out all references to his divine prediction of our entangled future lives…this was not going to be a coerced proposal. I simply needed to have an answer straight from her heart.

After nervously asking her to become my wife, tears began streaming down her beautiful cheeks as she leaned into me, wrapping her arms around my neck and burying her face in my chest. After a few moments she raised her head and whispered the one word that forever changed my life again: *"yes"*. That's all it took. The realization was almost too much for me to take in: Abby was going to be mine, a cherished and loved woman. I would do my best to see that she never suffered again. More than that – I wanted to give her all she ever dreamed of. And Jimmy would now get the father he always deserved, as well as a built-in playmate for life. Those were the promises I made to them. I would spend the rest of my life making it so. And that is exactly what I did.

Epilogue

The building was boxy, gray, and looked somewhat industrial. Modest landscaping around the grounds made a mostly futile effort towards hominess. Can't blame them for trying I guess. It was obvious that buildings like this most often erred on the side of function instead of fashion. It did however betray the notion that people here were thought of as mostly just marking off time, many of them perhaps unaware of esthetics anyway. Failing eyesight and foggy minds probably made the bland surroundings tolerable. *Depressing.* Entering the front doors immediately ushered in the smells of medicinal products and bleach. Add to that the more embarrassing odors brought about by those who couldn't always look out for their own personal hygiene very well anymore and you get the picture. The lady at the front desk was pleasant enough, but more business-like than personable. After a few perfunctory pleasantries, she directed me towards my destination, more than happy to get back to her crossword puzzle.

The long linoleum hallway was littered with various medical devices, most of which were completely foreign to me, and most of which were on wheels so they could easily be moved from room to room. Efficiency ruled over clutter. Stale fluorescent lighting was the crown jewel in this sterile kingdom of coldness and lightly veiled despair. Glancing into various rooms during my walk down the corridor revealed patients either lying still in their beds, or siting in chairs watching some mindless daytime television tripe. Not much in the way of academy award material on the docket for today. The hollow echo of my footsteps was reminiscent of a ticking clock, once again reminding everyone that time was slipping away - for *these* people more than most.

I finally arrived at room 13, took a deep breath, and peered through the window in the door. I'm not sure *how* I knew, but I immediately *did* know. Something was drastically different. Staring through the glass, I saw my father. Well, actually it wasn't my father, at least not the way I remembered him. He himself was staring as well, but not at me. His face was turned towards the window on the side of his room. The angle was such that I could see most of his face, and I had never seen such an odd combination of serenity tinged with grief. His shoulders, no longer broad and defiant, were now stooped in a relaxed posture of humility. In fact, his entire body language spoke volumes about this new man who sat before me: soft facial features weathered from aging, gentle brow devoid of all past malice, and elbows casually slumped at his side with no hint of arrogant or defensive posturing. The hands were the most curious things to me, until I realized what was happening. His palms were turned upward as he gently swayed forward and back, eyes periodically closing for various lengths of time as his lips moved silently. *He was praying.* That was surprising enough, but what was equally unexpected was that, with a little lip reading, I was nearly positive he had mouthed my name a couple of times.

The striking change in my father was stunning to say the least. I still had a vivid picture in my mind of an abusive man who cared for nothing but himself. No, it was beyond that: a man who used others for his own benefit. But this lonely figure sitting all by himself in an isolated room of a nursing home was really the polar opposite of the man I knew from my youth. I knew it instinctively. I knew it spiritually. A short phrase kept popping into my mind: *"put off the old man and put on the new"*. This man was *not* the man he once used to be. And I guess, like father like son, neither was I. J.C. had seen to that. Perhaps he'd seen to *both* of us.

I realized for the first time that, though I certainly had nothing to apologize for regarding my abusive upbringing, I had *every* reason to find guilt in my attitude towards this man. I had hated him with all my heart for decades. And not just with a casual hatred - it was a burning loathsome hatred that had seethed within me, keeping me in bondage all my adult life. But the new Spirit within me left no room for that kind of malice anymore. And it went further than that. I found an emotion stirring in me that I never thought was possible. My new heart found within itself the ability to actually *love* this man. I was just as amazed at *my* transformation as that of my father's. Everything Jesus had said was true.

I watched through the glass for a little while longer until my newfound sense of compassion could no longer restrain itself. I timidly prayed that I was not wrong about the character change I had witnessed in my father. This was a big step for me. When I reached out and opened the door, he immediately turned towards me in astonishment. The initial look of bewilderment was to be expected, our eyes had not met in decades. But the tears that began to stream down his face told me everything I needed to know, and his tears were soon joined by a river of my own as we embraced. J.C. was right...*God had done the impossible.*

OTHER BOOKS
BY CLIFF HULLING

Behind the Veil, living in the reveald wisdom of God – This book examines the startling difference between the wisdom of man and the wisdom of God. The Bible is clear: *"There is no wisdom or understanding or counsel against the Lord"* (Proverbs 21:30), but mankind has continually fought this concept, preferring to favor the values of their surrounding culture. Honest seekers of truth will find that the Bible is wildly counter-cultural and it presents us with a unique opportunity to swim upstream against the tide of a society that has gone wrong. Come and open-mindedly examine the scandalous yet wonderful claims found in the Bible. Peer behind the veil and into the revealed wisdom of God.

The Chosen Path of the Beatitudes - This book will help reveal the vital progression that helps establish a deeper relationship with God. The spiritual path of the Beatitudes is prescribed for all, but must be chosen by each individual. God does not coerce; He calls. And the journey He calls us to is certainly one worth choosing. Why should we resist the comforting call of Jesus? *"Come to Me, all you who labor and are heavy laden, and I will give you rest. Take My yoke upon you and learn from Me, for I am gentle and lowly in heart, and you will find rest for your souls. For My yoke is easy and My burden is light."* (Matthew 11:28-30) That's a deal worth taking. Honest seekers of truth - pack up your gear…we're following Jesus down the path of the Beatitudes.

Mr. Hulling's books are available on Amazon.com & cliffhulling.com

Made in the USA
San Bernardino, CA
24 May 2018